HOT POTATO

A SEACROFT NOVEL

ALLISON TEMPLE

HOT POTATO

As Seacroft's resident weirdo, Avery proudly flies a lot of freak flags. It's a constant battle to be taken seriously when everything, from his red hair to his sexuality, makes him stand out in this small town.

Small towns are also a terrible place to keep secrets, and Lincoln has a bunch of them. But his demons aren't going to hold him back from his dream job at the Seacroft Fire Department. His life is finally coming together, until the red-haired twink with the big smile and fast mouth calls in an emergency.

Pining for the hot firefighter is Avery's newest flag, even if he agrees to be "just friends." For Linc, every minute with Avery is a temptation. He needs to let go of his fear and admit the truth. Linc doesn't want to be Avery's friend; he wants to be his everything. But just as Linc is ready to risk it all, Avery gets an unexpected offer to spread his colorful wings and fly away.

Cover Design: Cate Ashwood Designs
Developmental Editing: Christa Soulé Désir
Copy Editing and Proofreading: LesCourt Author Services

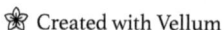 Created with Vellum

For the members of the Toronto Fire Department who came to my house that evening in August 2017, especially the firefighter who thought my painting of Kyle Lowry was really cool.
Little did you know, you'd wind up in a book.

Join the A-List, my monthly newsletter (allisontemplebooks.com/newsletter), for news on future releases.

1

_____

*A*very had always been good at numbers. Good at understanding how they fit together. In his life, he had several important numbers:

27—the decimals of pi he memorized in eighth grade to impress girls.

14—the age he realized he was way more interested in impressing boys.

9—(although it seemed longer) the seconds of silence between the time he said, "I'm gay," to his parents and when his dad said, "Get out."

3—the nights he slept at a shelter for homeless LGBT teens before his aunt and uncle found him and brought him to live at their house.

And now, two more numbers to add to the list with a certain immediate urgency.

5—how many minutes the internet said it would take to microwave a sweet potato all the way through.

4—(give or take a few seconds) the minutes it took Avery to fall so deeply asleep on his couch that he didn't notice the sweet potato catching fire and filling his kitchen and his open-concept living room/dining room with smoke.

Fortunately, the alarm he'd had installed the week before moving in did its job and went off, screaming like an air-raid siren.

Avery was upright and scrambling for the alarm panel before he was even fully awake. His pulse thundered, and his brain was goopy sludge as he stared at the keypad and tried desperately to remember the temporary code the technician had punched in.

Of all the numbers to forget.

"You'll want to change this to something you can remember easily, but that no one can guess."

Yeah, thanks for that. Avery had meant to. Too many numbers to pick from, though. So he'd procrastinated and figured he'd get around to it eventually. Except now the alarm whooped and made his head hurt as he futilely stabbed at keys and tried to think what combination the technician might have used. Nothing was working.

0000?

1234?

Was it even a four-digit code?

His pocket vibrated, and he fumbled for his phone. The screen showed the name of the alarm company.

"Hello? Hello?"

"Yes, hello sir, we're receiving an alarm signal from your property," the voice on the phone said formally.

"Yes. Yes," Avery gasped. "It's fine. Just a false alarm." He'd find a towel to wave under the smoke detector, open some windows—did his windows even open?—and it would be fine.

"False alarm?" The operator sounded uncertain, but what did he know? To him, Avery couldn't possibly be more than a flashing dot on a computer monitor.

"It's fine. Just my dinner. Nothing to worry about."

"So you don't require the fire department?"

Oh God, that would be the *worst*. Avery did not need the spectacle of first responders in front of his building.

On cue, flashing lights filled the small space at the top of the stairs to his basement apartment. Avery bounded up to the door and stared in horror at the big red truck parked at the curb.

"I'll call you back," he said into the phone.

"Sir? Sir?"

But Avery was already pulling open the door and running out over the lawn.

"It's fine, it's fine!" He held up his hands, warding off the uniformed firefighters who were coming across the yard. "It's just my dinner." Baked sweet potato stuffed with eggs. He'd seen it online and thought it looked good.

"Your dinner?" The woman pulled her helmet off. She wore her dark hair short, shaved on one side, and her glittering brown eyes scowled at him.

"It got away from me." Heat crept up the back of his neck as he met her eyes.

"Can we see it?"

"What?"

She took a step forward. "Can we come inside to make sure everything is okay?"

Oh no. "Sure."

Apart from his aunt and uncle, no one had been to his apartment yet. He hadn't imagined welcoming guests this way, but now this firefighter, along with another one, followed him back through the door.

"It's my dinner," he said again. "This is a lot of fuss for an overcooked sweet potato. It's really not necessary for you to come in, but—" He stopped so he could cough. His eyes stung, but he led them into the hazy space of his kitchen.

"Is it in the microwave?" she asked.

"Uh-huh. The internet said five-to-eight minutes. I poked

holes in it—the recipe said I should do that, but maybe I didn't—"

"Could you open the microwave?" She was giving him his personal space, but for something so simple, this lady was really determined.

"Oh, sure." When he punched the button to open the door, smoke rolled out like too much dry ice in a high school production of *Macbeth*, making Avery cough some more. As it dissipated, he saw the tiniest flicker of orange.

"Holy shit!" He reached into the microwave, only realizing at the last moment that grabbing an actual flaming sweet potato with his bare hand was probably a bad idea.

"Maybe you want to use a spoon?" the firefighter said.

"Right." Avery reached for the plastic soup ladle his aunt had bought for him.

"A metal one. So it doesn't melt."

The smoke was still pretty dense, which was lucky; it hid Avery's blush. He leapt for the cutlery drawer and pulled out the gravy scoop that he'd thought would be fun to own but didn't think he'd actually ever use. Definitely not in the first week.

He dragged the remains of his sweet potato out of the microwave, letting it settle into the spoon. The smoking thing was—oh, man, he could barely tell what it was. Maybe a root vegetable once, but now it looked like the kind of thing his uncle had used to start barbecues. Briquets. That's what he'd called them, right? Briquets.

The firefighter coughed. Avery realized he was holding the evidence of his incompetence right under her nose.

"Sorry." He dropped the whole mess in the sink and turned on the water. The charcoal potato hissed and steamed.

The woman peered into the microwave, like there might be more inside to worry about. Satisfied the danger had passed, she scanned his kitchen. "I'd open some windows if I were you. And you might want to go sit outside for a bit, until this all clears out."

"Thanks." In dismay, he followed her line of sight, surveying his half-unpacked apartment.

The other firefighter, who had followed his colleague in but so far hadn't said anything, was standing in the living room area, his back to them. He faced the *Winterlands* poster Avery had framed last summer after his trip to Raleigh MegaCon. As if he knew Avery's attention was on him, the firefighter turned. He jerked a thumb at the poster. "This is really cool."

"Oh, thanks."

"Do you play?"

Was it nerdy to say yes? Did it matter? "Yeah, I . . . It's signed by Colton McCluskey."

The firefighter's eyes widened. "The game designer? That's awesome."

"Okay. We're done here." The female firefighter came to stand next to him, but her intent gaze was still on Avery. "Be more careful next time, all right?"

His budding enthusiasm for his second-favorite topic fizzled as quickly as the sweet potato in his sink. "Yeah. I will. Thanks for coming."

Thanks for coming? Like he'd invited them over for dinner? Blackened sweet potato with a side of ash? If they weren't still standing there, he'd pull the neck of his shirt up and bury his face inside it like a turtle.

He trailed after the two firefighters as they headed to the front door. An elderly woman with her puffball dog stood on the sidewalk, gawking at them, while her dog shit on Avery's lawn.

His lawn. Shame tried to swamp him. Last week, he'd been so excited to live in a place where things could be *his*, even if he was sharing with the tenants in the two other units of the converted house. As he'd picked up the keys, he'd asked the landlord whether he could do some landscaping. Not that he knew much about landscaping, but he wanted to plant a few flowers or something, because then they would be his too.

Except he'd just proven he couldn't even be trusted with a microwave.

The fire truck took five full minutes to pull away and disappear down the street. Avery made himself stand there the whole time. This was his mess, and he'd own it right to the end.

Also, the lady firefighter had told him to hang out until the smoke cleared.

His phone rang.

"Hello?"

"Hi, Sweet pea, how was your day?"

Avery closed his eyes at the cheery sound of his aunt's voice. No doubt anyone standing within a hundred yards would be able to hear the kiddy nickname she insisted on using. He was twenty-six, for goodness sake. He was no one's sweet pea. "Hey, Aunt Brenda, how are you?"

"Oh, good, good. Monday, you know?"

For her, Mondays were the same as every other day of the week. She woke up with Uncle Theo at six-thirty every morning. They made breakfast and drank their coffee together. Uncle Theo read the newspaper, and Aunt Brenda checked her social media while Theo grumbled about not understanding the point of social media. Then, once her husband left for work, Brenda would go to her studio for a few hours before she went downtown for any number of committee meetings and bridge games, or to do the shopping. By the time Uncle Theo came home from work, dinner would be staying warm in the oven, and Aunt Brenda would be sitting by the fireplace or on the porch— depending on the weather—with a glass of Pinot Grigio and a book.

A wave of homesickness swept over Avery, even though *home* was only eight blocks away.

"Theo said you had to leave work early?" Aunt Brenda said.

He flushed. "Yeah, migraine. It wasn't too bad." A few hours with the blinds drawn and the nausea had subsided enough that he'd felt hungry. Hence the sweet potato.

"Well, you sound better. Make sure you eat something, okay?"

"I will." The heat crept up his ears and into his scalp. He couldn't tell her what had happened. When Avery said he wanted to move out, she'd taken it the hardest. If he admitted he'd already managed to get the fire department to his front door, she'd be over in a heartbeat.

She must have heard something in his voice, though, because she said, "Are you okay, Sweet pea?"

Avery glanced up and down the street again, then back at the entrance to his smoky apartment. "I'm fine. I slept a lot. Still waking up."

"Do you want to come over for dinner? It's almost ready. Theo should be home any minute."

The cozy image of them gathered around Brenda's perfectly set dining room table made his chest hurt. "No, I'll be fine."

"Are you sure? I made chicken and rice. Your favorite."

Avery sighed. He didn't live there anymore. He couldn't go crawling back any time something went wrong.

Down the street, a door opened, and an elderly couple and two little boys appeared. Avery had met the woman the week before. She'd been very friendly and only too excited to tell him about the two grandsons she babysat after school every day. Now, as her husband loaded the two boys into a small SUV, she waved at him.

Avery waved back, feeling defeated.

"Chicken and rice?" he said into the phone.

"And green beans. I could make a salad too, if you wanted."

She would too. He could get in his car, and she'd have a perfectly mixed salad in an equally perfect bowl on the table when he got to the house three minutes later.

"You don't have to do that."

"So you're coming?" Her excitement made him smile at least. If he could make his aunt happy, that had to count for something.

"I'll be right over."

Hopefully, by the time he got back to his apartment, the smoke would have cleared.

2

*T*he initial report on scene had been "nothing showing." Vasquez relayed the call back to the station as they'd pulled up to a nondescript house on a nondescript street in nondescript Seacroft, North Carolina.

"Dispatch, this is truck seven-two. We're on-site at 171 Sand Dollar Crescent. There is nothing showing."

Nothing showing. Lincoln Scott had been in Seacroft for two months. The town's false alarms—not to mention the bogus call-outs, which turned out to be a homeowner upset with the smell of their neighbor's barbecuing—exceeded the actual emergencies by so many miles, he could have driven to Florida and back a dozen times.

The house showed no sign of danger as he slid out of the truck.

"This'll be quick," Vasquez said, coming to stand beside him.

The house's front door burst open, and a kid with the reddest hair Linc had ever seen tumbled down the steps like he was being chased.

Maybe something was going on after all.

"It's fine! It's fine! It's just my dinner."

Nope. Never mind. Maybe Linc could rescue a cat from a tree somewhere close by to make the trip worthwhile.

Of course, Vasquez insisted on doing everything by the book, and, yeah, he'd heard the stories often enough in his training—the ones where a "nothing showing" call and a crew who couldn't bother being thorough resulted in an entire city block burning down—but this was Seacroft. If the town got any sleepier, they'd all be in a coma.

"Let's go." Vasquez motioned to him to follow as the kid led them back toward the front door.

"This is a lot of fuss for an overcooked sweet potato." The kid was breathless. As he calmed down from his initial panic, though, his voice dropped, settling on a decidedly adult register. He walked them down the stairs to a basement apartment, apologizing the whole time. With every step, the stench assaulted Linc's nose.

Maybe not a false alarm after all, because holy God, what was that smell?

He'd heard somewhere once that the Inuit people had hundreds of words for snow.

As a firefighter, he'd learned about as many for the smell of something burning. Smoke came in so many different flavors, ranging from the comforting smell of campfires with friends to the burning sting of a chemical fire.

This one, though, was epically bad. It started with campfire, then turned harsh, like the time Lacey tried to toast marshmallows in her room using a curling iron, burned her hand instead, and melted a hole in the carpet. Sweet, but in a way that clung to the hairs in his nose.

And the whole apartment was full of smoke.

Something might not be burning now, but it had been recently.

The guy was still babbling. While Vasquez appeared to be listening patiently, the collar of her jacket inched up her neck as her shoulders bunched. But every time he started running off on another tangent, she stayed all business, gently bringing him back around to the source of all the smoke.

For the briefest second, the kid's eyes flicked to Linc's, but they didn't focus before he was back to apologizing. The split second of missed connection caught Linc's attention, though, when he should have been scanning the small apartment, looking for any other sources of smoke or the potential for a flare-up.

The kid was a classic ginger. More freckles than skin that disappeared down his neck and under the collar of the ratty old T-shirt he kept pulling on nervously.

He opened the microwave door and more smoke billowed out. "Holy shit!" He dove for whatever was inside. Linc almost called out for him to stop, but then the red-haired man was fumbling with a soup ladle—Linc didn't miss the dry humor in Vasquez's voice as she pointed out something metal would be safer—and coughing while he tried to fish out the smoking thing in the microwave with a silver gravy spoon.

This guy was seriously high maintenance.

And cute.

Linc's amusement and boredom evaporated as cold fear shot through his chest.

The guy dumped the remains of his meal in the sink, letting the water run, and lifted his arms over his head before stuffing his fingers into his hair in dismay. He and Vasquez had their backs to Linc. He was only slightly taller than she was, even in her gear. With his elbows sticking out like that, it pulled the T-shirt taut over his back, making the flare of his shoulder blades and the dip of his spine visible, along with the edge of the elastic waistband of his underwear over the top of his jeans.

Linc flushed and spun, blinking rapidly. Arguably from the smoke, but who was he kidding?

Shut it down.

His lungs were tight, and not from the air.

He distracted himself with the poster on the wall. *Winterlands*. His favorite game. The poster was nice. Looked like part of the Destroyer expansion worlds. He'd lost a lot of hours to *Winterlands* over the years.

The apartment had gone quiet.

Linc turned back slowly to find Vasquez and the kid looking at him, heads cocked in opposite directions. The kid's throat bobbed up and down. Linc had the sudden, unexpected, and altogether amazing thought that he'd like to suck on it.

Panicking, he jerked a thumb over his shoulder and said, "This is really cool."

Yup. Very slick. In an emergency, you definitely wanted Lincoln Scott on your team.

As the truck pulled away a few minutes later, Vasquez elbowed him gently. "What was that about?"

Linc stiffened. "What was what about?"

She jerked her thumb over one shoulder and dropped her voice. "'This is really cool.'"

He shrugged her off. "The kid seemed stressed. I was trying to distract him before he lit something else on fire."

She laughed and shoved at his shoulder. "That was a new one for me too. A sweet potato? The thing was just gone. He must have had it in there for twenty minutes at least."

Linc turned his gaze out the window. Somehow, he doubted it. The kid—the guy—whoever he was, hadn't struck Linc as the sort of person who would let something go so easily. His speech had been precise, even if he used a lot of words. And someone who went to the trouble of framing a poster, instead of tacking it up on the wall, would also color-coordinate their underwear drawer and read all the instructions before doing anything, including turning on a microwave.

"It's your turn to buy the donuts," Brian said from behind the truck's steering wheel.

Relief slithered down Linc's spine at the change of subject, but it turned to annoyance as he caught Brian's grin in the rearview mirror.

"I *know* I bought them last time," Linc said. According to Seacroft FD's unwritten rules, if your call was a false alarm, you brought back donuts so the trip wasn't wasted. Linc felt like he'd bought donuts every damn day.

"I picked up an extra shift yesterday while you were sleeping," Vasquez said. "I bought them, then. So it's definitely your turn."

"But it wasn't even a false alarm. There was a fire."

Brian snorted. "No one is going to believe we got called out on a sweet potato fire."

Linc grumbled, but he'd lost. As the low man on the SFD ladder, he was pretty much everyone's bitch. If they said buy the donuts, he bought the donuts. If they brought him in for an extra shift to work the dispatch desk—the most surefire way the regular crew would get called out on an MVA or something requiring any real skill—then he'd sit there and answer the phone. He'd be polite when people called to ask if—*hypothetically*—they wanted to have a cookout with an open fire—*and this was a totally hypothetical question, I just want to know, officer. Do I call you officer?*—did they need a permit or could they just light a match wherever they felt like it?

Twenty minutes and a box of eleven donuts later—he'd ordered a dozen, but while Linc was okay with being the department's donut mule, but he wasn't going to risk letting someone else eat the double chocolate—they rolled back into the station.

"Are those donuts?" Sharon, the department's daytime dispatcher, came across the bay with wide eyes and grabby hands as Linc, Vasquez, and Brian finished putting their gear away.

Linc shoved the box at her. "Take your pick."

"So nothing to report from the scene?"

"Not a thing." Brian pulled out an apple fritter and stuffed half in his mouth. His wife was pregnant and had banned all sweets and junk food from the house. Once everyone else had a chance, he'd probably polish off the rest of the box.

"Just a college student who needs some cooking lessons," Vasquez said.

"I think he was older than that," Linc said, then immediately regretted it, because everyone's gaze swung to him.

"Oh, yeah?" Sharon winked as she chewed. "Was he cute?"

Good thing Brian had taken the box from Linc, because he would have dropped it. He forced himself to keep his breath steady.

"Is he your type?" Vasquez cocked an eyebrow at him.

"No." The answer came faster than blinking. Years of practice made the lie a reflex.

She waited, letting the question hang. Brian fished another fritter out of the box.

Linc started to sweat. "He's a kid. And he set a sweet potato on fire."

Very smooth.

"Scott! Vasquez! Lindsey!"

Saved by the chief.

"Gotta go." Sharon snagged a second sour cream glaze and scurried away.

The three of them turned as the SFD's chief strode across the bay.

"Yes, sir," Brian said around a mouthful of donut.

The chief glared at him before sighing heavily. "You three are officially our community-giving committee."

"Our what?" Linc said.

The chief's eyes narrowed. "Community giving." Each syllable was pronounced so slowly, Linc could practically hear the individual letters.

Brian and Vasquez both started speaking at the same time.

"Chief, I can't. You know I'm busy."

"I'm the worst possible person you could ask to—"

"Jess and the babies, they—"

"And frankly, I'm a little offended—"

"The heartburn, you don't even know—"

"Are you asking because I'm a woman? Because that's—"

"And the baby brain. Yesterday, I found her keys in the front door. She—"

The chief held up a hand. "This is not a democracy. Lindsey, your wife isn't due for another month. Vasquez, it is not because you're a woman, it's because you were standing here when I came looking for volunteers."

"But I didn't—" Vasquez started.

"Not a democracy." The chief's icy blue eyes landed on the box of donuts.

"Chief?" Linc said carefully.

"What?" He pinched a honey glaze between his fingers like the pastry was personally offensive.

"What exactly does the community-giving committee do?"

"Oh." The chief wiped his hand on his shirt and pulled a printed page out of his back pocket. "I got this request from the Seacroft Activator League."

"The what?" Did Seacroft have superheroes?

"They're one of those do-good charitable organizations that raise money and then give it to local groups. Mostly women with hearts of gold. They ask for donations. Run events. You know, fundraisers."

"My brother is the League secretary." Brian puffed out his chest. Vasquez snorted, and Linc suppressed his grin as he imagined another Brian, probably in a cape and a mask to hide his identity, studiously taking notes.

The chief glared at them all, and Linc buried his smile.

"And you want Scott, Brian, and me to organize something?" Vasquez asked.

Linc groaned inwardly. A bunch of ladies—and Brian's brother—in search of a fat check would probably expect the fire department to hold a car wash—ideally, a shirtless one.

"You were conveniently located when I went looking for volunteers."

"We didn't volunteer."

"Well, I volun-told you. Do whatever you want. Walk some dogs, do a boot drive—just get these ladies off my back. Scott."

Linc straightened. "Yes, sir?"

"Two of the department volunteers just quit. I need you on call tomorrow and Thursday."

"Yes, sir." He'd been hoping to pick up a few more shifts, but on-call paid half of actually being in the station.

"Good man." The chief eyed the box of donuts. "And next time, buy more fritters."

———

Looking forward to a few hours of sleep, Linc headed home when his shift ended. His anticipation turned to dread, though, at the sight of the red Miata in the visitor parking. Chelsea was here with Jordan, so there went his decent night's—or day's—rest.

He could hear them as he came up the hall, and it made the backs of his eyes ache. He was too old for this roommate crap. But housing was short in Seacroft, unless you had money to rent one of the teetering beach houses for the off-season—which Linc didn't—and the ad on Craigslist seemed welcoming enough.

For Rent: 1 br in 2 br apartment facing the ocean. Steps to amenities and services. Single 27yo guy looking for other single dude who isn't a jackass. Access to living room, kitchen, and all common areas of the unit. No laundry. Don't be a dick.

How bad could it be?

"Yes! Yes! Yeah yeah yeah yeah yeah." The woman's voice rose, and the space between the words melted together.

That bad.

As he entered the apartment, a framed photo of Jordan, his roommate, greeted him. In it, Jordan hang ten'd the photographer and clutched a parachute. The picture swung on its nail in time with the thumps coming from the other side of the wall, amplifying his excitement.

"Yes. Yes. Yes yes yes yes."

Linc pinched the bridge of his nose and slammed the door.

The commotion in the bedroom paused.

"Hello?" Jordan's voice called.

"It's me."

"Hey! I thought you were working a twenty-four today." Jordan was a paramedic, so he understood the pain of Linc's erratic schedule. Unfortunately, Jordan's coping mechanism for his own occupational hazards was getting busy with his girl-friend whenever he had a day off, even if the only overlap in their schedules was first thing in the morning.

Or maybe they were still going at it from the night before.

"Nope. I'm home now."

He could still hear their frantic whispering, although not as distinctly as Chelsea's enthusiastic cheerleading a moment earlier.

"We'll, uh, we'll be right out."

"It's fine. I'm going to bed." He poured himself a glass of orange juice and sucked it all down in one gulp.

"Oh, okay. See you later, then." More whispering followed by Chelsea giggling and some choked-off shushing.

They took longer than usual to get started again. Linc was nearly asleep before he heard Chelsea's high, happy sigh.

"So good, baby," Jordan groaned.

Linc found the pair of foam earplugs on his nightstand and stuffed them into place. They were imperfect. He'd tried sleeping with his gaming headphones, but he'd only succeeded in rolling onto them and snapping the mic off. He still hadn't had time to buy replacements and was stuck using a shitty in-line auxiliary cable mic for the last few weeks when he had the chance to game—which wasn't often.

"Spank me! Do it hard!"

He gritted his teeth, wrapping the pillow over his head.

He was going to have to do something about this situation.

3

*L*inc was still grouchy as he walked into the station. He hadn't gotten to sleep, *and* Jordan and Chelsea's orgasm Olympics only reminded him how long his own sexual drought had become. He'd been halfway to redownloading Grindr when fear got hold of his libido, and he'd canceled the app. Again.

And then his shift started out *really* well.

"Scott!" Vasquez threw a rag at him. It hit his chest with a wet splat, the water seeping through his SFD T-shirt. He growled. The bay doors were open, as they always were during the day. As he peeled the rag off, a stray breeze caught the wet spot on his shirt, making him shiver.

"What's this for?" He squeezed the rag in his fist.

"Chief wants you to wash the trucks." Vasquez's eye sparked with mischief.

"Again?" He'd washed them at the end of last week. By hand. With a bucket. And a ladder.

She shrugged, dark eyes twinkling. "The chief wants what the chief wants."

As if on cue, the man himself appeared in the open bay doorway, an insulated lunch bag in one hand. "Good morning."

"Chief," Vasquez said.

"What's the plan for today?"

"Scott's going to wash the trucks, sir."

The chief pulled his aviators off, glancing between them, then over to the gleaming red fire truck behind them. "Sounds good. They could use it."

They waited until he disappeared in the direction of his office.

"Chief wants me to wash the trucks, huh?" Linc said on a growl. "That's pretty convenient, considering he only just got here."

Vasquez's brows danced as she winked at him. "You heard him. They could use it." She squeezed his arm. "If you need any training on the proper procedure, I'll be in the gym."

"Yeah, yeah." Firefighting wasn't the worst job in the world. The *worst* job was serving pizza to drunk college students, who either had struck out at the bar and wanted to take anyone with a pulse home or wanted to pick a fight with anyone who looked at them funny. Linc had broken up more fights and fended off more horny girls (and guys) in the six weeks he'd worked there a few years ago than he ever had tending bar. By comparison, hosing down a fire truck in a sleepy town because he was still in the "how high?" part of the chain of command was practically relaxing.

And messy. Washing a fire truck by hand was tricky. Despite what the salad dressing ads said, the chore wasn't done with sponges and no shirts while the locals drooled. Usually, it involved high-powered washers and rubber boots. Shirts stayed on.

But Vasquez was entitled to her fun. No doubt the guys pulled the same on her when she signed on with the department.

Which was all well and good, except all but the most ancient of the department's stepladders had *conveniently* disappeared.

The remaining one was warped on one side, and the feet wouldn't sit level on the ground, so Linc set it up next to the truck. He put the bucket on the paint tray for access while he wiped down the cab's roof.

Except he didn't get that far. The second he set the bucket down, the tray collapsed, and the whole thing tumbled, dumping cold, foamy water on his head and his shoulders.

"Goddammit!" As water soaked through his pants and boxers, the wet spot on his chest didn't seem like such a big deal anymore.

"Oh. Um. Hi."

Linc froze, water dripping down his neck and along his spine. A pair of brown oxfords stood at the edge of the bay. Linc followed them to the cuffs of a pair of pressed khakis. Above the khakis was a striped button-down—equally well-pressed—and above that was a freckled neck, face, and the reddest hair Linc had ever seen.

"Can I help you?" It came out flatter than it should have.

Linc's visitor took a small step back. "Oh, um. Sorry. I'm not sure if I'm in the right place."

"It's the fire station. Are you trying to get to the fire station?" Linc's balls were shriveling in his shorts, even as something warm settled low in his belly when Red Hair swallowed.

His throat bobbed up and down over the collar of his shirt. "Yeah. The fire station. That's it."

Linc spread his dripping hands. "Then you've come to the right place."

Red Hair stood up straighter. "Oh right. I mean. I was—" He cocked his head to one side. "Were you at my apartment yesterday?"

Linc bit back an angry reply. He shouldn't blame Red for lousy timing. The whole prank had Vasquez and Brian written all over it. "*Winterlands*? Smoldering yam? That was you, right?"

His face fell. "It was a sweet potato."

"Is there a difference?"

"Sure! A yam is . . . " Red's brows bunched together, and a corner of his lower lip disappeared, snagged under a tooth. The thing in Linc's belly spread, and even his balls were less pissed off about their sudden dunking.

"Don't hurt yourself." He grinned.

The brows drew tighter, like Red was too absorbed in the question to notice Linc's amusement. "No, I actually used to know this."

Linc waited, suddenly interested, but the longer the silence stretched, the more Red's eyes started to dart nervously around him, much like they had the day before, as if he were trying to find an escape. Watching the distress spread over Red's face was almost painful, and Linc's instincts to help fired up immediately. "Did you get your kitchen cleaned up?"

"Hmm? Oh, yeah. Mostly. There's like this orange stain on the inside of the microwave that I can't get off. I tried everything. Baking soda. Lemon juice. I even tried steaming a bowl of water in it to see if I could loosen it, you know?"

"You shouldn't do that. It can explode. The surface tension traps the heat in the water until it superheats and then—" He made a noise like a small explosion and pushed his hands into the air in a burst.

Red's eyes widened as he followed the movement. "That's exactly what happened!"

Linc stiffened. Red was serious. He'd managed two microwave-related incidents in the last twenty-four hours. How was this guy living on his own? How had he not died in the first week?

Although, the unpacked boxes scattered around the apartment had said maybe the week wasn't up yet.

A breeze wafted through the bay, making Red's hair wave across his forehead. The spring air still held an edge of overnight chill, and Linc shivered as the damp material of his T-shirt stuck to his chest. Red's eyes were wandering again, and his lip rocked back and forth under his teeth.

"Was there something you needed?" Linc said.

"What? Oh. Yeah. There's, um—one sec." Red spun and hurried back to a blue Mazda parked at the curb. He pulled open the back door and returned just as quickly, this time with something between his hands: a casserole dish, covered in a blue-and-white dish towel.

"I, uh—" Red's cheeks turned pink under his freckles, and Linc's pulse picked up at the sight. "I wanted to say thank you for . . . I know it wasn't exactly an emergency, but—"

Linc gaped, flustered that he could react to something as simple as a blush. "Oh. You don't have to do that. It's our job."

"No, I know." The pink was turning a bright red, and the heat seemed to be radiating over Linc's skin too, even though they weren't touching. God, if they touched—

Red kept talking, the damn casserole still clutched in his hands. "But it . . . I wanted to. It's not every day you have a fireman—" His gaze flicked upward, and Linc flinched for the split second their eyes met until it passed beyond his shoulder. "I mean, firepeople in your living room. I thought you might—"

"Scott!" Vasquez's call rang out behind him. "Quit flirting and get back to work!"

"Oh, he wasn't—I mean, we weren't—" Red backed away, but Vasquez's voice kept Linc rooted to the spot as she approached them.

"Hey! Sweet Potato! Nice to see you. Any more culinary mishaps?"

"Um—" Red glanced away, hands trembling around the dish. Linc lunged forward to catch it. Their fingers brushed for the briefest second, until cold radiated through his palms and into his wrists, distracting Linc from the sensation of their touch.

"What's in here?" The pan in his hands was icy.

23

"Lasagna." Red brightened, probably relieved he didn't have to tell Vasquez about the exploding water bowl. Linc decided not to ask him why he happened to have entire casseroles of lasagna in his freezer just waiting to be handed out yet didn't seem to know how to operate a microwave. God forbid he ever try to cook one of these things himself.

"That's really nice of you," Vasquez said to Red, then looked Linc up and down. "What happened to you?"

"The paint tray on the ladder wasn't secured, and the bucket fell on him."

Linc and Vasquez swung their attention back to Red, who was blinking and blushing while his mouth worked open and shut like a dying fish.

How long had he been standing there?

"Scott, do we need to review ladder safety?" Vasquez smirked.

Linc's eyes narrowed, still aware of Red's presence. "I think we have to talk to someone about making sure we take shitty equipment out of service."

Her smirk stretched. "Or maybe you need to remember the importance of inspecting your gear before you tackle a job." She clapped a hand on his shoulder, smacking the soggy T-shirt against his skin. "It's fine. It's a rookie mistake. They're expected."

"Rookie mistake? You're the one who—"

"Are you leaving?" Vasquez called out after Red, who was halfway to his car. Linc ignored the stab of hurt. He hadn't even said goodbye.

"Yeah. I, uh, I have to get back to work." Red glanced over his shoulder, hands stuffed into his pockets. They pulled the khaki tight over the swell of his ass, and Linc's pulse thundered in his throat, as he glued his gaze to the asphalt at Red's leather shoes.

"Have a good day. Thanks for the food!" Vasquez nudged Linc.

"Yeah, thanks."

Red did a funny kind of hop, back arching like he'd been electrocuted, before he finally pulled his hands free of his pockets and gave them an awkward wave. "Thanks for, um, coming . . . to my house. Last night. Thanks!"

His shoulders were hunched as he continued to the car, and he didn't say anything else before he pulled away and drove off.

Linc didn't realize he was staring again until Vasquez took the pan from him.

"You got a crush, Scott?" She bumped a hip against his.

Panic tightened its grip on his sternum. He covered it by peeling his wet shirt off and tossing it at her. "That guy doesn't need a boyfriend—he needs a babysitter."

She arched an eyebrow. "The way he was looking at you, I'm sure he'd let you sit on him. Or he'd sit on you."

Linc's brain turned into a sludge of slow-moving images, illustrating what Red in his lap would be like.

"Scott. Vasquez." The chief stood at the far end of the bay. His words made Linc jump. "How is the community-giving plan going?"

Linc swallowed. "Fine, Chief."

"Good to hear. Anything else we need to talk about?"

Linc glanced at Vasquez, who made a few kissy noises. He glared at her, and she shrugged.

"Not a thing, Chief," Linc said.

They'd eat the lasagna, and Linc would probably never see Red again.

4

By the time he parked his car at the office, Avery had only replayed the conversation at the fire station a hundred times in his head. The whole scene had started like something out of porn, with the sexy firefighter "accidentally" dumping the bucket of water on himself, molding his T-shirt to his ripped torso until Avery could count every ridge of his six-pack.

Of course, then Avery went and made it weird by staring like a creepy stalker, then even worse when the firefighter somehow knew about the exploding bowl, making Avery look like an *incompetent* creepy stalker. By the time he managed to snag his watch on his pocket trying to wave goodbye, he'd given up any hope of class or credibility.

Just another in a long line of good-looking guys who would only ever see Avery as a loser who couldn't make his body parts work in sequence or operate a microwave without risking life and limb.

He let himself in through the back door, hoping to sneak in without his uncle seeing him—which of course meant Uncle Theo was literally at Avery's desk.

"Where's the MacPherson file?" Uncle Theo asked. He was

wearing his favorite green tie, featuring the rainbow tie clip Aunt Brenda bought him for their first Pride march.

"MacPherson?" Avery didn't have any clients with that name.

His uncle blinked up at him, frowning. "Who's MacPherson?"

"I don't know."

"Then why did you say that name?"

Avery tried to keep up. "You said it first."

"No, I didn't."

They did this a lot. Avery wracked his brain to come up with the most likely candidate. "Do you mean McLellan?"

Uncle Theo pulled open a file drawer and riffled through it. "Isn't that what I said?"

Avery had long ago learned not to bristle when his uncle did this. The company was Uncle Theo's, so all the information in the building was his. "You said MacPherson."

"Well, I meant McLellan. He called this morning. They got an audit notice in the mail. You finished their submittals, right?"

"Of course." The question wasn't an accusation. Just his uncle being thorough.

"Great, then where's the file?"

"It's on the computer."

Uncle Theo pushed the drawer shut. "What?"

"It's all online. Don't you remember? We switched to digital records for McLellan at the end of the last fiscal year."

His uncle harrumphed. "Well, I don't recall that."

"I know. I'll show you where it is on the cloud."

"The cloud? Clouds are made of water vapor."

"And water evaporates. I promise you, it's totally backed up and safe." Sometimes, he thought Uncle Theo would still be running his business with a slide rule and punch cards if Avery wasn't there to drag him into the twenty-first century.

They were almost to Theo's office when Meredith, the firm's administrator, rushed through the door. "Sorry I'm late. Kevin lost a tooth this morning, and then Carrie threw up, so the house was all blood and vomit, and then I had to wait until my mom could come take over."

Uncle Theo waved her off. "It's fine. Avery's just arriving too. Late start for every—" He turned, narrowing his eyes. "Wait, what are you doing here? You were supposed to be at Aulderson's at nine."

Busted.

"I was."

"You should have been there all morning."

"Well . . . " Avery chewed on his lower lip. He should have been going over *this* on the drive back, trying to figure out how to break the news to his uncle, instead of replaying how the T-shirt hugged the firefighter's torso as he'd turned to find Avery there, gawking.

Uncle Theo crossed his arms. "Tell me."

Avery slumped. "Pro-Count."

"Oh, no." Meredith put a hand to her mouth to cover her gasp, like he'd said the Auldersons had joined a cult—which they basically had.

Uncle Theo grumbled. "That's it, then?"

"I tried," Avery rushed on. "I said we could do more than just his bookkeeping. That there were lots of things we could do to help him grow the business."

"That's not what we do." Uncle Theo shook his head.

"But we could!"

His uncle was already disappearing into his office, closing the door behind him. Avery wanted to go after him, but he'd tried and failed too many times already. Uncle Theo would never listen in his disappointment.

"It's okay." Meredith squeezed his elbow. "You didn't do anything wrong."

Avery hung his head. "I know. But that's the third client we've lost since Christmas." And the fifth in the last six months.

The cult of Pro-Count was spreading. Once one business owner realized how easily he could do his own books with the right software package, he couldn't keep himself from bragging to his buddies, and then they told their friends, and they told theirs.

And soon Avery, Meredith, and Uncle Theo would be out of a job.

"I just wish he'd let me try new things." It didn't have to be major. The clients who had gone to paperless filings were still with them. And while Avery wasn't officially licensed yet—he kept meaning to register for his ethics exam, but he also kept falling asleep trying to read the manual—he'd slipped in a little consulting for a few of them, and they seemed to appreciate it.

"He will. He'll come around sooner or later." Meredith went to the office's small kitchen and started the kettle.

Sooner would be better. Aulderson, a heavy machinery repair company, was one of their bigger clients and had recently bought a smaller company in South Carolina. Converting them to a consulting client instead of only bookkeeping would have been great, but the office manager had shaken her head. *Cash is tight. The owner thought, with what we save in going to Pro-Count, we'd have more for advertising in the new region.*

Avery could have told them Uncle Theo hadn't raised his fees in years, and what they'd save would be gone in the first quarter of next year if they spent it on advertising, but that would have been petty, and he was trying to save face.

"You have to trust him." Meredith's kind smile stopped below her eyes. She'd worked for Uncle Theo for nearly twelve years, but Avery was family. If they lost more accounts and had to find ways to save money, they both knew which would lose their job first.

Or it might be both of them. Avery'd been doing the firm's own books for two years. He knew what was there and had a good guess about how much Uncle Theo had tucked away for retirement. He and Aunt Brenda didn't need much. Their house was paid for, and they didn't travel a lot. If things at the firm really took a nose dive, Avery was confident his aunt and uncle could live on what they had for a very long time.

Meredith was opening the mail. "I guess we won't be donating to the Activator League's fundraising drive this year."

Avery took the paper she was holding. "We have superheroes in Seacroft?"

"No, silly. They raise funds and then give them to local charities. My sister volunteers with them."

"Oh." He scanned the page. They did seem to be asking for money, something he and Uncle Theo didn't have a lot of right now. Then he brightened. "Maybe I could do their books? If they're fundraising, they probably need an accountant, right?"

Meredith patted his cheek. She couldn't be more than ten years older—although he would never ask, because Aunt Brenda, and even Avery's mom before her, had always said you don't ask a woman's age—but she often felt more like another aunt than a friend or coworker. "That's a sweet idea. I can ask if you want me to. Oh! How was your first weekend in your new apartment?"

"Awesome!" She hadn't asked about yesterday, so he didn't have to lie about the firefighters the way he had at his aunt and uncle's the night before while sneaking the lasagna out of the freezer.

"Yeah, what did you do? Sleep in?" She sighed. "I would love to sleep in."

Meredith's kids were four and six. Their age was partly to blame for the lack of sleeping in, but Meredith and her husband had also enrolled them in everything imaginable. Basketball, soccer, Tae Kwon Do. Every day she was rushing off from work to drive them somewhere, and weekends had to be equally busy.

It sounded awesome. When Avery was growing up, his mother signed him up for an art class once, but, like Bible study, he hadn't been able to sit still long enough to participate. Art classes stopped. Bible study had not.

If Meredith wasn't working here anymore, how would her family pay for all those sports?

"Are you okay?" The hand moved from his cheek to his shoulder.

"Yeah." He waved vaguely around his head. "The migraine yesterday must have been a bad one. Still feeling a bit off."

He'd feel worse if she lost her job.

He had to talk to Uncle Theo again.

———

The sum total of callouts at the fire department the next day was three false alarms, one "heart attack" that turned out to be indigestion after a chicken-wing-eating contest, two lost cats, and a little boy trying to burn the edges of a "treasure map" with a magnifying glass who instead succeeded in lighting the lawn on fire.

On Linc's drive home, his phone rang. His sister's name on the screen made him wince. Linc had only discovered she and their other sister had moved to Wilmington six months earlier, after he'd accepted the job at the SFD. He hadn't expected them to be so close, but then he would have known they'd moved if he spoke to them more often.

He let the call go to voicemail this time too, but as soon as the phone went silent, and he breathed a guilty sigh of relief, the ringer picked up again.

Call from Lacey Scott

That couldn't be good. He was still a few minutes from home, so he pulled over on the side of the street and took the call.

"Hello?"

"They're letting him out."

Good thing he stopped, because his whole body went on alert. His mind raced and his fingers went numb on the wheel, while his heart pounded in his chest and his tongue went thick.

"Hello?" Lacey's voice was annoyed.

"I—I'm here." He struggled to get even those words out.

"Did you hear me?"

He nodded, swallowing hard, then remembered she couldn't see him and said, "Yes."

"Yes? I call you to tell you our shithead father is getting out of prison, and all you say is yes? What the hell is that, Lincoln?"

If she was using his full name, he was fucked. She had always been the mother figure in their little trio of feral siblings.

"How—" He had to clear his throat again. "How did you find out?"

"Smug bastard called me." The phone filled with the familiar snap of a gum bubble popping. Linc hadn't seen her in years, but that sound said she was working on her gum like an angry beaver on a log.

"Just like that?" His stomach turned. Their father's sentence had at least a few more years to go.

"Good behavior or some shit, I don't know."

Good behavior. That fucking sperm donor wouldn't know good behavior if it folded his laundry and brought him breakfast in bed.

Linc had tried that so many times as a kid. None of it helped.

Get your hands off my goddamn son, you pervert!

The only time Linc's dad ever tried to be a father was the worst day of Linc's life.

"Does Lilah know?"

"No." The word dripped with sarcasm. "I called you first because I love talking to your voicemail, rather than speaking to the person who lives in my house."

"Well, fuck, Lacey. It was just a question." Sometimes he felt guilty for not calling more. Other times, she talked to him as if he were a five-year-old, and he didn't feel so bad after that.

The phone crackled to silence. The gum snapped. Lacey sighed. "Sorry. I'm a little freaked out. I haven't ever told the kids about him. I just said he lives somewhere else. What am I supposed to say now?"

"Tell them you're adopted." He'd wished for that so many times.

"Linc." Her voice was sad now, the earlier anger totally gone. "What if he comes here?"

"Did you ever tell him you'd moved?"

"No."

"Then how would he know where you are?"

"You know he could find out."

He could. Their father was mean and devious. A few questions to the right neighbor or an old friend were all it would take to figure out what became of his children.

If he cared enough to ask.

Hopefully, he wouldn't. In the seven years since his arrest, Gerry Scott had hardly spoken to his three kids. He might have called Lacey to gloat about getting out, but Linc had no reason to think his dad would try to see any of them face to face.

"Do you think you could come down here? When he gets out? Just for a few days. Until we know it's safe?"

Linc's earlier panic had settled into a sick laundry-machine twist in his stomach, but her question pushed it out of his guts and over his skin like a dozen spiders. He glanced out the window, at the quiet, normal town around him. "I can't. I just started this job. I can't take time off yet."

More silence. No gum this time. Guilt followed the panic spiders.

"I gotta go to work," Lacey said. Linc felt shitty he couldn't be who she needed. "I'll call you if I hear anything else."

"Sure." He didn't want her to call. If she did, it would be

about their dad, and Linc . . . He couldn't deal with that. He had half a mind to go back to his apartment, pack up all his things, and start driving north. Pennsylvania wasn't too bad. Upper New York state got cold in the winter, but he'd managed before. He could drive until he ran out of gas or until he spotted a "Help Wanted" sign in a place that looked like it paid more than minimum wage and wouldn't care about his . . . busy . . . past employment history.

"Okay," she said. He'd almost forgotten she was still there.

"Okay."

The call went dead. His throat hurt. He couldn't even be kind enough to say goodbye to her.

The guilt wound its way around to anger, like usual, and he glared out the windshield as he started the car. He hated this feeling. For months after that night in Raleigh when he was nineteen, the shame gnawing at him literally made him sick. He couldn't eat anything, couldn't sleep. He saw his dad around every corner and jumped every time his phone rang, even when the call turned out to be his sisters. Every time he felt eyes on the back of his neck or thought he smelled his father's brand of cigarettes, he'd packed up and moved on.

But that was before. He wasn't running. Not again. He had time at least. If his dad didn't know Lacey and Lilah were in Wilmington, no way he'd know about Seacroft. Linc could make a plan, apply for jobs, find a new place to live. No need to skip straight to sleeping in his car again. He'd done that before often enough; he knew exactly how to fold his knees and twist his spine to fit his six-foot-one frame without being completely bent out of shape in the morning. But he wasn't eager to do it again.

As he pulled in, a quick check of the apartment building's parking lot showed no signs of Chelsea's Miata or even Jordan's battered pickup truck. Hopefully, Jordan was working and Linc would have a few hours of peace.

Except, by the time he found himself inside, he wasn't tired anymore. His mind jumped all over the place from Lacey's angry voice on the phone to the sickening crack of Mickey's ribs under his dad's booted foot.

And then to Red, with his sweet face and nervous smiles. And Vasquez, sniffing around Linc's sexuality. She didn't strike him as the kind of woman who wanted a gay best friend to keep in her purse, so what the hell was she playing at? She had no right to poke into his personal life.

He turned on the Xbox. Linc hadn't played *Winterlands* in at least a year, but the poster in Red's apartment got him thinking about it again. It worked best in a two- or three-player format. You could bring your own partners or join a queue and get matched with another singleton looking to kill an hour or two with a stranger while fighting murderous trolls and seducing the occasional elf.

A new player's name flashed on the screen.

AveryCNC.

Linc put on his headset and waited for the connection.

"Hello?" The reception was good. The guy's voice was clear.

"Hey, you looking to play?"

"Hello?"

Linc grimaced and pulled the mic dangling from the headset closer to his chin. He really needed to get a new one. "Hey. Wanna play?"

"Yeah! I'm Avery. What should I call you?"

"Abe." His screen name was GatorAbe24, picked up in part working for an office cleaning company in Tampa and in part from his friends' insistence on calling him Abraham Lincoln growing up.

"Nice to meet you, Abe. Avery and Abe. The A-Team!" Avery's enthusiasm was goofy, but it also made Linc relax. Sometimes the strangers you met were weirdos who only grunted into the headset. Avery sounded young, but also human, and that was enough for Linc.

The screen flashed. *Would you like to proceed with AveryCNC?*

Yes. Linc thought he would.

They started one area away from the furthest dungeon Linc had ever reached. Whatever Avery's age, he'd racked up an impressive amount of points and gear. His avatar was a human warrior with bright orange hair streaming down his back over heavy leather and mail.

"You're pretty gnarly-looking," Avery said. Linc's was a half giant, dressed in furs and carrying a spiked mace.

"He's okay." Linc's giant took a step toward the path leading into a dark forest.

"I just got new armor last week. Killed this mage on a mountaintop, and this half-naked elf popped out of nowhere and was all 'would you like his armor?' I didn't even know it was part of the area, but I looked it up online and apparently it's one of those Easter—Hey, where are you going? It's this way." Avery the warrior disappeared off the right side of the screen.

"But the path is up here."

"There's a shortcut, duh."

"Really?" Linc followed after him. Navigating through the Wood of Infidels had taken the better part of a week last time, and this kid knew a shortcut?

As it turned out, the kid knew a lot of shortcuts. Over the next two hours, they moved ahead three areas, killed a dragon, stole its hoard, and shortcut their way to Hell's Garden. Linc hadn't played this long with anyone in ages, and Avery's steady narration of tactics and awkward jokes was entertaining. The tension from earlier—Vasquez's teasing and Lacey's call—slid off Linc's shoulders.

"This is as far as I've ever gotten," Avery said as they made their way up a dark path. His warrior was carrying a shiny new shield.

"What happens here?"

Avery sighed. "There's this zombie mage that keeps freezing

me and then eating my brain. I've tried everything, all the spells I can find, and I can't figure out what I need to beat him."

Linc's stomach growled. The sun was going down, and his eyelids were heavy.

"Maybe we should stop here," he said.

"Oh." Avery's voice was disappointed. Even his warrior seemed to slump a little.

"For tonight. Are you around to play again sometime?" Linc hadn't found someone to play with regularly since starting at the SFD, and Avery was a welcome reprieve from the outside world.

"Yeah, sure! I can be here most nights after work." The warrior did a small dance in a circle.

"Cool. My shifts are a bit all over the place, but what time zone are you in?"

"Eastern, you?"

"Same." Strictly speaking, you didn't always ask that. Some people got really uptight about sharing personal information.

Avery was apparently not one of those people, because he said, "Really? That's so cool. I'm in North Carolina. That's what the NC in my screen name is for."

"Oh, yeah?" Nerves prickled down his neck. Asking for a time zone was stretching it. Avery sharing more was unusual, but what were the odds they'd be in the same state?

"Yeah, it's this really small town. You've probably never heard of it. It's called Seacroft."

Linc froze, staring at the red-haired warrior on the screen as nervous suspicion shivered over his spine. He played back Avery's happy chatter. Never mind the poster on the wall in the nondescript apartment on the nondescript street while the guy with the red hair flailed and blustered over his smoking microwave. Wasn't he the reason Linc turned the game on in the first place today?

"Red?" he whispered.

"What? What's red?"

Shit, it totally *was* the same guy.

By his hip, Linc's phone buzzed, and Lilah's name showed on the screen.

"Abe?"

"I gotta go. Sorry. Maybe I'll see you online tomorrow?"

"Oh. Yeah, sure. No problem. See you tomorrow."

Linc hung up and saved the game, shaking his head. This would make the best story the next time Red called the SFD on a cooking mishap.

Or not. Linc stilled. Maybe he didn't have to say anything. In fact, maybe this was his solution. If he spent time online with Avery, he wouldn't have to worry about Vasquez's teasing. He and Avery could be faceless acquaintances, away from scrutiny, and no one would ever have to know.

5

*A*very stared in dismay at the flat-pack boxes sticking out of the back of his Mazda. They fit, barely. Driving with the open hatchback on the highway had been kind of terrifying. The trip home took him nearly three hours, because he'd been too worried about the packages shifting if he drove above the speed limit.

So, now, at almost five o'clock, he had an entire couch to unload and assemble, and he wasn't sure he'd be able to get the boxes out of the car and down the stairs by himself. The guy at IKEA who'd helped him load up had asked if he had anyone to assist him at home. Avery assured him he did, but when he'd called his aunt and uncle, they didn't answer. Then he remembered Uncle Theo had taken Aunt Brenda away for the weekend to celebrate their anniversary.

Avery chewed on his lip. He could wait and get them to help when they got back tomorrow, but he wasn't comfortable leaving the packages in the car overnight if he couldn't lock it. Seacroft was pretty safe, but the risk seemed unnecessary. He could already picture the cop's patient annoyance as Avery explained why he thought no one would steal his couch or his car, but why he also hadn't done anything to secure either. He'd seen that kind of expression a lot in his lifetime.

While he tried to puzzle it out, a car drove by. It got to the curve of the dead-end street but came back around before stopping opposite Avery.

"Do you need a hand?" The firefighter—the one with the shrink-wrapped abs—was leaning on his elbow in the car window.

Scott. The woman firefighter had called him Scott. Because calling him Shrink-Wrap would be weird.

"What are you doing here?" The question wasn't weird, but maybe kinda rude. Aunt Brenda had taught him better.

Scott grinned like he thought Avery was funny, not impolite. "I was in the neighborhood and saw you standing there."

"Are you lost?"

Scott laughed. The warm sound made some of the anxiety prickling over Avery's skin settle. Lots of people laughed at him, but Scott's laughter had none of the normal patronizing tolerance.

Scott pointed at Avery's car. "Do you need a hand with those?"

He wanted to help? Like some fairy futon godfather? Avery was shaking his head before he could think. "Oh, no, you don't have to do that."

But Scott was pulling his car to the curb and getting out as if Avery hadn't said anything. His jeans and plain navy tee fit him like an Instagram model. Avery's heart thudded in his chest. For a while the previous summer, Avery had been obsessed—but not in a weird way, Avery was just a big fan, and anyway he'd been busy crushing on an older guy named Oliver who ran a juice bar in town—with Damian Marshall, the movie star with a huge online following. One day, Damian had posted a video on Instagram walking his dog. He was all soft brown hair and toothy smiles for the people asking for autographs.

Scott looked exactly like that as he came toward Avery.

"Whatcha got?" He placed one large hand on a box.

"A sofa?"

"You're not sure?" Scott's grin was still all patient amusement, rather than the waning indulgence Avery had grown used to.

The unexpected thrill of someone who genuinely seemed to want to help, instead of feeling obliged—because sometimes it seemed like Avery needed help with literally everything—made him stand up straighter. "No, I'm sure. It's a sofa. Just—" He waved at all the flat-packs. "A sofa in pieces."

"So let me help you."

Avery eyed him. The "in the neighborhood" bit still seemed sketchy somehow, but Avery wasn't getting any weird serial-killer vibes either. And the boxes weren't going to unload themselves. "I'll go unlock the front door."

By the time Avery got back, Scott had pulled out all but the biggest box and stacked them on the lawn. He hadn't even broken a sweat.

"You take those." He nudged the two smallest boxes. Avery nearly protested. He was small, but he wasn't a weakling. He could pull his weight. But then Scott bent and hefted the two longest boxes, one under each arm, biceps bulging.

"Um . . . " Avery swallowed hard at the firefighter straining and looking so social media-perfect on Avery's front yard.

"Lead the way," Scott said.

Avery nearly dropped his boxes, fumbling with the door to his apartment. Scott expertly maneuvered his two boxes through the exterior door without even breathing hard or anything.

"You lived here long?" Scott asked.

"A couple weeks." Avery set his load down on the floor by the TV stand. The top box slid, and he had to catch it before it knocked over his Xbox.

"Where were you before?" Scott set his own boxes down.

They leaned solidly against the wall as if they'd always been there.

"I've lived in Seacroft since I was fifteen." He didn't want to admit he had only just moved out of his aunt and uncle's house at twenty-six years old. Well, technically, he'd been to UNC Wilmington for college, but that was only a hundred miles away, and he'd been home almost every weekend for the whole four years.

The apartment had gone quiet. He realized Scott was staring.

"Where are you from?" Avery's question was a hushed croak.

"South Carolina. Near Columbia." Scott spun on his heel and went to the door. His back in the smooth stretch of his T-shirt was beautiful. When he reached the first step, he glanced over his shoulder. "Are you going to help me with the big box?"

Avery leapt into motion. "South Carolina. I went to—" He bit his lip, because the rest of the story was embarrassing and too personal to share with someone he'd only met recently. Avery had a tendency to overshare, but he was working on it.

The only place he knew in South Carolina was a Bible camp north of Greenville he'd gone to a few times as a kid. The last summer, he'd kissed a boy for the first time. The experience had scared him so badly he'd called his parents in tears, begging them to let him come home.

He didn't know it then, but two years later, he'd be begging them to let him stay. In both cases, his mother had cried and his father had been intractable. Both times, Avery lost the argument before he'd barely started. He'd often wondered, especially in the first months at his aunt and uncle's, if things would have been different if he'd been allowed to come home from camp. He'd kissed that boy more than once that summer. By the time he got home, he knew what it meant for him and what it would continue to mean for the rest of his life.

Of course, Scott knew none of this, and he was standing next to the sofa box in the yard, waiting for Avery with no pity, no sympathy. Which was a little bit awesome. Not many people in Seacroft didn't know at least part of the story of how Theo and Brenda brought their disaster of a nephew to live with them in the middle of the night.

The box was heavy. Or Avery thought so, anyway. Scott barely looked like he noticed. If it weren't so long, he'd probably carry it himself.

"Did you measure to make sure it would fit?"

"No?" Avery nearly dropped his end of the box. "Was I supposed to?"

Scott grunted. "I guess we'll find out."

Avery had a moment of panic at the bottom of the stairs, where they had to get the box turned around, or even stand it on end, and slide it through the door. He envisioned having to carry it all back up to his car, drive the two hours back to the store, and try to return it. Did he even have the receipt? He'd meant to remember where he'd put it and not just toss it onto the passenger seat as he'd driven away from the loading area, but—

In the end, Scott, managed to work some wizardry and angle the box through. It involved sliding Avery's dining room table against the wall, but better that than navigating the return.

"I think I'm going to have to live here forever," he said.

"Why's that?" Scott had his hands on his hips, looking pleased with himself.

"Because I'll never figure out how to get it back up the stairs without you."

Scott grinned. "It's not that hard. It's about finding the angles and using all the space, not only what's right by the door."

"You sound like you know what you're talking about."

"I worked for a moving company for a few months." He let out a long breath. His torso was the perfect shape: wide through his chest and narrowing through his waist and hips. "Can I get a glass of water or something?"

"Oh my God. Yes. Of course you can! Sorry." Avery only

managed to tear his eyes away from his ogle-fest when he stumbled over a box. He nearly smacked his head on the kitchen counter, except suddenly Scott was there, and instead, Avery face-planted directly into the chest he'd just been gaping at. Scott was marginally softer than the counter, but he was definitely warmer and smelled great and—

"You okay?" Scott's voice rumbled amazingly through him, sending little sparks over Avery's cheekbones.

"Fine." Except he had nowhere safe to put his hands, just pecs and chest and—"I'm fine." Man, Scott smelled good. Somehow, Avery got himself disentangled while only making things thirty percent more awkward in the process. "I have juice, almond milk, and I've got—" he spun around, "—one of those countertop water carbonators, but I haven't had a chance to set it up yet."

He was such a dork.

Scott was not only new in town, but also apparently completely oblivious to Avery's ridiculousness, because he said, "Juice," without any other snide comments or judgment.

"Great." Except not so much because he opened the door and remembered his idea of juice was not the same as other people's. "Uh—"

"Something wrong?"

He could say he was out, but what he was actually out of was almond milk, so he literally had nothing else to offer him except —"I have carrot turmeric ginger, or kale and spring pea."

"Is that juice or a salad?"

"It's juice. I . . . made it myself?"

Dork. Dork. The dorkiest dork to ever—

"Water's good."

At least, he had clean glasses.

"Thanks for your help. I can take it from here." If he cut off this encounter now, Avery could be satisfied he'd managed to only embarrass himself a little. He didn't meet Scott's eyes, patting a box that leaned against the counter. It slid out from under his hand and hit the floor with a solid thump that would have broken any toes in the way.

"These things can be pretty heavy. Definitely a two-man job." Scott polished off his water, a tiny trickle of it sliding down his chin before he wiped it away. Avery wiped at his own face on reflex.

"Scott, you don't have to stay."

"What did you just call me?"

Avery's heart fluttered in his chest. "Scott?"

"How'd you know my last name?" His brows knit together, and his lower lip pushed forward. He had a good lower lip. Full and softly pink.

Avery blinked. "Sorry?"

"My last name is Scott."

Oh, no. Here it was. Things had been going so well. Here was the moment where Avery made it awkward. "But the fireman—the lady—the lady fire—the firelady, she—"

"Vasquez?"

He was having trouble breathing. "Is that her name?"

Not-Scott put his hands on Avery's shoulders. "Hey. Hey, it's okay. It's not a big deal. My name is Lincoln."

"She—the . . . Vasquez. She called you Scott. At the fire station, when I was there." Dropping off lasagna like a society matron. "I'm Avery, by the way."

Not-Scott's shoulders relaxed. "I forgot she talked to you." His smile was nice. The good bottom lip shone a bit, and Not-Scott's teeth were white, with only one a little crooked, like it wanted to make sure his face wasn't totally perfect.

"You do that a lot," Not-Scott said.

Lincoln. His name was Lincoln.

Avery's throat was so dry it could be used to start a fire. Who needed a microwave? "Do what?"

Lincoln's grin spread. He wasn't quite clean-shaven, and soft, brown stubble ran along his jaw. But the hair wasn't exactly brown. Or not only one kind of brown. So many. Coffee. Chocolate. Darker chocolate. Avery was better at numbers than colors.

"The thing where you stare at me so hard it looks like your head is about to explode."

Avery's gaze slipped to the floor. "Sorry if I'm making it weird." He always made it weird.

He expected Lincoln to take off, tell him to have a nice life, but instead, his broad hand appeared in Avery's line of sight. "Let's try this again. Hi, Avery. My name is Lincoln."

Avery's grin was a relieved reflex as he shook Lincoln's hand. "Lincoln. Like Abraham Lincoln."

Lincoln let go of Avery's hand. "Most people just call me Linc."

"Nice to meet you, Linc. Most people call me—" He faltered. Most people called him Avery. His father called him disgusting.

"Red?"

"What?"

"Most people call you Red?"

"Why would they do that?"

Linc's skin was darker than Avery's—honestly, everyone's skin was darker than Avery's; he could get a sunburn sitting too close to the TV—but it showed a faint tinge of pink now. "Because of . . . " He gestured toward Avery's head. "Because of your hair."

Avery frowned, like he'd never heard that reference before. The discomfort creeping over Linc's face was fun to watch, but Avery couldn't keep the charade going long. He burst into laughter as he bumped gently against Linc. "Yeah. I get that one a lot. Red. Rusty. Rooster. Carrots. Ginger. Ginger beer. Ginger muffin."

"Ginger muffin?"

Avery clacked his mouth shut. Back when he'd attempted Grindr that one and only time, he'd been bombarded with messages from guys as far away as Florida and Missouri. Gay men, or the ones on Grindr anyway, *really* liked a guy with red hair. He'd heard all the names. Not that Linc needed to know. Or that Avery should be bringing up his misadventures with gay dating apps to a near-stranger. A straight near-stranger, most likely. Avery risked one hopeful glance, looking for any signal that Linc was on his team, but you couldn't exactly identify gayness by the way a man stood in your kitchen.

Weird. He was making this weird. The longer he didn't say anything, the worse it would get. He moved their glasses to the sink. "Should we get started?"

———

Linc hadn't even planned to be there, but Jordan had come home from a long shift and said he and Chelsea were going to need some "personal time" that afternoon—all Linc needed to hear to make a beeline for the door.

Except where did he go in the middle of the day in a tiny town he barely knew? He'd been working so much, he still hadn't figured out how to make friends outside the fire station. Brian's weekends were filled with his wife and their upcoming offspring. Vasquez didn't talk much about her personal life, but she undoubtedly spent her downtime karate-chopping boards with her bare hands and bench-pressing St. Bernards.

And somehow he'd wound up driving past Avery's house for no good reason other than he didn't know where else to go, and Avery had been there, staring at the flat-packs as if strategizing his next Jenga move, and Linc saw an opportunity to be useful.

It turned out to be harder than he expected. The couch was . . . Well, to start, the thing wasn't even a couch. As they opened boxes, metal springs and frames appeared, along with cushions and hinges. Avery said it was a futon.

"So, if I have company, they have somewhere to sleep." He

smiled widely, like he already had a list of people waiting for an invitation. But where had those people been as Avery stood there, trying to figure out how he was going to get all of this down to his apartment?

The two of them got it organized with only minimal swearing, and somehow what looked like a gigantic pile of random parts took shape. Avery was pretty good to have around. Linc was handy with tools, but the little stick figure drawings in the instructions frustrated him.

"You've got it upside down," Avery said.

"No, I don't." Linc lined up the two parts of the frame.

"No, you totally do. See?" He pointed at the stick man, who held what was either a screwdriver or a really skinny dildo and was jamming it into one end of the slats. The stick man had a weird smile on his face while he did it too.

"What does that even mean?"

"Look." Avery rattled the page in front of him, as if that would help, then leaned over the half-assembled sofa to point at the piece Linc had just fit into place. His T-shirt rode up while he stretched, revealing a half-moon of skin along the small of his back. He didn't seem to notice, but Linc sure as hell did. The skin was pale and smooth. Running a hand over it, just to see if it was warm or cool to the touch, would be so easy. He glanced away quickly, looking anywhere but at Avery, who was still innocently trying to explain the basics of furniture assembly. "You see these grooves? They're supposed to go on the bottom."

Linc narrowed his eyes, struggling to regain his calm. Avery sat up on his heels, letting the T-shirt shimmy back down over his torso and pulling at it so it covered his body. Now instead, it sagged at the neck, exposing a line of freckles and a few coppery hairs just below his throat.

Linc coughed, focusing on breathing and doing normal things acquaintances did. The longer he glanced between the page with the happy Scandinavian dildo man and the frame on the floor, the more it looked like Avery was right.

Which was how it went. Linc did most of the heavy lifting, while Avery pointed at pieces and gave instructions. When Linc tried to guess what came next, he almost always got it wrong or backwards. And every time Avery pointed out that he'd missed a step, he did it with this endless patience, like he didn't care how long this was taking or that Linc had basically invaded his house out of boredom.

The sun went down. The futon got made.

And it was purple.

Avery wore a wobbly frown. "It looked gray in the showroom."

"It's pretty purple." Linc tried not to laugh at the open disappointment on Avery's face. "Do you want to take it back?" A mountain of cardboard was neatly cut down and stacked by the door—Avery's doing. No way could they pack the bits of the futon back.

"No." Avery flopped down onto the new piece of furniture. Linc half expected the whole thing to collapse back into its original pile of bits and hardware, but it didn't even creak.

"We did a pretty good job."

Avery spread his arms over the back of it and grinned enthusiastically up at Linc. "We did. I'm so glad you were in the neighborhood."

When had someone been so happy to be in Linc's company? Smiled up at him like Linc had anything more to offer than a history of moving a lot and vague answers about his background?

Avery said, "Do you play?" before Linc could work out his words.

"Play what?"

Avery knocked against the framed poster over his head. "*Winterlands*. You sounded like you knew it when you were, um, here. That other time." The color was back on his cheeks. It seemed to be automatic with him. Speak. Blush. Speak. Blush. After years of keeping secrets, being around someone so open all the time left a nervous giddiness fizzing under Linc's skin.

"Yeah. I've played before." *Say it. Say it.* He should tell Avery he was GatorAbe24. "I haven't played for a while, though. It's been more first-person shooters lately. When I have the time. I work a lot."

Avery's eyes bugged wide. "It must be so cool to be a firefighter. So exciting."

"It's fine." Better than anything else he'd done since that night in Raleigh. The year he'd spent on the firefighting foundations course was the longest he'd lived anywhere in seven years. "Firefighting isn't like how you see it on TV, though."

"Oh, I know that." Avery's head bobbed, then stopped suddenly. "What's it like?"

Linc grinned. Now would be a good time for a drink. A beer would be traditional, after assembling a couch/futon/bed thing. But since all Avery had was salad smoothies in a bottle, he went to the sink and poured himself another glass of water. "It's good. A lot of waiting, which is what you want, really."

"Oh, I hadn't thought of that. Yours is one of those jobs that you always hope people won't actually need, right?"

"Something like that." He'd become a firefighter because he wanted to help people, and he hadn't been smart enough or had enough money to become a doctor. And how was he supposed to do a four-year degree and med school when the idea of signing a one-year lease left him feeling trapped? Signing on to sublet a room from Jordan was about as permanent as he'd gotten in ages.

"No one wants my job," Avery said with a big sigh. "Or they think it's something they can do by themselves on the computer."

"What do you do?"

"I'm an accountant."

He choked on his water. "Sorry. That wasn't what I was expecting."

"I know. It's boring. Or it's not as sexy as being a firefighter, anyway." He waved his hand in Linc's direction, making his skin tickle under the cotton of his shirt. Avery didn't appear to have any delay between his brain and his mouth, whereas Linc weighed every single word. Especially words like *sexy,* because he never knew when they could be used against him.

He kept his expression neutral. "Do you like being an accountant?"

"Sure. I get to meet lots of people in town and really make a difference in their businesses." His smile was coming and going like a yo-yo. "Unless we go out of business. Not that it matters to you. Sorry. You don't want to hear about that."

Linc thought about asking, but the naked distress on Avery's face hurt to look at. Instead, he said, "And what else do you like to do?"

Avery's expression lit up. "Gaming! We could play some *Winterlands*! Oh man, I just got to a new area. Wanna see it? I can order some takeout."

Linc swallowed, and his stomach growled. Food sounded good. *Winterlands,* though . . .

He'd have to admit he was Abe first.

Or he could say nothing and watch realization dawn as he logged in under his username.

He hadn't expected this to become an issue so quickly. Linc liked the tiny safe space of having Avery to talk to in the game. Especially with the specter of Linc's dad looming suddenly. Keeping his identity online a secret for a little longer wouldn't hurt, and he needed what *Winterlands* offered: the chance to breathe and not choose every word carefully.

But Avery was still standing there, lower lip snagged under one tooth, waiting expectantly for a reply.

Say it. Just say it.

Linc jerked a thumb over one shoulder. "I should go, actually. I have to work tomorrow, and it's getting late."

It couldn't be later than eight o'clock.

"Oh, sure. You didn't mean what I would like to do right now. I get it." Seriously. One second, Avery's face was practically glowing with excitement, and the next Linc might as well have said puppies were the devil and Avery believed him. "But maybe we could play sometime? You could come here, or online or . . . ?"

No, Avery's emotions were more than a light going on and off. A whole movie played over his eyes and cheeks and lips. The compulsion to make him smile was a weight between Linc's shoulders.

"Yeah. I'd like that." He glanced at the empty fridge. "Or we could go out. Have a beer."

Avery's eyes went so wide, his eyebrows practically disappeared. "Are you asking me on a date?"

If only Linc still had some water, so he could choke on it again. "Wh—Wha—"

Avery's gaze slipped away, and he gnawed on his lip. The movie on his face started playing over again. Embarrassment, disappointment. Now Linc was responsible, and that made it all so much worse.

"I'm sorry," Avery said slowly. "That was the wrong thing to say, wasn't it?"

"No. No, I—" The need to run before Avery asked too many uncomfortable questions was at war with the need to fix the hurt look on Avery's face. But he had secrets. Things he couldn't say, no matter how much Avery's disappointment made him uncomfortable. Avery might not care, but other people would, and Avery seemed sweet, but also like the kind of guy who didn't keep secrets well. And that train of thought just made it clear Linc was definitely better off keeping Abe a secret for the time being. At least if Linc had to leave town, he'd still have Avery to talk to online.

"It was. You're straight. I knew you were straight. I just—and then you—" Avery was shifting his hands back and forth like the scales of justice, and the wrinkles in his forehead were getting deeper all the time.

Say it. Say it. A new chant. Not about the game and Abe, but about something bigger and so much scarier. "I meant we could —" Linc scrambled for the words that would make this better and keep himself safe. "We could hang out sometime."

The wrinkles smoothed out, the blush appeared, and Avery's happy smile came back. "Like friends?"

For the first time in a very long time—maybe ever—Linc thought he'd missed an opportunity, and the realization made his eyes sting. He should say no, he didn't want to be friends. Not because he didn't want to hang out with Avery again. Shit, they both could pretty obviously both use a buddy, but . . .

His skin. His cheeks. The soft way Avery's lips parted as he waited for Linc to say something. If Linc were being honest with himself—and he was hardly ever honest with himself—he wanted so much more than a few video games and some bar snacks. He didn't even know this guy, but you didn't have to know someone to want to kiss them and suck on their bottom lip until they moaned.

Linc clenched his jaw and forced a grin. "Yeah. Exactly that. Friends. My roommate's having a birthday party next week. You could come."

Avery's delighted smile sealed Linc's fate.

6

On Monday, Avery joined a gym. He'd been meaning to for a while. He'd tried running, but the best place to run was the beach, and he hated when sand got in his shoes. And he'd tried one of those high-interval training classes last fall, but he'd pulled something in his shoulder so badly, he hadn't been able to put his own shirts on without Aunt Brenda's help for a week.

But this wasn't one of those gyms. This was a plain old boring one with treadmills and weight machines. Old people and teenagers. Yoga classes.

And Linc. Who wore baggy shorts and a T-shirt so tight it might as well have been a tattoo.

"Oh, no." Avery stumbled on the treadmill.

He did his best not to watch as Linc made his way through the cardio machines toward the weights. Of course he would go there. A guy built like him . . . You didn't get that from the elliptical machine. He could probably snap Avery in half. Or bend him over that bench and—

Avery leapt off the treadmill like it had caught fire and stumbled to the water fountain to refill his bottle.

He hadn't talked to Linc since Saturday. Not after the whole

You want to go on a date—oh, no, you didn't mean a date, it's only that I can't read basic social cues so I can't even tell you're not gay. Linc had been super nice from the beginning, what with the whole some-assembly-required thing, but then, of course, Avery had gone and made it weird.

The thing was, Avery didn't want to date him. Not really. Sure, Linc was hot like whoa, but that just made anything happening between them all the more unlikely. Because Avery was a red-haired mess who had been a late bloomer in every way that mattered. He wouldn't even know what to do with a man like Linc. No, he *would* know what to do. Porn wasn't healthy sexual education, but in terms of illuminating the possibilities of two bodies together, Avery had some really good ideas. Only Linc would want someone experienced, someone who knew what they liked in bed, and Avery—

Well, shit, Avery was a twenty-six-year-old accountant who hadn't been naked with another guy since college.

His water bottle overflowed.

On Tuesday, Mrs. Henderson, who owned the flower shop, said she was signing up for Pro-Count. She only reconsidered when he sat her down and explained his idea to increase her business by building better relationships with the local day spas. (Somehow Seacroft had six—Avery had no idea how the town could support them all, but apparently his neighbors really liked their massages and pedicures.) But then Uncle Theo got that look on his face which said he wasn't happy with how Avery handled it because "That's not what we do here," and Avery went home in a funk.

His apartment was quiet. He hadn't been prepared for how quiet it got when you lived alone.

He turned on his Xbox, slipping the headphones over his ears. The white static before the game's soundtrack started helped settle him. He brought up *Winterlands*, which he hadn't played since the week before. He could play the one-player campaign, but he'd already beat it nine times, so he dropped into the queue, looking for other players.

GatorAbe24.

Avery's pulse went sparkly. He'd liked playing with Abe. *Abe.* What a weird name. Like he was eighty-nine years old. His voice hadn't been old, though. Low. A little husky, but some of that had been distortion. Having him in Avery's ear had been nice. Almost intimate, in the quiet space of the apartment.

He clicked on Abe's avatar, then gripped the controller too hard while the little circle spun on the screen as the game connected. He was about to give up and go try the single-player quest again when the message changed.

You are now connected to GatorAbe24. Would you like to proceed?

"Hello?"

The headset crackled, then, "Hello?"

"Abe?"

A pause.

"Avery?"

Even though Abe couldn't see it, Avery grinned. "Hey! How have you been?"

Another pause, then Abe cleared his throat. The sound coming through Avery's headset echoed like Abe was talking through a tin can. "Pretty good. You?"

"Yeah, not bad. Work's busy. Things are good. I joined a gym, I—" he bit his lip, "—I'm talking too much."

Another crackle.

"It's fine. You don't talk too much."

He sagged against the couch cushions. "Have you played since last week?"

"No. You?"

"Nope. I thought about it, but I kinda liked playing with you and—" He was rambling again. He'd gone to play a few times, actually, but they were heading into new territory now, and somehow, even though he didn't know him, Avery wanted to go there with Abe. He'd liked the calm way he'd talked last week. A lot of the time, when Avery played with strangers, he got these hyperactive dudebros who wanted to curse at the screen and mash buttons until either they or the monsters were dead. Abe had been methodical and a good listener, following Avery's instructions on navigating the Winterlands to a tee.

Kind of like the way Linc had been so helpful with the futon Avery was now sitting on. Avery liked working through the illustrated how-to guide, but a lot of the time he got overwhelmed with all the bits and pieces, or he'd lose a screwdriver, or wind up with extra parts at the end. Linc was slow and asked good questions, and the whole thing had come together perfectly.

"Still there?" Abe said.

"What? Yeah. Yeah, I'm here. Should we play?"

Playing together was like last time. Easy. So much easier than talking to people in person. Neither had cleared this place in the game before, but Abe had good instincts.

"Have you ever tried the Winter Haven expansion pack?" Avery asked as they trudged up a mountain.

"No. I heard good things, though. Everything they let McCluskey design is awesome."

"It really is. I got him to sign my poster last year. I went to Raleigh MegaCon. It was amazing. He was just there! Like at a table. You could talk to him and everything!"

The split second of silence before Abe responded was enough to make Avery tense. Was that too nerdy to say?

"That sounds pretty cool."

"Yeah, I thought so. Man, you should have seen it. There was a firefighter in my apartment last week. He was totally geeking out over the poster."

This time the pause sounded more like Abe was choking. "A firefighter? Everything okay?"

"Yeah. Just a cooking mishap. But then he came back again.

I'm not even sure why. I must have seemed really helpless, so he came back to check on me."

Abe laughed. The closeness of it, even though they were separated by however many miles of cables and internet frequencies, made Avery warm.

"He sounds like a considerate kind of guy." Something in the way he said it—half serious, half laughing—made the hairs stand up on the back of Avery's neck.

"Yeah. I mean, they probably all have to be nice, right? Like professionally, I mean. They wouldn't be great firefighters if they made people feel shitty when they're also dealing with an emergency."

"True. But that doesn't mean he has to be friendly, or comment on the stuff in your apartment. I think a lot of them would stick to keeping it professional. Is there a fire and how do they deal with it?"

"Oh, that's a good point." Like Linc's partner, Vasquez. She had been super professional—and kind of scary. Her attention never wavered from his sweet potato and the microwave. Linc, though, he'd looked around, actually noticed things. Maybe that meant—

Out of nowhere, a troll appeared and pushed Avery off a cliff.

"Holy shit!" Abe laughed. He had a nice laugh. Avery didn't mind giving up a life for that laugh.

———

Linc woke up two hours before he wanted when his phone rang. Of course, at two in the afternoon, a phone call wasn't completely out of line, but Linc had a twenty-four-hour shift starting at nine and, in a perfect world, he'd like to be asleep until four o'clock. Six would have been even better. But the phone screeched and would not be ignored, particularly when the display picture showed Lilah's face.

"What's up?" He rubbed a hand over his face.

"Linc?"

He sat up straight, blinking hard to clear the rest of the sleep out of his brain. "What's wrong?"

"What if he comes here?"

He sighed. Their desperation must be maxing out if they were calling him.

"He won't."

"You don't know that." His baby sister's voice wobbled, making his heart hurt.

"Where's Lacey?"

"At work."

By benefit of being the youngest, Lilah had lived under their father's reign of terror the shortest amount of time, something Linc almost envied. But she also had no memories of her father before he'd become so angry. Before their mother walked out and too many years of lost jobs and bad get-rich deals made him mean about things that most parents would shake their head about and go, "Kids. What can you do?"

"Look, he won't come to Wilmington."

"You don't know that."

"Even if he does, he won't come right away. He'll go home. See his buddies." The ones who weren't dead or also in jail, anyway.

"But you could come here. Get a job in Wilmington. Then we'd all be closer and safe."

"I just started here. I can't pack up after a couple months."

"Right." Her voice wobbled. "Sure."

He closed his eyes. Even the first few months after he left, talking to them had been hard. Impossible to see them too, because at some point someone would mention their dad, and then he'd have to … He was still too afraid and too ashamed, even now, to look them in the eye. They didn't know he'd been there with Mickey. He hadn't even gone home. Instead, he'd hitchhiked to Charleston, made up a lie about a job on a construction site, and never looked back.

Eventually, over the years, the requests for visits dried up. He missed it at first, but then his absences became one more thing he and his sisters didn't talk about, until they had nothing left to talk about at all. If he told her, she might understand. She was his sister, after all. If he told her he was gay, she might still love him, right?

You worthless fag. Not worth the dirt on my boots.

His father's words, not meant for him, still haunted Linc. People got hurt when he was too selfish to think about his actions.

The SFD got called out on three false alarms that night. Linc bought a lot of donuts which did nothing to stop the ache behind the backs of his eyes.

The sun rose, and he stood at the edge of the bay watching it, trying to clear the unease settling in his stomach like cement. His dad was coming. No matter where Linc lived, he'd have to face him. Have to tell his family the truth, and then risk seeing the same disgust on their faces he'd seen on his dad's seven years ago.

He blinked as the sun peeked over the roof of the town hall, and shafts of red-orange poured over the pavement. The beams were the color of Avery's hair, and the pink in the sky was—Linc shook himself. He couldn't be thinking like that.

"Hey, rookie!" Vasquez called. "Kitchen needs cleaning."

The task was simple enough but would keep him focused. Linc ignored the light creeping toward him and disappeared into the station.

7

On Friday, Avery had an actual fight with his uncle, the first in a long time.

"We are accountants," Uncle Theo said from behind his desk.

"Accountants who don't make money!" The way they were going, they'd have to let Meredith go by Labor Day.

"It's a downswing. We've been through them before. It'll work itself out."

"It won't. We're losing clients. We need to evolve, or we'll both be out of work by next year."

"I've been running this business for twenty-seven years. I know what I'm doing."

"But if you'd just let me try to—"

"Avery." Uncle Theo leaned back in his chair, hands on his stomach. "If you think it's time to move on and work somewhere else, I'll understand."

That shut him up. "Are you firing me?"

Uncle Theo swore he wasn't, but the damage was already done. He didn't want Avery. Avery was being a nuisance. Why couldn't he just trust Uncle Theo to run the business? Why did he have to mess everything up?

He was still upset when he got home, and the anxiety of his argument was compounded by the anxiety of having actual plans on a Friday night for once. He was going with Linc to his roommate's birthday. Well, not *with* Linc. But sort of. Because Linc was coming to pick him up at the apartment, which meant they would be arriving together. Well, not *together*, but still better than arriving alone and not knowing anyone and—

He showered until his skin was flushed and pink, and the whole bathroom was so steamy the water practically dripped down the walls. Avery washed his dishes. Since he still had a few hours to kill, he also cleaned out the fridge and mopped the kitchen floor. Not that Linc would see the inside of his fridge . . . or probably care about his floor, but Avery was too full of nervous energy to sit down.

Which was how he didn't hear his phone ring, or even the knock on his exterior door.

"Hello?"

Avery froze. Aunt Brenda stood in the doorway.

"Uh. Hi. What are you doing here?"

She lifted two large plastic shopping bags. "I brought you some things."

He sighed. "You talked to Uncle Theo, didn't you?"

"Well, he is my husband. We talk all the time." She bustled around his apartment, unpacking paper towel and air fresheners.

"Yeah, but he told you, didn't he? About what he said?" He pulled a toilet brush out of the bags she'd set on the counter.

"I don't know what you mean."

He stared at her, and she smiled innocently back until he finally dropped his gaze. "Can I get you something to drink?"

She patted his hand. "A cup of tea would be lovely."

He set the kettle on, and they pretended to keep busy, putting away housewares and making small talk about the goings-on in town.

"The Activator League is missing a few bachelors for the auction."

"The what?"

She swatted at him. "You know. We're fundraising for the new animal shelter."

"With a bachelor auction?"

"Don't underestimate the appeal of a handsome man."

Avery never underestimated the appeal of a handsome man. He might be a mess, but he wasn't oblivious to a good-looking guy when he saw one.

Like Linc. Who was straight and hadn't asked Avery out on a date, but was still nice enough to invite him to hang out like they could just be buddies, even if Avery would have to learn how to stop yearning from afar.

Jesus. Was he yearning now? Hadn't he learned his lesson last year, when he'd spent a month reading signals into every smile from Oliver that turned out to be nothing more than professional courtesy? Avery needed to pull himself together.

When the tea was steeped, he stood, hands wrapped around a mug and said, "Tell Uncle Theo I'm sorry."

"You?" She scoffed. "Why should you apologize? You're not the pig-headed dinosaur who won't listen."

Whoa. He'd never heard her say anything against her husband in the last eleven years.

"No, it's my fault. I pushed too hard. It's his business. I need to trust he's doing what's best. If I don't, then—" The words were harder to say than he'd expected. "Maybe I should be looking for a job somewhere else."

She had him wrapped up in her arms before he'd even finished speaking. "Oh, honey. You know it's not like that. He loves you. We both do."

"I know."

"He would never want you to leave."

"I know." He closed his eyes. They had come for him. For

three nights, he'd been too ashamed to reach out to anyone, sure his whole family had forsaken him. And then Theo and Brenda had appeared, almost from nowhere, and held him close and cried, and they'd brought him home and kept him safe.

"Am I..." a deep voice said behind them. "Am I interrupting something?"

Avery untangled himself from his aunt in a second, practically climbing over the counter. "No! Hi! You're here. You're—"

"Sorry," Linc said. "The door was open."

"Oh, of course. No problem. We were—" *We were hugging it out to help me deal with my abandonment issues.*

"I should get going. I didn't realize you had company." Brenda's smile was sly, and it made him flush.

"We're not dating. He's just taking me out for a drink."

The kitchen plunged into silence. Linc's eyes were wide. Aunt Brenda's mouth hung open. Avery's face was so hot it could melt wax.

"Um," Linc said.

"I mean—"

"Of course." She kissed his cheek. "Don't stay out too late."

Linc and Avery stared at each other, the creepy crawly feeling under Avery's skin growing with every second, as they listened to the sound of Aunt Brenda's feet on the stairs.

"Bye, boys," she called from the exterior door, then left.

The faucet dripped in the kitchen.

"So..." Avery said.

Linc said, "Your mom seems nice."

"My who?"

Linc jerked a thumb over his shoulder. "Your mom? Seems nice. She looks exactly like you."

Avery's chest squeezed. "Thanks."

Linc opened his mouth, like he could tell he'd said something wrong, but Avery grabbed his keys off the counter and pushed toward the door. "Ready to go?"

Jordan had chosen a bar called the Dugout. Linc was very familiar with the atmosphere, having worked in his fair share and having fished his dad out of a few more. Dim and a little grimy, but that gave it personality. He'd driven by another bar downtown a few times. Where the Dugout used neon beer signs to entice customers to enter, the one downtown had posters in the window advertising live music and cocktails.

Without a chaperone, Avery was likely to get jumped in a place like the Dugout, or at least lost in the press of bodies at the bar. Maybe somewhere that served cocktails while a bearded guy with a guitar played soft music was more Avery's speed.

Of course, that sounded an awful lot like a date, which was not what Linc and Avery were doing. They were friends—could only be friends—and that was how they were going to stay.

Avery's mom had definitely seemed like a white wine and snacks type of lady, though. She was probably responsible for the lasagna. Although something in Avery's face, when Linc had said she seemed nice, spoke of a pain beyond his embarrassment over blurting out they weren't on a date.

They ordered drinks and found Jordan and Chelsea huddled in a booth with a bunch of people Linc didn't know. Avery stuck close to Linc as they squeezed into the round booth. Introductions were passed around, but Linc forgot almost everyone's name, except for Derek, who sat across the table from them. Derek was loud, dominating the conversation. He was the kind of guy who thought he was hot shit, but also felt the need to prove it by jumping into every conversation to give his take on things.

"Linc is a firefighter," Chelsea said to the woman next to her.

"Really?" Her friend, who had introduced herself as Emma, sat up a little straighter. She was petite and wore a low-cut top that showed off her cleavage. As she looked Linc up and down, she pulled her long brown hair back, baring her shoulders.

Linc smiled. She wasn't the first—or the last, probably—woman to like his profession.

"A firefighter?" Derek said from across the table. "That must make you popular."

Linc ignored him.

"Do you rescue many people?" Emma asked, eyes wide.

"Not really. It's mostly property damage and close calls."

"That's how we met," Avery said.

Linc grinned at him. "Yours was a very specific kind of close call."

"Do you want to dance?" Emma said.

Linc sipped his drink and shook his head. "I'll pass."

"I'll dance," Avery said. Linc had to slide out of the booth again to let them by, and Chelsea and Emma both grabbed Avery's hands, giggling as they led him away.

Linc downed the rest of his beer as the three on the dance floor picked up the rhythm of the meat-and-potatoes rock playing over the sound system.

"What's his name again?" Jordan asked over Linc's shoulder.

"Avery."

"And how do you know him?"

Linc smiled as he flagged down a server to order another beer. "We met at work."

"Oh, yeah?" Derek said, a gleam in his eye. He hadn't even made it to ten o'clock, and the flush in his face said he was already halfway to loaded. "Was there a fire at the massage parlor by the highway?"

Linc stared at him. A tiny spark of fear lit up in his chest as Derek's grin spread. Linc's dad had smiled like that on more than one occasion, when he knew he was facing down a weaker opponent.

"Don't be an asshole, Der," Jordan muttered.

"What? It's funny because—"

Linc tuned him out. On the dance floor, Chelsea, Emma, and Avery were moving now. Or the girls were moving anyway. Avery was . . . well . . . The white boy had rhythm—except he was clearly listening to music no one else could hear. His joints popped and flailed, bobbing totally out of sync. If more people were dancing, he might have been a safety hazard, the way his elbows stuck out and his head rocked in every direction. But Chelsea and Emma seemed to have taken it upon themselves to form a protective perimeter, dancing just out of reach but also keeping any other dancers at a safe distance to avoid injury.

"So, Linc," Derek said. "They got you doing any calendars?"

Jordan laughed and shoved at Linc's shoulder.

"Calendars?" Normally, Linc would joke along, but Derek's face pissed him off and they'd only just gotten here.

"Yeah, like those sexy firefighter calendars. Take your shirt off, hold a puppy in front of your junk. Chicks love that kind of thing." His eyes narrowed. Yeah, Linc knew that look. He was testing him, looking for soft spots. Linc had been hiding for a long time—and he used more than a puppy to do it—but he'd never met anyone who zeroed in on him so fast. Was he slipping? His mind raced back through the very short list of things he'd said and done since arriving and turned up with nothing.

Maybe the problem wasn't something Linc had done, but who he'd come with. The thought made him sick. "You lived in Seacroft long?"

"Oh, yeah. My whole life." Derek was wiry, with scruffy brown hair, and a beard that covered too much of his neck and not enough of his jaw.

"So, you've met Avery before?"

Derek smile was lazy, his eyes like a snake's. "Ever since his aunt and uncle smuggled him in like a refugee, back when we were in tenth grade."

"Smuggled him in?"

Derek sneered. "I heard his dad used to hit him or something, and he wound up here."

Linc barely registered the last part. His pulse boomed in his ears as his whole nervous system went on alert. On the dance floor, Avery's red hair bobbed in and out of a growing crowd of people. Was that what he hadn't said when Linc had asked about his mom?

"Hey!" Two new people arrived at the table and were greeted with cheers and hugs. Linc excused himself while the new arrivals distracted Jordan and Derek. He'd meant to head to the bar. Instead, his feet brought him to the edge of the dance floor.

"Linc!" Chelsea flung her hands over his shoulders, pulling him out toward where Avery and Emma were still dancing. Linc wasn't much of a dancer, usually preferring to stay at the edges and let people who knew better do their thing.

The last time he'd danced with someone—*really danced* —had been Mickey.

The bar spun in a haze of bright lights and a bass line. But Chelsea and Emma didn't seem to care he didn't bring a whole set of moves with him. Emma, in particular, was happy to do all the dancing for him. She swayed her hips and lifted her hair off her shoulders. He knew the smile in her eyes. In the past, on other nights, in other bars, he might have even encouraged it. It would give him room to breathe. She turned her back to him, letting their bodies bump against each other from time to time. If he put a hand on her hip or on her shoulder, she'd know the invitation, and no one, not Derek or anyone else, would bug him for the rest of the night.

But as Emma dipped lower, Avery's wide smile came back into focus. He was still giving it his all. His hair was slicked down to his forehead, and he looked like he was having the best night of his life.

If only Linc had half the guts to be himself in public that

Avery did. Then someone like Derek would have no power over him.

He took a deep breath and stepped to the side, away from Emma, so the four of them almost formed a little square, with Linc between Emma and Avery, and Chelsea across from him.

Emma moved in again, but this time she spoke over the music and into his ear. "You guys are so cute together."

Despite his burgeoning courage, if he'd been moving his feet at all, he would have tripped. "What?"

She winked at him. Then Avery bumped his hip, but the surprised expression on his face said he hadn't meant to do it. Linc had to put a hand on Avery's waist to keep them both from careening into Chelsea. When he glanced over his shoulder, Emma was still watching them, her lower lip caught between her teeth as she smiled.

"Sorry," Avery said breathlessly.

Linc growled softly in the back of his throat. Avery's body under his hand was warm and alive.

Friends. Just friends.

Unfortunately, the dance floor continued to be the safer option. Back at the table, the more Derek drank, the louder he got, and the more Jordan drank, the less he seemed to care what his friends said or did.

"You're a great dancer," Avery said, cheeks flushed and eyes bright.

Linc sighed. Even if they were only friends, two guys dancing together in a place like this would raise a few eyebrows sooner or later—and not just from Derek.

Avery leaned into him, the perspiration on his skin glowing in the dim bar light. "I'll be right back."

Linc watched him go. A line of sweat trailed down the back of Avery's shirt, drawing Linc's eye to the curve of his ass as he made his way through the crowd.

He jerked back. He needed to get off the dance floor.

A cheer went up at Jordan's table, where they had moved on to tequila shots.

Maybe they should go. If Derek was drinking tequila too, he might get even sloppier, and Linc hadn't liked the way his eyes kept drifting to Avery on the dance floor.

Except Derek wasn't at the table anymore. A quick check showed he hadn't joined the dancers either. Linc's gaze swung in the other direction, toward the washrooms. And Avery.

His heart stopped. In the dim back hall, Avery's red hair shone like a campfire. And the dark shape of Derek's body surrounded that glow.

Linc was already moving. Derek had a hand on the wall, planted just above Avery's shoulder. The gesture could almost be intimate, but Derek was definitely going for intimidating.

As Linc weaved around people and chairs, the tightening of Avery's jaw and the way his eyes narrowed became more obvious. Derek said something and laughed, and Avery shoved at his chest, making Derek stumble back. His eyes rounded in surprise, but just as quickly, he was moving forward again, big fists crumpling the material of Avery's shirt.

Linc nearly threw the last person between him and them out of his way. He definitely took hold of Derek's shoulder and pulled him back roughly. "What the fuck are you doing?"

Derek swayed, bleary eyes unfocused. "Hey. Fireman. Avery and I were just getting reacquainted. It's been a long time."

"Fuck off, Derek," Avery spat, and Linc had to give him credit for holding his ground. But his eyes held real fear too, underneath the green sparking with little copper flecks.

"I think we should go," Linc said.

"Aw," Derek pouted. "Coming to his rescue? That's real cute. You two make a cute couple."

From Emma, the words seemed sincere. But Derek undoubtedly meant it as a threat.

Avery ducked down, slipping below Derek's arm. Linc would

have preferred Avery to get behind him, but instead, he turned so they stood shoulder to shoulder.

"You're still an asshole, Derek."

Derek sneered. "And you're still a twinky little queer."

Linc grabbed Avery's wrist, pulling him away, because the other option was punching Derek's lights out, and then he'd have to call into the station the next morning and explain why he'd been arrested.

8

———

$\mathcal{A}$very stumbled out onto the street. Linc's grip on his arm was tight, but the pressure helped combat the panic still pumping through his veins. Without Linc's hand on him, he might have fallen.

Actually, without Linc, he'd still be reenacting that terrible high school tableau in the back hallway smelling of decades-old cigarettes and urinal cakes. He'd surprised himself by pushing Derek away—a new development in the years since he'd been the weird gay kid in school, and Derek had been the homophobe slacker who saw an easy target he could pick on.

They passed two storefronts before Linc slowed down. They were both breathing hard. Avery's clothes were sticking to him.

"Are you okay?" Linc asked, hands on his hips.

"Fine." His insides were basically liquid, but he'd learned years ago that the feeling wouldn't actually kill him.

"Did he hurt you?" Linc's chest heaved.

"No."

"Avery."

"I'm fine." He stepped back, and Linc stumbled forward, like he was on a string. They stared at each other. A new nervous something beat in Avery's chest, but it disappeared just as quickly when Linc turned on his heel and walked a little farther up the street. Avery gave him some space.

He'd been having a good time, overall. Seeing Derek again had tripped him up a bit, but he'd been easy enough to avoid on the dance floor. And Avery had actually been having a lot of fun once Linc had joined him.

Oh, man, had it been fun. Dancing Linc was—well, he was hot, okay? All muscle and stubble. Avery never imagined he might be able to dance with a guy in Seacroft without getting decked, but with Chelsea and her friend for camouflage, pretending they were dancing together had been pretty awesome, even for a little bit.

Of course, then stupid Derek had gone and ruined it. His slurred threats brought back all kinds of uncomfortable teenage memories: Avery pressed against a locker or against the wall of the building, with no one to help.

Except Linc had stepped in, like a hero in a movie. Only Avery didn't really like playing the damsel in distress, or the way the tension wasn't sliding out of Linc's shoulders as he continued to pace on the sidewalk.

"Are you okay?" Avery asked.

Linc whirled, charging back toward him. "You know him, right?"

"Sort of. It's not like we're friends or anything. He's a high school bully whose life never went anywhere."

"It's not okay for him to treat you like that."

"I know. That was pretty cool when I shoved him though, right?" Avery tried for a charming—or maybe goofy—smile, but Linc either didn't notice or was still too mad to care.

"He knew you."

"Everyone knows me." Avery sighed. He didn't want to talk about this, but Linc was so upset.

"Why?"

He shoved his hands in his pockets. "Can we walk and talk?"

Linc was already pacing, but if Avery was moving too, he'd feel less like everyone in town was staring at him right now.

He started up the street, and Linc joined him, shoulder to shoulder.

"The lady at my apartment tonight?" Avery said.

"Your mom?"

"She's not my mom. She's my aunt."

"Okay." Linc strung the word out slowly.

"I grew up about an hour from here. When I was fifteen, I came out to my parents. They were super religious, super conservative. I knew they weren't going to be happy about it, but I guess I thought they'd tell me they would pray for me, and then we'd go on with our lives." A stupid hope, but they were his parents. The alternative had been unthinkable.

"And?" Linc said.

"And, instead, they kicked me out."

Linc whistled softly. "Just like that?"

"It took my dad nine seconds to decide he didn't have a son anymore." And maybe another thirty seconds before Avery fully understood the words that had just come out of his dad's mouth. His mom cried, but she hadn't done anything to stop her husband as he spewed hate at Avery.

"Jesus, Red, I'm sorry."

Avery put everything he could manage into a backpack while his dad had shouted at him through his bedroom door. He'd walked maybe ten blocks, on an evening a lot like this one, before he'd realized he wasn't going to call anyone to help him or give him a place to stay. Shame. Fear. Call it what you want— he couldn't drag any of his friends into this, too afraid their parents would see him the same way his dad had.

"My aunt and uncle brought me here to live with them," he said eventually. Linc was keeping pace with him. While Avery didn't want to look at him, the angry tension wasn't bleeding off him anymore. "It was a bit of a thing. I came in the middle of the school year. My first day at Seacroft High was a Wednesday. I was suddenly just there, and because of the way I look—" he waved a hand over himself, "—and the way I talk, it was hard to blend in. I don't know who found out what happened with my parents, but by Friday, it was all over the school. So... yeah." All these years later, he could still recall the exact sequence of events in those first days at a new school. Avery risked a glance at Linc. "They all know me. This whole town. If I didn't go to school with them, they know Uncle Theo through work or my aunt through one of the billion committees she's been on. But I'm sorry you had to get mixed up in it." His throat hurt. He'd been so excited for tonight, and now his baggage had ruined it.

They walked a few blocks in silence, leaving downtown and moving into Avery's residential neighborhood. The longer Linc didn't say anything, the more anxious Avery became. His story wasn't uncommon, but this version was his, and now he'd let it out, he needed to know what Linc thought.

"Did your dad hit you?" Linc said finally.

Avery tripped over a seam in the sidewalk, but Linc caught him; his strong hand on Avery's biceps kept him from face-planting on the concrete.

"What? No. Why would you ask that?"

Linc's mouth was pressed into a grim line, and he wrinkled his nose, but eventually he said, "Derek might have said—"

"Derek doesn't know shit." *Fuck him.* This was supposed to be a fun night. A friendly night. And now Avery had gone and told Linc the whole sad story, and Derek was responsible for all of it.

"Sorry. I just . . . My dad used to . . . He's in jail. I just found out that he's being released."

That brought Avery up short. "Oh." He walked ten more steps, waiting for Linc to say something else. It felt awkward, like he was prying, but at the same time, Linc had brought it up. "Why?"

Linc shrugged. "Good behavior, I guess."

"No." Avery chewed on his lip. "I mean, why was he in jail?" The idea of someone hurting Linc, hitting him like he'd been afraid Avery's dad might have, made Avery feel sick.

More silent footsteps. Ahead, a possum ran across the street, illuminated by a streetlamp, then disappeared into the bushes that lined a dark house.

"He beat up a guy outside a gay bar in Raleigh."

Avery's blood went cold. "He—?"

Linc's face had gone pale. His lips were thin, and his eyes were haunted.

"Did you—" Avery started to say, but Linc interrupted him.

"I'm not like that."

"Not . . . " Not gay? Not a criminal? Not—

"An asshole. Like Derek. Like my dad. I don't care if you're gay."

Avery sucked in a breath. He hadn't even considered Linc might have a problem. He'd been way too nice. About everything. But that he needed to say it out loud basically sealed any of Avery's secret yearning down tight.

"I know you don't care," he said quietly. "But I appreciate you saying so. What happened with your dad?"

They turned the corner. Avery's house was at the end of the street.

"They gave him nine years. It wasn't his first conviction, but all the previous ones were for stupid shit. Theft. Small con jobs, stuff like that. But it meant they could put him away for longer after . . . " Linc blew out a big breath and laughed, shooting a quick glance toward Avery. "Sorry. Didn't mean to turn this into a competition as to whose dad was a bigger shitball."

Avery bumped his shoulder against Linc's. "Is it weird if I say it's kind of nice? I mean, not like *nice* nice. But . . . yeah. I get it."

They were at the curb, walking toward Avery's front door.

"Do you have any more family?" Linc asked.

"Besides my aunt and uncle?" He fumbled for his keys.

"I was thinking more like siblings."

"Oh. No." He'd wondered about that sometimes. If he'd had a brother or a sister, would they have stood up to his parents for him? Or would they have turned their backs and pretended he didn't exist too? "You?"

"Two sisters. We don't—we don't talk much. They're in Wilmington."

"That's where I went to college." He flipped the light on in the apartment. "Can I get you something to drink?"

"Beer?" Linc's eyebrows rose hopefully.

"Oh." Avery poked his head into the fridge, but he already knew he didn't have any beer. "I've got homemade pumpkin spice concentrate or almond milk."

Linc laughed, even as his nose wrinkled. "Water is fine."

As Avery returned with two glasses, Linc was sitting on the purple couch, arms spread over the back.

"This is looking good," he said brightly.

"Yeah." Avery handed him a glass. The couch was too small for Avery to sit without getting closer to Linc than platonic personal space would allow. He pulled over a chair from his small dining room table. "I hope your friend didn't mind that we left early."

"Fuck him. If he's hanging out with dickwads like Derek, then he doesn't get to dictate what we do." Linc rolled his head on his shoulders, then, as if a new thought had occurred to him, said, "And fuck me too."

Avery coughed on his water as all kinds of awkward and awesome images flooded his brain. "Excuse me?"

Linc sighed like he hadn't noticed anything weird. "Because I have to go home and sleep soon. My shift starts early. And Jordan and Chelsea will be home late and still feeling the party and—" His eyes narrowed, and he swallowed. "They aren't very discreet, and the apartment isn't exactly soundproof."

"Oh." Avery's skin heated as he realized what Linc was saying. "Oooh."

Linc tipped his glass toward him. "Yup."

"You could . . . " Avery swallowed, tamping down the sudden excitement that buzzed under his skin. "You could stay here. I can pull out the couch."

Linc shook his head. "It's okay." But his body settled farther down into the cushions, arms and knees spreading wide.

"No!" Avery popped up to his feet. "No, it's totally okay! I mean, that's why I have it, right? So people can sleep on it. And you should totally be the one to break it in!"

Linc coughed. "Break it in?"

Of course, *he* didn't notice when he said something inappropriate, but as soon as Avery let out an accidental innuendo, Linc caught on immediately.

"Sorry. My tongue works really fast. I mean—it's not—oh, no. Sometimes my mouth will—" He sighed. "Sleep. Would you like to sleep here? If I can stop talking, I promise it will be quieter than birthday sex and—oh my *God*."

Linc was laughing so hard, his T-shirt rippled over the muscles in his stomach, a spectacle hard to look away from.

Avery hurried down the hall before he burst into flames. Sleep. Linc would need a pillow and some blankets to sleep. Avery pulled open the hall closet and—

The closet was empty. Of course. Because hall closets didn't miraculously come full of spare blankets and pillows when you moved in. Not like the closet at Aunt Brenda's that was always stuffed with clean sheets and towels. You had to buy things like that, and Avery had not.

"It's really great of you to let me crash here," Linc called from the living room.

"Of course." He was really nice, right up until the point he had to tell Linc his options were to sleep on the couch with nothing but a towel for warmth, or sleep with Avery in his bed.

78

He shut the closet and rested his forehead against the door. Linc in his bed was . . . Well it just wasn't a possibility. Because how would you say that? *Hey, I know we just bonded over our shitty dads, and I get that you're straight and all, but would you like to sleep with me?*

Avery would totally say that. And then Linc would look at him like an adorable puppy who couldn't keep track of his feet —because most people looked at him like that, when they weren't whispering about his history—and the whole "good friend" moment would be ruined.

His bed was big enough. Avery couldn't believe he was considering this, but he'd bought a big queen, because adults had queen-size beds—not the narrow single he'd still been sleeping in when he'd left Brenda and Theo's. He and Linc could fit in it without it being weird. The sheets were new and the comforter was—

The comforter.

He stumbled down the hall to his room and yanked the comforter off the bed, leaving the flat sheet in a wrinkled heap. He grabbed one of his two pillows, then slowed long enough to fold the comforter to make it neat and approximately closet-sized. If Linc knew Avery had pulled the damn thing off his bed, he'd be all nice and polite and say that wasn't necessary and he should go home.

"Here we go," he said as he came back up the hall.

"Thanks." Linc's expression was blank, like he hadn't noticed anything.

They got the futon unfolded without too much fuss, and Avery did a mental happy dance when all the bits held together.

And then Linc took off his shirt.

Be cool. Be cool.

Being cool had never been Avery's skill set.

"Well, I'm going to go brush my teeth. There's a spare toothbrush under the sink— " he bumped his hip on the corner at the end of the hall as he retreated, "—if you want it."

Linc smiled, the bland friendliness totally at odds with his pecs and his abs and his altogether too—

Avery closed his eyes and fled.

———

Linc slipped into his apartment early the next morning. He'd slept well. Really well, in fact. It felt like almost the first decent night's sleep since arriving in Seacroft.

So, of course, Jordan was sitting on the couch watching TV and slurping down cereal as Linc arrived.

"Hey, man." Jordan smiled around a mouthful of Cheerios. Linc grunted and headed toward his room. He needed a change of clothes, and then he was leaving for work.

His stomach growled as he came back toward the door, so he went to grab something to eat as well.

"Have a good time last night?" Jordan said.

"Not really," he said while his head was still in the fridge.

"What? Why not?"

Line rested his forearm on the top of the fridge door and glared at his roommate. Jordan was on the couch, wearing only his T-shirt and boxers. The spoon was halfway to his mouth, and it dripped milk in his lap.

"Your friend Derek," Linc said.

Jordan grinned and pointed the spoon at him. "Oh, yeah. He can be too much, but he's actually a lot of fun once you get to know him."

"He's a bigot. He cornered Avery on the way to the bathroom."

Jordan's face fell. "He did?"

"Yeah." Linc grabbed a yogurt and slammed the fridge door.

"He was probably just playing around. He can get weird when he's drinking."

"He wasn't playing."

Jordan gaped at him.

Linc waited for him to say more, but when nothing came, he shook his head. "Whatever. I'm going to work. Enjoy the hangover."

"Hey, come on." Jordan at least had the decency to set his breakfast down.

"It wasn't cool. And if you can't see that, then that's going to be a problem."

"What do you mean?"

Fuck, he hated having to spell out stuff like this. You heard all the time about gay rights progress. They could get married. They qualified for benefits. But then assholes like Derek cornered Avery in a bathroom, and their antics were laughed off as drunken shenanigans.

Until it turned out to be something more serious, and Avery was left lying on the ground with a split lip and broken ribs.

No, not Avery—Mickey.

People like Derek were why Linc couldn't be completely honest with himself about who he was, let alone honest with someone like Avery.

"It's not safe, okay? Because it's impossible to know when a joke is going to be something else. You can't take the risk. It's not safe for people like Avery. For people like—"

He'd been so caught up in the tangled image of Mickey and Avery, one blurring with the other, that he'd nearly said *people like us*.

Jordan's eyes bugged out of his head, and Linc was ready to leave. This queer education session had not been on his plan for the morning. "People like what?"

"Nothing." He needed a new apartment. New roommate. New life. Everything.

Jordan wouldn't be put off that easy. "Like who? Like you? Are you gay?"

The denial was there, on the tip of Linc's tongue, like so many times before, but he couldn't find the energy to spit it out.

Jordan's eyes widened. "But you don't—"

"Please don't finish that sentence."

They stared at each other.

"It wouldn't matter if you were."

Linc squared his shoulders. "Look. I didn't come home last night because I'm tired of living on the set of your personal porn channel. And now this thing with Derek? If you're going to have people like him in your life, then maybe it's better if I find a new place."

Jordan's head was bobbing like he'd fixed it on a spring now. "Yeah. Yeah, of course. I mean . . . Don't move out. I'm sorry. I never thought about—I'll talk to him. Let Derek know he can't be like that anymore. Don't go."

That wasn't comforting. Derek would need more than a stern talking-to in order to complete his personality transplant.

"I'll think about it."

"And Chelsea and I can be quieter, man. Sorry. I didn't realize it was bothering you so much."

"It would bother anyone."

"Yeah." He was back to the bobblehead again. "Yeah. I'm sorry. I'm a jerk. I'll talk to Chelsea. And to Derek. And then it'll be cool, right?"

Linc grimaced. "Let's just see how the next week or two go."

He drove to the fire station and pulled in as Vasquez was getting out of her car.

"Hey, rookie!" He glared at her, and she held her hands up, backing away slowly. "Rough night?"

The night part had been good, what with the sleeping and all. The parts around it, though, had been less than awesome.

Well, that wasn't true. Dancing with Avery had almost been

fun. And their conversation on the walk home had been hard, but Linc hadn't told anyone about Mickey. Ever. Not even the half-complete version he'd shared with Avery. Talking about it brought a gentle current of relief Linc hadn't expected.

"This town has a cute exterior and a nasty underside," he said.

She snorted. "I'm a Latina living with my girlfriend. Tell me about it."

He stopped short. "You—" He bit his tongue, because anything he said would get him into way too much trouble.

She whirled on him, eyes narrowed, hands balled into fists. Veronica Vasquez would eat him alive if he said anything that could be considered ignorant in any way.

"You're a lesbian?"

Her lips thinned.

He was fucked.

"I'm bisexual. Not that it's any of your business."

"And you—" He swallowed, thinking of Derek's nose in Avery's face, of the resigned way Avery talked about his parents like what had happened was sad but totally out of his control. His throat hurt, like it had as he'd begged his dad to let Mickey go. "You're okay? Here?"

She glared at him. Despite her tough exterior, her knees wobbled in her dark cargo pants. "We know where to go and who to stay away from."

"Like the Dugout?"

She snorted. "Rednecks and losers who peaked in high school. Skip that place unless you want tetanus and the shit kicked out of you." Vasquez pursed her lips as she eyed him up and down. Linc shrank back, because he didn't like how much she was seeing. "So you got skin in this game or what?"

He fumbled, struggling for the right thing to say. One bisexual coworker did not make this a friendly place. "A friend of mine had a run-in there last night."

"Yeah." She patted his shoulder. "Best not to go there unless it's daylight. Most of the rednecks will be at work, and the unemployed ones usually aren't mean enough to start shit on their own."

He nodded. Hate always found safety in numbers.

"Who's your friend?" she asked.

"Hmm?" he said, still reframing what he knew now about this town and about Vasquez.

"Your friend from the bar? The one who had some trouble. Seacroft isn't exactly queer Mecca. I thought Wanda and I knew all the local gays."

"Wanda?" He nearly choked on a laugh but caught it before it could escape and get him castrated.

"My girlfriend. She's Polish."

"Wanda is a Polish name?"

"Well, it's not Cuban."

"Is your family Cuban?"

"A few generations ago, yes. But you're avoiding my question. Who's your friend? Or is he in the closet too?"

He ignored the "too." "It's Avery. The guy from the microwave fire."

Her eyes rounded. "Sweet Potato! You and the sweet potato kid are a thing?"

"We're not—" He bit his lip because the words had come out too loud, and Brian was walking toward them. "We're just friends."

She arched an eyebrow. "He's kinda cute. If you like that wide-eyed twink thing."

He did. Avery was exactly what he liked, although he'd never put it in so many words. The wide eyes to the nervous chatter, the purple couch, and the awkward dancing. Avery was appealing in every way, right down to how his blankets smelled. Linc had woken up to scents of soap and sleep and all the tempting imaginary softness of Avery's body pressed against his, even on the futon two inches too short for Linc to stretch out on comfortably and—

He was saved from having to say anything further as Brian held up a blue sheet of paper.

"Hey! I found the perfect thing for our community team."

They were a pretty ragtag team.

"Should the rookie be taking minutes?" Vasquez asked, and Linc exhaled in relief.

"This won't take long." Brian shook the page again. "My brother's charity group. They have a bachelor auction coming up and still need some bachelors."

Linc and Vasquez both took a step back.

"What?" Brian asked.

"I'm not doing that," Linc said.

"Me neither," Vasquez said.

"Why not?"

Linc scrounged around for an excuse. "It's sexist." The truth was, he sucked in front of crowds. He could storm into a burning building, but getting up in front of people who expected him to be interesting sounded like hell.

"It's not sexist."

"It's totally sexist. Bachelor auction?" Vasquez scoffed. "Where are the bachelorettes?"

"So, you want to volunteer?" Brian asked.

"Hell no."

"Why not? Come on, Martin's in a tough spot. They need at least two more people if they have a chance of hitting their fundraising goals."

"It's demeaning. Buying people is demeaning."

"Yeah," Linc said, grateful that she could put it into words better than he could.

Brian wasn't giving up, though. "Come on, guys. Martin really needs the help. I bet they'd even take Vasquez and overlook she's not a bachelor."

"Why can't you do it?" Linc said.

Brian scuffed his shoes on the concrete. "It's Jess's due date."

Linc and Vasquez had a silent argument using only their eyes. He begged her to step up, and she fuck no'd him until they both sighed and turned back to Brian.

"Couldn't we, like, just give them money?" Linc asked.

"Give them money?" Vasquez laughed. "What money? The county won't even pay for the groceries in the station kitchen."

More throat-clearing and gazes that bounced off anything but one another's faces followed the question.

"What if—" Linc scratched his chin. "What if we all went and chipped in some money and bid on someone? We could get them to help around here for a day. Wash the trucks. Do the food run."

"Is that—" Brian said slowly. "Is that less demeaning than getting Vasquez to auction herself off?"

Vasquez sighed. "We'll go bid on someone. But I'm bringing a date. And so is Scott."

Linc's stomach bottomed out, but Brian smiled widely. "You got a girlfriend? Someone from town? How did you meet?"

"Jesus, Brian. You've got two babies on the way. You don't need to baby me." He glared at Vasquez and then at Brian. His team seriously sucked.

"Aw, rookie." Vasquez pinched his cheek until he pulled his head away. "You're everyone's baby. Better find someone to sit beside you. Don't want you getting lonely."

But the only person Linc wanted to sit beside him was the one person he couldn't ask.

9

"So, Sweet pea." Aunt Brenda ladled more gravy onto Avery's plate. "How's the apartment? Need anything? I saw a salad spinner on sale this week."

"I already bought one." And he'd used it too. Watching the little droplets of water hit the sides of the bowl was super satisfying. He'd eaten a ton of lettuce, but the extra salads were worth it.

"How are things at work?"

"Fine." He glanced at Uncle Theo, opposite him. Two men in navy suits had been in Uncle Theo's office for more than an hour that afternoon. None of their clients dressed that well, which meant they were lawyers or bankers. Neither option sounded good, but Avery couldn't share that kind of information with his aunt. If Uncle Theo wasn't talking about it, Avery was going to have to hold his tongue.

"I had lunch at the diner with Penny and Carol Anne today," Brenda said.

Avery let the familiar chatter wash over him as they talked about the diner Penny's husband owned and how Carol Anne's grandson would be going into fourth grade in the fall.

"I think you'd be a big hit," Aunt Brenda said, but he was on his third bite of pot roast before he realized she was speaking to him.

"I'm sorry, I didn't hear you. A big hit at what?"

"The auction."

He glanced at his uncle, who only shrugged into his mashed potatoes. "Better you than me."

"What auction?"

Aunt Brenda cocked her head. "Weren't you listening? Are you feeling okay?"

"I'm fine. Just zoned out for a sec. What auction?"

"The bachelor auction for the Activator League. You'd be perfect. Anyone would love to spend time with you."

Not really. Either they called him a weird little queer or they tolerated him like an overexcited kindergartener, but no one wanted to spend time with him.

Well, except for Linc. If Linc bought him, then Avery would—

He cleared his throat. Having those thoughts at the dinner table while his aunt and uncle were waiting for him to say something was just gross.

"Why can't you do it?" he said to his uncle.

"I'm already spoken for." Uncle Theo winked at Aunt Brenda, who blushed and tossed her napkin at him.

"I don't know." Avery poked at his dinner. The portion he'd already eaten formed a lump at the bottom of his stomach.

He had no trouble picturing how it would all go wrong. He'd walk out on the stage in his best suit, maybe with a boutonnière pinned to his lapel. The announcer would give a short speech about what a catch Avery was and bang his gavel.

And silence would roll in like storm surge in a hurricane.

It would be the longest, most horrible moment of his life. Longer than the silence before his dad started cursing his name as he'd packed his bags. Avery heard him the first time, but his dad insisted on making it clear how disgusting he thought Avery was, how morally corrupt.

He and his dad were never close. Avery had always been a sensitive kid, prone to emotional outbursts and choosing brightly colored clothes when his dad wanted a son who would grow up to be a man's man like him. An upstanding pillar of the community, he'd say. He probably hadn't even been surprised when Avery came out, although he would have never voiced his suspicions beforehand. But once Avery said the words, he'd made his opinion very clear. Avery was broken. An abomination no moral person would ever want to be with.

No one would want him. The auction would be no different.

"No," he said.

"But it's for charity," Aunt Brenda said.

"I know." He shrugged, keeping his eyes on his plate. If he looked at either of them, they'd know what was going on his head. They might not be his parents by birth, but they were by everything else.

"Sweet pea." She put a hand over his. "It's not like that. Just people from town raising money. Worst comes to worst, your uncle and I will—"

"Please don't." If she said it, his insides would shrivel up into nothing. They'd bailed him out enough. If he couldn't even get someone to bid on him at a damn bachelor auction, what hope did he have of ever being a fully functional adult?

Uncle Theo and Aunt Brenda were having a wordless conversation, as they did sometimes when Avery was at maximum Averyness and they didn't want to upset him more.

He hated that they still had to do that.

"We could always make a donation," Aunt Brenda said.

"I'll think about it," Avery mumbled into his potatoes.

He got home earlier than normal. Even once the auction thing was set aside, conversation hadn't come easily, and they'd said their goodbyes on the front porch before the sun was fully down.

It sucked that he couldn't put his baggage away and help them. The business didn't have any money for charitable donations. So what if no one bid on him? At least he could say he'd done his bit for the community. And that's what he wanted, right? To be part of the community.

He slumped onto the couch and turned on the Xbox. He hadn't played in a few days, but when he logged onto *Winterlands*, Abe was there.

"Hey," Avery said when they got connected. "Haven't seen you online in a bit."

"Yeah, sorry. I've been working a lot." His voice was scratchier than usual, like the connection was really bad. The line crackled, and the words cut off. "—playing much lately?"

"Not really."

"Ready to keep going?"

The last time they played, Avery had been mangled and stomped on by a zombie troll.

"You're leading the way this time."

Abe laughed softly in Avery's ear. "Whatever you say."

Twenty-six minutes later, Avery had been stomped on twice, fallen into the same crevasse three times, and started an avalanche that swept them both back to the bottom of the mountain.

"You okay there, Red?" Abe asked. "Usually I'm the one causing trouble."

"What did you just call me?" Avery's attention prickled.

"Red?"

He swallowed hard. "How did you know to call me that?"

The pause seemed to go on too long, sixteen seconds at least, followed by a crackle, like Abe was moving his microphone. "Because you have red hair."

His pulse thumped in his throat. "How do you know?"

"Because I can see it? On the screen, I mean. I can see your avatar's red hair on the screen."

Oh. Avery half laughed, half sighed. "Right. Sorry. I'm being weird."

"No you aren't. Everything okay?"

Avery bit his lip. He shouldn't be unloading on Abe; he barely knew the guy. People didn't make random online gaming friends to share their problems.

"You still there?" Abe said.

He wanted to tell Abe everything because he needed to tell someone. About the auction and why he couldn't do it. About work and how Avery was starting to feel like he was suffocating. And about how Linc had slept on his couch under Avery's comforter, and that evening had been the most intimate moment of Avery's life though they weren't even in the same room.

And, as weird as it sounded, he kind of trusted Abe. He wasn't about to give him the address to Avery's apartment, but they could talk.

"Yeah. I'm here. Sorry. Just have a lot of stuff on my mind."

"Game stuff? Or life stuff?"

"Life stuff. I don't know. Work. Family. And there's this guy."

"A guy?" Abe jumped on that last comment quickly, and Avery's heart caught in his throat. He hadn't meant to bring Linc into this. He shouldn't have said anything. Bringing up his sexuality to a stranger online was a near-surefire way to never hear from him again.

"Yeah. I don't know. He seems nice." And straight. *Nice and straight.*

And Abe seemed like a really nice guy too, so Avery would be sad to see him go. But getting randomly paired in a video game was not an invitation to unload on him when they'd never even met face-to-face, especially about Avery's weird crushes.

This time, the silence was so long Avery had to double-check the screen to make sure Abe was still connected.

"Avery, I—"

An alarm shrieked over the headset, so loud that Avery pulled the earphones off and threw them across the room. Avery stared at the headset, listening to the muffled shrill. When the noise stopped, he carefully lifted it back up to his ear again.

"Abe?"

No sound came from the Abe's mic. A few distant voices, maybe, like a conversation in another room. On the screen, Abe's gnarly warrior stood at attention, patiently waiting for direction.

"Hello?"

But Abe didn't reply.

———

The Xbox at work was a bad idea, an unnecessary risk. But sometimes the nights got quiet, and Linc could only listen to Brian talk about prenatal reflux and stretch marks for so many hours while the console sat quietly by the TV, untouched and offering a refuge. The temptation of talking to Avery outweighed the chance of being discovered and having to answer unwanted questions from his team, at least until the alarm had sounded and Linc didn't even have time to say goodbye before he'd needed to run for the truck.

And there's this guy.

Avery's words echoed in Linc's head. If Avery had met someone, Linc would—really, what could he do but wish him well? But if—and this possibility made Linc's heart race and his stomach turn—Linc was "the guy" in question . . . The conflicting urges to both throw himself at Avery's feet and pack up his car and leave town were equally strong and terrifying.

He needed to call Avery after his shift to explain the Abe

thing once and for all, but he was sore and stunk like sweat and smoke. He went home and showered, then collapsed into his bed. The next thing he knew, fourteen hours had passed, the sun was up, and he had another twelve-hour shift starting at the station.

When he finally found a minute to call Avery, it felt like ages since they'd been online, and Linc half expected Avery to ignore him or pick up the phone and hurl accusations that Linc definitely deserved. So, of course, Avery answered the phone with a cheery "Hey there!" Linc didn't deserve that simple kindness.

"Hey. Um. How you been?"

"Good. I'm just between meetings. Going to see Mr. Graves at the equipment rental. What's up?"

Linc sighed. Now was not the time to admit his creepy misstep. "Nothing. Just wanted to know what you were up to." Yeah. Smooth. "Maybe I could come over later?" If he hoped to be Avery's friend, better to have the awkward conversations face-to-face anyway. He'd tell Avery, and they'd laugh about it and then move on.

"Oh." Avery's voice brightened instantly. "Yeah, that would be awesome. I could make us dinner. How do you feel about chard?"

"Like a barbecue?"

Avery laughed. "Not really. Maybe you could grill it. I'm not sure. I could look it up? I— Oh, shit. I'm going to be late. I'll see you tonight?"

"Yeah." Linc smiled over the phone. Maybe Avery would understand. Abe wasn't that big of a deal. Not like the other things Linc wasn't ready to talk about. "See you, then."

Linc had spent a lot of time moving. He'd worked odd jobs, never staying anywhere more than six months at a time. At first, he'd worried the police might catch up with him, and make him testify. But his dad pled guilty, skipping the need for a trial.

Nevertheless, all the moving around, even in the years after, meant his social life took a hit. Making friends was hard when you were always the new guy, and practically, being a closeted drifter meant his love life was nonexistent aside from rare hookups with strangers he never saw again. He'd been okay with that for a long time.

Which was why he had to salvage this growing thing with Avery if he could. Avery, who was queer and who might be patient enough to wait as Linc struggled through his identity. He'd like to get the chance to run his fingers through Avery's glowing ember hair and suck on his bright pink bottom lip.

He stuffed that thought aside. Avery might not speak to him again after tonight. Better to not get ahead of himself.

Linc knocked on Avery's apartment door. When he got no reply, he tried the knob, and the door swung open.

"Hello?" he called from the top of the stairs.

Nothing.

"Avery?"

He made his way down to the small entranceway that opened into the kitchen. The lights were out, the TV off.

"Avery?"

The thump of feet running up the hall broke the silence. Linc turned just in time to catch a glimpse of Avery's pale legs in striped boxers before he disappeared through the bathroom door, slamming it shut behind him.

"Av—" The sound of vomiting cut off his question. Instinctually, he gripped the counter as his body threatened to run away. The choked gagging sounds from the bathroom continued, punctuated periodically by heaving gasps.

When quiet filled the apartment again, Linc waited, but Avery didn't come out. Linc glanced at the door. He should go. But he needed to make sure Avery was okay.

The toilet flushed, and the door swung open with a gentle creak, but thirty seconds later, Avery still hadn't reappeared.

Linc approached the bathroom. The smell of bile made his

stomach roll. As he entered, Avery was on his knees near the sink, head pressed to the floor. Linc was beside him in a second.

"Avery?" He put a palm on Avery's shoulder, and Avery hissed and shifted, like he might try to crawl away, except he had nowhere to go.

"Hey. Hey," Linc said. Avery curled in tighter on himself like a turtle. "What's wrong?"

He was dressed only in a faded blue T-shirt and his boxers. His body was totally rigid under the thin cotton.

"Migraine," Avery gasped. He moved slowly, like every muscle hurt.

"What can I do?"

"Stop." Avery's voice was whisper thin.

"Stop?"

"Stop breathing so loud." He groped at the vanity, and Linc slipped an arm under his shoulder to help get him up. The breathing thing took care of itself, because the wet putty color of Avery's face trapped the air in Linc's chest.

"Okay. Okay." How was he supposed to help if he couldn't speak? He'd never known anyone who got migraines. Not like this.

Avery lurched away from him, stumbling back to the toilet and retching again. His spine bowed, and his muscles bunched.

When Avery was left gasping over the bowl, Linc helped him up again, half carrying him down the hall.

"What do you need?"

"Meds. Above the sink."

This Linc could do. He helped Avery back to bed, Avery's eyes squeezed tight the whole time.

Fortunately, the medicine cabinet over the bathroom sink only had one prescription bottle, half-hidden behind all kinds of weird supplements that Linc had never seen before with names like *Power* and *Peace*. He didn't spend much time considering those, though, instead taking the pill he needed and filling a glass of water before he went back down the hall.

Avery's eyes were still shut, and Linc was afraid to say anything and make the migraine worse. He put the pill in Avery's palm and set the cup between the fingers of his other hand.

"I'll just throw the water up again." Avery slipped the tablet between his pasty lips, and Linc winced at the crunching sound as Avery chewed it and swallowed hard.

"Can I do anything else?" Linc asked, but Avery moved very slowly, until his back was to him.

Which was how Linc found himself all alone in Avery's apartment. He was too worried Avery might choke on his own puke, or stop breathing altogether, to leave. Avery's phone was on the counter, and Linc tried to get the number for Avery's aunt off of it, but it was password protected.

Linc used his own phone to look up treatments for migraines online, but the remedies were pretty much the ones he already knew. Quiet. Dark. Rest. Hydration, if water could be kept down. Prescription medications could help sometimes.

Nothing to do but wait.

Eventually, the battery on his phone died, and the sun started to set. Avery was still sleeping. Linc should leave. In some ways, he should be grateful. He'd been spared his awkward conversation for another day.

The bedroom door opened. Linc tensed, waiting for another round of "run and puke," but it didn't come. Instead, Avery stood silently in the hallway, one hand in his rumpled hair. He'd pulled on a pair of gray sweats that still matched the color of his skin, and he had a ragged blanket wrapped around his shoulders.

"Hey," Linc said, sitting up on the couch. "Feeling better?"

Avery's face was shadowed and hard to see clearly, which made Linc realize he'd been sitting in the dark. He hadn't turned a lamp on in case Avery came out of his room, but between the late hour and the basement apartment's few small windows, the natural light still managing to seep in was thin.

"Uncle Theo?" Avery said, his voice rough.

Linc frowned. "No. It's . . . It's Linc."

Avery padded forward. He didn't even acknowledge Linc had spoken. He came to stand at the side of the couch. His eyes were barely open, his mouth slack.

"Do you need something? Glass of water?" Linc asked.

Avery sat down silently, pulling the blanket tighter around his shoulders. His hair was mashed down on one side, and Linc nearly reached out to straighten it, but then Avery tipped over to the side. Suddenly, his head was in Linc's lap as he snuggled down like a puppy finding the best place to nap.

"I'm glad you're here."

"Um." Linc sat there, arms raised, like Avery might burn him if he put them down. Avery sighed, his whole body going soft against Linc's, and he started to snore gently.

"Okay . . . " Linc glanced around the darkened room. He had no way to escape, not without waking Avery, and he had no idea what to say, or how to explain what he'd been doing, camped out in the living room while Avery suffered silently down the hall.

Looked like he had a few awkward conversations in his future.

10

$\mathcal{A}$ very came back to functionality and general awareness like he was swimming backward up a garden hose. Man, what a bad one. He'd felt the migraine coming on just after lunch and let Uncle Theo know he was heading home. By the time he reached his car, the auras started. Before he'd gotten home and out of the daylight, the orbs in his vision were so intense he could barely get his apartment door open.

Somewhere along the way, he'd thrown up. He could taste it in the back of his throat. Hopefully, he'd made it to the bathroom this time. But he'd also managed to take one of the fast-acting pills and keep it down, if the bitter residue crushed between his molars was any indication.

The pain in his head was gone, though, mostly, which left him with the general sensation of having been hit by a school bus and then stepped on by every member of the Power Sound of the South. He was warm, though. Comfortable. His cheek was resting on . . . not his pillow. Something too firm for that. And something heavy was draped over his midsection.

He opened his eyes. On the TV, two actors carried out a scene. He flinched at the flashing lights, but the migraine had settled and did not rear back to life.

Avery blinked, taking stock. Coming back was always a slow process. But honestly, given how he'd been prepared for his eyeballs to burst and his ears to start bleeding at any moment not that long ago, he felt pretty okay.

Except then he realized he couldn't hear a word the actors were saying.

Not a single thing. Their lips were moving, and Avery could hear none of it.

"Oh my God!" He pushed himself up, flailing and rolling.

"Whoa!"

"Oh my God!" He flopped over, tumbling to the floor. He was scrambling back to his feet in a second.

"Avery?"

"I can't—" He put his hands over his ears. "I can't—"

"What's going on?"

"I can't hear them. I can't hear!" He turned and—

Linc stood there in his SFD T-shirt. His eyes were wide and scared, his hands out like he was ready to tackle Avery if needed.

"What's going on?" he asked.

Avery pointed at the screen, gasping. "I can't—I can't hear what they're saying." The doctors said he shouldn't be worried about side effects with his migraines, but they didn't know. They'd never felt the pressure. Never heard the ringing that said the bomb in his brain was about to detonate at any second.

"I can't—I can't—" He was hyperventilating.

"Hey. Hey. It's okay." Linc wrapped his big arms around Avery and held him close.

"I can't hear." Tears pricked in the corners of his eyes.

The shoulder under his cheek rumbled with laughter, and Linc's fingers tunneled into the hair at the nape of Avery's neck, massaging at the bottom of his skull.

"Can you hear me?" From this angle, Linc's voice was deeper than usual.

Avery blinked. "What?"

"You can hear me, right?"

"I—" He pushed himself up so he could see Linc's face. "Yes."

"So . . ." Linc smiled widely. "Is it possible you're okay and I muted the TV?"

Avery gasped. "I—you—" He glanced at the TV where the actors were still mouthing their lines. "But why would you do that?"

"Because I didn't want to wake you up?"

Avery slumped back onto the sofa, burying his face in his hands. "Oh my God."

"Are you okay?" Linc was next to him in a second, his big hand on Avery's back. The warm pressure was helpful, giving him something else to focus on while his heartbeat and breathing came back into orbit. Except then he remembered the warm arm around him, holding him close until his skull stopped trying to drill holes in his brain.

He almost shot off the couch again. "We were cuddling!" And they were sitting in the dark. "Why are there no lights on?"

"You were—" Linc pulled his hand back, rubbing his palms over his knees. "You were in pretty bad shape. I was trying to avoid bright lights and loud noises."

"So, you've been sitting here for—" He glanced at the display on the microwave. "Oh my God, it's after nine. How long have you been here? What are you even doing here in the first place?"

"I—" Linc grunted and leaned over toward the small light that sat on an end table. "Can I?"

"Yeah."

The light clicked. Linc's cheeks were flushed, and a day's growth of stubble shadowed his chin.

Avery smacked his lips and remembered his mouth still tasted like barf. He rose to get a glass of water, then froze, slow horror spinning him back to Linc.

"Did you have to clean up my puke?"

Linc ran a hand over his hair. "No, you made it to the bathroom."

"Oh man." He covered his face with his hands again.

"What? It's fine."

"No, it isn't." He remembered a little now. Linc's phone call that morning. The warm, buzzy feeling at the thought of seeing him again. Linc's gentle hands as Avery had tried to crawl out of the bathroom because he couldn't get his muscles to pull him upright again after throwing up his lunch, probably most of his breakfast, and half his stomach lining. Linc tucking him into bed —oh God, he'd tucked Avery in like a child.

"How did I end up in your lap?"

Linc let out a soft laugh, his eyes skipping away for a second. "You kind of just did? You came out of the bedroom, you were— I don't know. I'm not sure you were actually awake."

"The meds make me foggy." Better than hemorrhaging out his eyeballs, but it did tend to lead to some awkward situations. Like forgetting "mute" was a thing TVs did. Or waking up with his head mere inches from Linc's dick without so much as a "How's your day been?" first. "I'm really sorry. About the forced cuddling."

Linc's smile widened. "It's okay. I'm glad you're feeling better."

They stared at each other for a minute. Avery licked his lips, and Linc followed the motion before glancing away again and sinking down on the couch.

"Can I get you something to drink?" Avery said.

"Water's fine."

"I have beer."

Linc paused. "You do?"

"Yeah." He shrugged, trying to look cool about it.

"You didn't have to."

"I wanted to." Good thing the migraine had passed, because his face was flaming, and the heat and the pain would not have been a good combination. But he *had* wanted to because he wanted to see Linc again. Wanted him to be comfortable here. The desire was pathetically small, but he needed to know he had something to offer.

"Oh, I got us a date," Linc said as Avery went to the fridge, making him bobble the beer.

"What?"

Linc cleared his throat. "Not like that. My coworker, Vasquez —she and her girlfriend said they'd be up to hang out sometime. Maybe go find a bar where people don't corner you on the way back from the toilet."

Avery swallowed. "Is that the firefighter who was here the day you came?"

"Yeah."

"Oh." He handed Linc the beer.

"Something wrong?"

He had no delicate way to say this. "She's kind of intimidating."

Linc chuckled. "I'll protect you, Red. Don't you worry about that."

———

"You didn't pick him up?" Vasquez said over her rum and coke.

Linc snorted. "Why would I do that?"

"Maybe he doesn't know how to get here?"

"He's lived here for years."

Wanda's eyes widened. "You're dating a townie?"

Vasquez elbowed her gently. "I told you they weren't dating."

For the twentieth time since he'd taken Vasquez up on her offer to get together, Linc regretted the choices he'd made since coming to Seacroft.

An increasingly familiar redhead appeared in the bar's doorway.

Well, except that choice. After the migraine incident, Linc's brain was full of things he shouldn't want to remember. The soft hair in his fingers, the warmth of Avery's body curled up against Linc on the couch. He'd enjoyed that a lot. Far more than he had any right to.

"Hey, guys!" Avery waved, eyes darting around them like a frightened squirrel. Linc shifted in the booth to give him a safe place to sit, away from Vasquez's toothy smile.

"Hey, Avery, nice to see you again," she said and introduced Wanda. She was not at all what Linc expected: blonde, with big glasses embellished with pink rhinestones. She wore a floral print dress and strappy sandals, while Vasquez sat next to her in a T-shirt that said *I Can Do It Bleeding*.

"It's nice to meet you," Avery said. He folded his hands on the table in front of him like a student waiting for the lesson to start. So tempting to poke him in the ribs, make him squirm and get him to relax, but as aware as Linc was of Avery, he was even more conscious of Vasquez's eyes on him as they did the small-talk thing.

"So how did you guys meet?" Wanda said.

"Oh, we're not together," Avery said. Linc risked a glance at Vasquez, who raised her eyebrows at him, inviting him to say something.

His toes curled in his shoes.

"But you still met," Wanda said.

"Hmm?"

Linc groaned inwardly. Of all the times for Avery to finally find a way to control his endless stream of words, it had to be now?

He leaned in to whisper low in Avery's ear. "I can't actually tell her how we met. We're not allowed to talk about callouts."

Avery swung his head, his mouth so close to Linc's cheek that breath puffed over his skin. "Callouts?"

"It violates privacy laws for me to talk about how you can't be left alone in the kitchen."

Avery sat back just enough for his green eyes came into focus. "Oh." The eyes widened. "Oh!" He turned back to Vasquez and Wanda. "I set a sweet potato on fire in the microwave and Linc saved me."

Vasquez choked on her drink.

"You okay?" Linc asked sweetly.

"Mm-hmm." She licked her lips. "That's exactly how I remember it too."

Wanda laughed. "Linc says you grew up here?"

"Yeah." Avery cleared his throat. "Should we get some drinks?"

Wanda slid out of her seat. "We have to order at the bar. I'll go with you."

Avery cast a nervous glance at Linc, but what did he want him to do? The bar, called Fitz's, was one Linc had previously dismissed as being too fussy to bother. Truly, they had way too many different kinds of beer on tap, but it also didn't contain the kind of lowlife his dad or Derek might call a friend. And no one had given Vasquez and Wanda a second look when they'd walked in hand in hand, so Linc figured it must be okay.

"He's cute," Vasquez said when Avery and Wanda were out of earshot.

Linc sighed. "We're not together."

"I wasn't implying you were. But first off—" Vasquez ticked points on her fingers, "—he's cute. That's not an opinion, that's a fact. They put faces like his in Apple ads. Second, I don't know for sure how you swing, but if you were even the littlest bit not straight, he'd be a good choice. And lastly, as Seacroft's resident bisexual, I assume everyone is queer by default until they tell me otherwise. So far, you have neither confirmed nor denied."

Linc scanned the room. The place wasn't busy, in part because they'd decided to come on a Wednesday when he and

Vasquez were between shifts. Also, Wednesday was a very un-date night, which seemed important.

"So you're telling me most of the people here are bi?" he said.

Vasquez's glass was mostly empty, but she snorted into her ice. "Oh, hell no. A town like this, people practically wear their heterosexuality on their sleeve."

Avery returned. He and Wanda both had two sets of drinks. Wanda set the fresh rum and coke in front of Vasquez and kissed her cheek. Avery set a beer in front of Linc. No kiss, which bugged Linc more than it should.

"Wanda works for a tech start-up in Atlanta!" Avery said enthusiastically. "They've done two funding rounds this year!"

Linc sipped on his beer, forcing himself not to wrinkle his nose. The beer Avery brought was darker than Linc usually liked and tasted like grapefruit. He had no idea what it was, just like he had no idea if funding rounds were a good thing.

"They make an app that converts recipes into grocery lists. Isn't that cool?"

Linc sipped another mouthful of the bitter beer. That would sound cool if he cooked. Or shopped.

"We're working on expanding into nutrition tracking."

"Should we let the two of you chat?" Vasquez scowled. "Scott and I can go play some pool."

Wanda shoved at her playfully. "Ronnie, don't be jealous. You'll get wrinkles."

Vasquez gasped. "You bitch."

Avery's glass clanked down on the table, splashing liquid over the sides. "Your name is Ronnie?"

Vasquez saluted him. "Veronica Maria Vasquez. But my friends call me Ronnie."

"I call you Vasquez," Linc said.

She winked at him. "You sure do, Scott."

"Avery's an accountant," Wanda said.

"Is that right?" Vasquez leaned in. "You enjoy that? Got any good stories? Someone cooking the books? Carrying off Grandma's life savings?"

"Oh, um . . . " Avery glanced down at his shoes.

"Back off, baby," Wanda said. Linc flinched. If he ever thought about calling Vasquez "baby," he'd have twenty seconds to live.

From Wanda, Vasquez was totally unfazed. "Back off? Why?"

"Because you're intimidating when you meet new people."

"What? I'm not intimidating." Vasquez pouted. "You want intimidating, you should meet Wanda's mom. The first time I went over to her house for a family dinner was like supper at the CIA."

Wanda laughed. "My mom's a corporate litigator."

"You'd think I was trying to steal her daughter's identity."

"And instead you stole my heart." Wanda giggled until Vasquez kissed her. The gesture was completely at odds with Vasquez's hard-ass persona at the station. Also weird they were so comfortable with PDA when Linc wouldn't even admit how much he wanted—

Shit. Maybe getting together like this was a bad idea. He'd only meant to find something fun and safe for him and Avery to do, but he felt like Vasquez was turning the whole thing into an object lesson about how safe it truly could be. Literally no one cared as she and Wanda nuzzled at each other.

For his part, Avery was watching Wanda and Vasquez closely. One corner of his lip was stuck beneath his teeth and his eyes were wide. The emotions on his face were always plain to anyone who bothered to look, but these made Linc's chest hurt. Desire washed through Avery's eyes, but not in the creepy horny way guys got when they watched two women kissing. More like . . . want. Longing. Like he wanted someone to bury their face in his neck the way Wanda was doing with Vasquez right now.

Double shit.

Linc turned back to his grapefruit beer before Avery's eyes could meet his. He didn't want to be the next person Avery saw after all those feelings . . . except he did. So much it made him ache. Damn Vasquez for putting the idea in his head.

———

The situation got worse two days later, when Linc—or, actually, Abe—and Avery were back in the Winterlands. Avery blasted the zombie troll with a blue-orange fireball that consumed it.

"What the hell was that?"

"I played a couple trials on my own the last few days. Learned some new spells."

"You played without me?" He shouldn't get so worked up about it. Avery didn't owe Abe anything. No player etiquette said they needed to wait for each other. But, still, Linc was weirdly annoyed that Avery would be alone long enough to learn these new tricks. Did he have no other friends to spend time with? Linc should have found a way to see him again.

"You've been busy. And you kind of disappeared on me last time. Was that an air raid drill?"

"Oh yeah. Sorry about that. Didn't realize it would be so loud on your end." Linc's teasing outrage died. What was he supposed to say without giving himself away? He should have said something by now. The longer he didn't, the more he risked making something small into a bigger deal. But Avery kept up his happy chatter, telling Linc all about the spells he'd learned. Linc didn't get an opportunity to say anything before they were already in the Winterlands.

They reached the top of the mountain, and the game zoomed back out to a map, asking if they'd like to proceed to the Diamond Mine or the Crystal Pass.

"What do you think?" Avery said.

Tell him. Tell him.

Except how was he going to tell him now? *Hey, I know you think I'm some online stranger, but surprise! I'm your new friend. I just didn't think you'd care, so I didn't tell you before. Also, I might be into you, maybe, but only if you can handle that we can't be together like that in public, even though everyone thinks we're together anyway.*

He was fucked. And he'd done it to himself.

"Abe?"

Linc's throat was dry, but he swallowed hard. "Avery, I—"

"Ohhhhh . . ."

The low moan echoed up the hall and set Linc's teeth on edge. He hadn't seen much of Jordan since their conversation the morning after his birthday, partially because Linc was working and partly because he suspected Jordan had moved his sexual escapades to wherever Chelsea lived.

"Ohhhh . . ."

But apparently the reprieve was over, and the timing could not be worse.

"What was that?" Avery said.

Heat spread over the back of Linc's neck. "You heard that?"

"Yes. Yeah. Just like that." Chelsea's words were so clear they might as well be coming from inside Linc's bedroom.

"Is . . . Is someone there?" Avery asked.

Linc exhaled forcefully. He could explain this without coming off as some internet weirdo who played games online with strangers while his roommate had orgies in the next room. Right?

"It's the neighbors," he said. "Newlyweds."

Avery gasped. "It's not even dark out."

Linc buried his face in his hands. Down the hall, the distinct sound of springs squeaking sang out, punctuated by male groans and a female repeating, "Do it," over and over.

"When the mood strikes, right?" He tried to laugh, but it came out sounding forced.

"I guess so . . . " Avery sounded uncertain. Linc nearly teased him for it. Hadn't he ever had a little afternoon delight?

Except what if he hadn't? *Oh, fuck.* Linc's dick perked to life like it had been asleep for a hundred years.

"Do it. Do it. So good. Do it," Chelsea chanted.

Avery snorted. "They sound like a sports ad."

Linc couldn't speak. He was picturing Avery's freckly white skin, laid out for him. Big, wide eyes looking at him so trustingly. Innocently. Like he'd never been touched ever, not even in the afternoon.

"Oh fuck," Linc said.

"Abe?"

Double fuck. He shouldn't be thinking about Avery like that, especially not when Avery thought he was someone else.

"I have to go."

"What? We just got started."

"Sorry. There's a, uh, a thing I have to do. I forgot about it."

He and Avery—along with Jordan and Chelsea—were all fucked, in one way or another, but only Linc was going to pay for it.

11

The suits were back. Avery watched from his desk as they talked to Uncle Theo. They'd been there for almost an hour. Every so often, one of them would pull a piece of paper from a briefcase and slide it across Theo's desk. Each time, Avery shivered at an imaginary nails-on-a-chalkboard sound.

"Who do you think they are?" Meredith whispered.

Avery chewed on his lip. Bankers. Lawyers.

He froze.

Buyers?

What if Uncle Theo was trying to sell the business before it went under?

He smiled at Meredith and shrugged. She eyed him—she always knew when he wasn't quite telling the truth—but turned back to her desk and the solitaire game on her computer.

They were so screwed.

His phone rang. He was so busy staring holes in the back of the suit jackets in Theo's office he nearly threw it on the ground before answering. "Hello?"

"Hey. Is this Avery?" a woman's voice said.

He straightened. "It is."

"Oh, great. It's Wanda. Do you have time to talk? Privately?"

He glanced at Uncle Theo. With no way to resolve that situation quickly, he put his hand over his phone and whispered to Meredith, "I'll be right back."

"Bring me a coffee with lots of cream," she said.

He left the office and walked out onto the street. "What's up?"

Wanda's voice was perky. "It was really great to meet you and Linc the other day. You guys are a lot of fun together."

"Oh, we're not—I mean. Linc and I aren't—"

"Oh, no." She laughed. "I didn't mean it like that. Just that we had a good time. With you. Both of you."

He relaxed as he crossed the street to the diner for coffee. "Oh. Yeah. You guys too."

"Are you working today?"

"Yeah." He glanced back at the storefront Uncle Theo rented more than twenty years ago to house his business. Would the new buyers let them stay there? Would they expect Uncle Theo and Aunt Brenda to move to be closer to some kind of corporate head office? Would Avery like working in a big office? There'd be more people to talk to, but they wouldn't be obligated by familial commitments to listen to anything Avery had to say. Not that Uncle Theo paid much attention these days, but Meredith was always happy to lend an ear as he babbled about his ideas.

"So, listen," Wanda said. "We were talking today. The company has expanded a lot."

"Your company? The app company?"

"Yeah. Heath, the founder, he's a really smart guy. He's so passionate about helping people eat better, you know?"

"Okay?"

"Heath's a great entrepreneur. He's so awesome at meeting people and sharing his vision. But he sucks at the details, you know?"

"Not really." Avery was all about the details.

"Exactly. We need some help, as we get bigger. Someone to manage the numbers. Heath's all about the ideas, and I handle the development, but we need someone to do the reporting, keep the books, that kind of thing. I thought you might be interested."

He hiccupped on a gasp. "Are you—" He swallowed. "Are you headhunting me?"

She laughed like he'd said the funniest thing in the world. "Well, I'm telling you we might have a job opening for someone with your skill set. You'd have to apply, just like everyone else, but I really liked talking to you the other night. I'd put in a good word for you with Heath."

She totally *was* headhunting him. Wait till Uncle Theo heard about this!

He stopped, and his gaze toward the office turned guilty.

"I can't," he said, pulling open the diner door.

"Oh." Wanda sounded disappointed.

"I think I told you I work for my uncle." He rubbed a hand over the back of his neck.

"Yeah, but—"

"I just—now's not a good time." Give it a couple months, when the firm had been absorbed into some big accounting company slowly turning Avery into a soulless cubicle drone. But right now? He couldn't leave while he still had a chance to save the firm.

"I'm sorry," Wanda said. "I hope I didn't make this awkward. I thought—"

"Yeah. Of course. No problem. Hopefully we can still hang out." In the course of the last few weeks, his social circle had tripled, assuming not taking this job didn't totally botch his relationship with Wanda and Vasquez. Oh, God. What if it got awkward with Linc? He and Vasquez worked together. Could the four of them still be friends? He couldn't lose Linc over something like this.

Not that Linc was even his to lose. Not really.

He ordered coffees as Wanda said, "Listen. Don't say no right now, okay? We want someone to start soon, but it doesn't have to be tomorrow. Just think about it. I'll text you a link to the job description."

He should say no. Uncle Theo and Aunt Brenda had done everything for him.

"Yeah. Sure."

"Great. It's awesome. You'll love it, I promise."

They hung up as Avery headed back into the office.

"Where did you go?" Uncle Theo was standing at his desk. No sign of his suited visitors.

Avery lifted the two cups. "Coffee break." He winced when he realized he hadn't bought one for his uncle.

Theo pursed his lips together. "Anything new come in while I was in my meeting?" he asked Meredith. She glanced at her computer screen, which still showed her solitaire game, and glumly shook her head.

"Ah, well. Maybe tomorrow, huh?" He pulled his glasses off his face and wiped them on his tie.

Avery bristled. He didn't want Meredith to get in trouble, but things had to be pretty bad for Uncle Theo to just turn away when she obviously wasn't working.

"Can I talk to you?" Avery said.

His uncle smiled blandly. "Of course."

Avery rarely got angry, but agitation sparked along his nerves as he followed Theo back to his office.

"Who were those people?" he asked as he closed the door.

"Who?" Uncle Theo said.

Avery's eyes bugged. "Who do you think I mean? The two suits. They've been here twice now."

His lips thinned. "I'm not ready to talk about that."

"Not ready?" Avery's voice rose. He didn't mean to, but Uncle Theo was killing the business and he didn't seem to care.

"You know things have been tough lately."

Avery snorted. "You could say that."

"So we're making some changes."

"You're finally going to listen to me?"

He sighed. "In a manner of speaking."

That didn't exactly sound like a yes. "What does that mean?"

"I hope you understand I've worked hard for what we have. It took me a long time to build up the business."

Impatience, along with the lingering anxiety from his phone call, made Avery twitchy. He and Theo kept having this conversation. Avery made suggestions and Uncle Theo talked about the good old days without ever actually listening. Avery had hoped he could help Uncle Theo see reason, but he had also hoped his parents would accept his sexuality. Maybe hope wasn't enough.

"The business is dying. We need to do something now. How much longer are you going to be able to keep paying Meredith?" He'd never spelled it out quite like that. If Uncle Theo wouldn't change for him, maybe he'd change to save Meredith's job.

"It might still be—"

"It's not a dip! We're not going to get better if something doesn't change. Why won't you listen to me?" Wanda would listen to him. He should tell Uncle Theo he'd been headhunted.

"Sometimes change is difficult."

It could be. He didn't know what it would be like, working somewhere else, but if he was valued there, if he could make suggestions and be heard, then maybe it was time.

"I applied for another job," he blurted.

"Oh." Uncle Theo leaned back in his chair like Avery had punched him, which was pretty much how Avery felt too. As soon as the words were out of his mouth, he regretted them.

"Uncle Theo, I—"

"It's fine. It's what I told you to do, isn't it? A young man like you. Understandable you'd want to try somewhere else. A sleepy place like this can't hold much interest long-term."

He wanted to cry. Or throw up. Or both. He'd give himself another migraine, but maybe he deserved that. "I'm sorry."

His uncle nodded. "Just an application for now, right? Let's not tell your aunt until it's official, okay?"

Oh, God. Aunt Brenda. She'd be heartbroken. First he'd moved out. Now he was going to quit his job.

"I might not get it," he said quietly.

Uncle Theo shook his head. "You will. You were always too smart for this place."

Avery spun and left the office before he could hurt either of them more.

Meredith was watching from her desk. Uncle Theo's office was pretty soundproof, but she'd know they'd been arguing. Avery couldn't meet her eyes. He packed up his laptop and headed out the door. As he hit the street, he pulled out his phone and dialed Linc's number.

"Hey." Linc's voice was deep and so welcome amid Avery's swirling thoughts.

"How's your day going?"

"Pretty shit-tastic, actually. You?"

Perfect. "What time does your shift end?"

"Nine."

"Meet me at Fitz's."

"What? Why?"

Avery gritted his teeth. "Because I think I just quit my job, and I need to get drunk."

———

Linc's day had been both epically shitty and longer than it had any right to be. His evening the day before started with two phone calls in quick succession from his sisters. First, Lilah tried to cajole him into going to their nephews' end-of-year school play. She played it off super casual, like he came down for visits all the time, but somehow that only upset him more.

Lacey called minutes later, like she'd been waiting for Lilah to hang up so she could have her turn. One of her kids wanted to know why she'd never mentioned "Grandpa" before. Linc hadn't known what to say there either and was left feeling more and more useless.

Then he'd gone to the station for his shift, only to discover the workout room had been TP'd. Vasquez and Brian lurked by the door, smothering grins.

"Must have been some kids playing a practical joke." Brian's belly shook over the top of his belt.

"You can clean it up though, right, rookie?" Vasquez winked. Linc glared and grumbled until the alarm sounded. The mess in the workout room was long forgotten because the next fourteen hours were the longest of Linc's life.

The apartment fire was two towns over. Ten stories, all of them ablaze. The local department was already on the scene, but the SFD had been called in for backup. People were scattered everywhere. Some of them looking dazed and scared, others sobbing and calling out for loved ones. Linc, Vasquez, and Brian could do nothing but keep throwing water on it with the other trucks and keep it contained to the structure and none of the other buildings or infrastructure in the area. These people's homes were gone, no matter what the firefighters did.

The station was quiet when they got back, but everything smelled like smoke and ash. Linc ached, and getting their gear checked and stowed seemed to take forever. After that, he was too tired to shower or do anything but fall into one of the bunks in the dorm room and crash. Except he'd only gotten about an hour of sleep before they went out on three consecutive false alarms. He'd been dead on his feet and crashed again for another hour, then woke when Avery called. "I need to get drunk."

He was already at Fitz's when Linc walked into the bar.

"Hey!" He waved, nearly knocking his pint glass over. For a guy who'd had a rough day, he looked awfully happy to see Linc, which pleased him so much more than it should have.

"Get started without me?"

Avery waved at the bartender and pointed at Linc. Another pint was delivered promptly.

"Cheers!" Avery held up his glass, and Linc clinked their pints together. Beer sloshed over the top of his, dribbling over his hands and Avery's too.

"Oops." Instead of wiping his hand on a napkin, or even his shirt, Avery stuck his beer-soaked fingers in his mouth one at a time, gazing absently around the room.

Linc exhaled and focused on taking his first sip without spilling because watching the finger that went between Avery's lips would only lead to bad—*so good*—things.

"So you quit your job?" Linc said.

Avery wrinkled his nose. "No. Maybe?" He rested his forehead on the bar, and Linc winced because bars in places like this were generally disgusting. Avery might as well be lying on the floor.

Linc poked at his cheek, watching it dimple under his fingernail. "Wanna talk about it?"

"Only if you tell me about your shitty day first."

So he did. More than he really should have, but he needed to talk to someone. The fire. The TP—which seemed so minor now, but he was fully sick of being treated like the newbie. The endless false alarms.

"Do people in this town not know we have to come out every time we get a call?"

Avery clinked his glass. "I'm glad you came out." His eyes widened. "Er . . . Not like that! You're not—I mean . . . " He

117

glanced around them, as if Derek or someone like him was waiting for any hint of gayness so he could pounce.

The only one pouncing on Avery would be Linc, especially when he got that flustered expression on his face.

Shut up. Shut up.

"So tell me what happened," he said.

It didn't seem all that bad. Avery's uncle sounded very old school. If Avery wanted to do something different, he should.

"You're young. If you need a change, that's not a bad thing."

Avery poked Linc's biceps. They were most of their way through a second pint. "I'm not that young. I can't be much younger than you. Why does everyone always think I'm a kid?"

"I'm twenty-six," Linc said.

"So am I."

Huh. Linc expected him to say twenty-two or twenty-three. But then, if he'd finished college and had already worked for his uncle for a few years, he couldn't be that young.

He clinked their glasses together again. "To twenty-six."

"I don't even know what I'm so upset about," Avery said, the words coming out in a breath. "I mean, he's my uncle. He's not my dad."

"Your dad's an asshole."

"So is yours. Theo's not. He's a good guy. He's just . . . He's stubborn, you know? But they've done everything for me. Everything."

Linc sighed. If his dad had been any kind of halfway decent human being, Linc would have done everything for him too. He'd waited for years for his old man to make a single good decision. In the end, the only one he made was pleading guilty when they'd arrested him and not dragging out a trial.

"Okay." Linc blew out a breath and flagged down the bartender. "Shitty day's done. Nothing left to do but drink."

Easy. So easy. The bar was busy but not crowded. No one bothered them. Linc told Avery about some of his noteworthy past jobs (*I dropped one of the boxes when we loaded it into the moving van and it was full of decapitated Barbie dolls*). Avery told Linc about the time he dressed as the Brave Little Toaster for Halloween (*I was in college. It was supposed to be ironic*). The bartender brought another round.

"I'm glad you called," Linc said.

"I'm glad you answered." Avery grinned. They faced each other, knees nearly touching. Avery had his elbow on the bar, head in his hand. He looked sleepy and happy, like he had waking up in Linc's lap after his migraine. Linc wanted to run his fingers through his red hair. Fuck, he wanted to kiss him. But not here. They couldn't do that here. And not while "Abe" was still between them.

"There's something I need to tell you." Yes. Now. He needed to get it off his chest, and then they'd be fine. Abe had been necessary when he didn't know Avery, when he'd needed a friend and didn't know if the red-headed stranger could be it. And now . . . now they were friends and maybe they could be more. Linc just had to tell Avery about Abe. Then they could kiss.

Avery sat up, green eyes blinking hard. "Oh, yeah?"

"You might not like it." *No.* This was a bad idea. He couldn't hurt Avery. Couldn't see the trust break on his face.

Avery's eyes clouded and slid beyond Linc's shoulder. Linc took another sip of his beer. Avery would understand. The Abe thing was barely even a big deal, wasn't it? Not like Linc was catfishing him or something. And then they would be okay and there could be kissing and other stuff. Oh, the other stuff. Linc probably shouldn't admit how much he wanted that.

One more big mouthful of beer and he was ready.

"Avery, I—"

Avery's face had gone pale, and he swayed on his barstool. His eyes were all droopy, but they focused intently on something across the room.

Linc started to turn, but Avery's hand shot out and buried itself in his shirt.

"Don't look," he hissed.

Linc leaned forward. "Don't look at what?"

Avery slid in so their knees bumped against each other. "Just. Do it slowly, okay?"

"I don't understand," Linc tried to whisper, but the bar was busy and the music loud. He was so close, the freckles on Avery's nose were blurring together.

"Turn around and look at him."

Their eyes met. Avery nodded seriously. Linc held his breath and gripped Avery's shoulder. "Okay. Slowly." He pushed around on his barstool. Avery's hand was still in his shirt, so he only got a quarter of the way. His own hand gripped Avery's arm, and he couldn't help letting his thumb brush over the soft skin above Avery's watch. He tried to smile reassuringly. "I'm not going to be weird, okay?"

Avery licked his lips, and you know what? Fuck it. Whoever was here, Linc didn't need to see. He could just go back to Avery's apartment and—

Avery let go and gave him a little push, so the stool spun the rest of the way on its own.

Linc scanned the crowd, but he didn't see anyone he knew.

"I don't—" He shook his head.

Avery's chin on his shoulder was a surprise. His breath in Linc's ear made him shiver.

"That guy."

Linc squinted, like that would help. "Who?"

A hand slithered along his ribs, then appeared on the other side of Linc's body and pointed in the direction of four men sitting around a table. Linc hadn't noticed them before.

"Which one?"

"The one with the hair." Avery slid in closer.

Of the four men seated at a table across the room, two were

dark-haired, two fairer. The one with the hair had to be the guy with the man-bun piled up on top of his head.

"Who is he?" Linc said as he turned back. His fists clenched. If that guy had hurt Avery before, even made him feel uncomfortable, Linc would not be okay with that.

Avery darted another nervous glance beyond Linc. "His name is Oliver."

The beer sloshed in Linc's veins as he looked Oliver up and down one more time. "I could take him."

Avery squeezed his knee and shushed him. "Someone will hear you." His hand on Linc's thigh was warm and soft.

"I could. Stupid little man-bun. I could totally take him."

"It's not like that." Avery rested his forehead on Linc's shoulder. "I maybe spent a month or two last year pretty sure we were into each other. Turned out it was only a one-way thing."

Linc stiffened. He put a hand over Avery's, but he didn't take his eyes off Oliver. "What happened?"

"Nothing. I mean—" He sighed. "I thought he felt something, he didn't. It was kind of awful, but the whole thing was my fault."

"He led you on?"

"No!" Avery unwound himself, and Linc missed the contact. "Just a misunderstanding. He was super nice, right up to the end."

"What happened at the end?" Linc's pulse thumped in his ears. Maybe he was going to have to talk to this guy after all.

"What? No. I ruined it. He was into someone else. The guy sitting next to him." He glanced away, putting his hands over his cheeks. "Can we change the subject?"

They could, but changing the subject didn't mean Linc would stop thinking about it. Oliver sat at his table, getting cozy with another guy, a few years older and built like a tank. Solid muscle and dark eyes were the first things Linc noticed. If he was the kind of guy Oliver was attracted to, then Oliver was a bastard for letting Avery think otherwise.

Oliver put his hand on the dark-eyed man's back, and his thumb swept up and down with casual affection, like it didn't matter who would see. The easy gesture was so unfair when Linc had been trying hard to keep some platonic distance between himself and Avery.

"Are you still interested in him?" he said.

Avery shook his head, while beer sloshed over the sides of his glass. "No. He's too old. I knew that then."

Linc wasn't. They were exactly the same age. They'd be so good together.

Avery did his best to make Oliver's arrival seem like no big deal, but his smiles weren't as bright, his gestures less animated. He held his beer between his hands instead of drinking it. The sight of him deflating, when they had been doing so well, made Linc finish the rest of his pint faster.

He checked over his shoulder again. Oliver had his head tipped back, laughing at something the other blond man was saying.

Avery's face was still sad. "I have to pee." He pushed himself off the stool, then frowned when Linc did the same. "What are you doing?"

Going with him? Trying to put the smile back on his face? Hooking up in a bathroom wasn't his favorite way to get busy, but for Avery, he'd do it.

Linc sat back down. "Nothing."

When Avery was gone, Linc finished his beer and ordered another one. He stared at Oliver. The unfairness thrummed beneath his skull. This guy was here, enjoying himself, showing off everything he had, while Linc couldn't get what he wanted.

He pushed off the stool, but instead of heading toward the bathroom, he weaved his way across the bar toward Oliver.

12

*W*hen he came out of the bathroom, Avery first noticed the two empty seats where he and Linc had been.

Avery scanned the space, but before he could find Linc, his eyes landed on Oliver. A year later, Avery's insides only shrank in embarrassment a little over what happened between them—which really wasn't anything at all. He'd meant what he'd said to Linc. Oliver really was too old for him. But though Oliver had been understanding, Avery couldn't help replaying the horror of that moment over and over, pointing out every single way he'd been so wrong about the situation.

But he didn't have time for that, because the next thing Avery saw was Linc, practically standing nose to nose with Oliver, an accusatory finger digging into his chest.

Avery moved through the crowded bar like he was on rocket roller skates.

"Hey!" As he approached them, he forced as much confident cheerfulness into his voice as he could.

Oliver's smile was the same genuine one he had always used with Avery. Last year, Avery had mistaken it for interest, when, really, he should have known it for the simple human decency that Oliver meant it as.

"Hey, Avery." Despite his bland friendliness, Oliver's eyes darted nervously to Linc, who was crowding way too much into his space.

"Big mistake." Linc swayed on his feet, and Avery's breath started to come quickly. He glanced at the men still seated at the table, watching this development with interest. Avery shook his head. He shouldn't have drunk so much. He didn't know the names of Oliver's friends, but he'd seen them before, back at Oliver's shop before he'd closed it. The blond one was watching them with sarcastic amusement twisted on his lips. The brown-haired man sitting next to him had the same nervous smile that Avery was pretty sure he was wearing. And on Oliver's other shoulder was the big one, the one with the buzz cut and the black eyes who was Oliver's boyfriend and who—Avery didn't doubt for a second—could crack a tree in half over his knee with the right motivation.

Motivation like Linc spoiling for a fight for no obvious reason.

Avery slipped an arm around Linc's waist. "Hey, buddy. Time to go."

"It's not right." Linc shook his head. His eyes were glassy, and his beautiful mouth was pressed into a firm line.

"I know," Avery said, but he didn't know. It didn't matter, though. What mattered was not adding to the Oliver wing of his personal hall of shame.

"Hi, Avery. Do you know this guy? Everything okay?" Oliver asked, because of course he would. Oliver would always be one of the nicest people Avery knew—hence his hopeless crush the year before.

"Yeah, fine. Guess we should have stopped before that last pint." He tried to communicate telepathically to Oliver to stop being so concerned and let them go already.

Linc's long arm settled around Avery's shoulders. "That's right." He pulled Avery close. "We're going home. Your loss, you jerk. I get to go home with him."

"Oh my God." Heat poured over Avery in an eruption. Was that what was going on? Linc somehow thought he was defending Avery's honor?

This was Avery's reward for being incapable of filtering a single thought before it went straight from his brain to his mouth.

"This is so awkward and amazing," the blond man behind Oliver said, then laughed when the brown-haired man beside him jabbed an elbow in his ribs.

"Can we call you a cab?" Oliver said, but Avery shook his head, already backing away.

"It's fine. We're fine. I'm—" He stumbled as he bumped into another patron. "Sorry." The man he'd run into looked bored, which was okay because the warmth of Linc's big body pressed against Avery's was slowly melting his brain. Not to mention the four sets of eyes on them meant Avery's joints and his heart felt like they were about to crumble to sand and pile all over the floor any minute now.

"He hurt you," Linc said fiercely in his ear.

Avery pulled him tighter, flashing one last apologetic smile at Oliver, hoping desperately he wasn't close enough to hear. "He didn't. It's fine. Let's go."

"I was trying to—" Linc lurched, like he might break away and go another round with Oliver.

"I know. You did an awesome job." He patted the hard width of Linc's chest.

"You deserve someone better." They were almost to the door. Avery fished his phone out of his pocket to call a cab. His apartment was close enough, but he couldn't make it that far dragging Linc with him.

"No, I don't." Being with someone like Oliver, who was smart and funny and so considerate—Avery couldn't imagine anything much better. He'd seen Oliver and his partner around town, and between that and local gossip, he knew they were disgustingly happy. But as far as boyfriend material went, Oliver was the prototype.

"No. Hey. Hey." They were outside, and Linc pulled him around, putting a hand on each of Avery's shoulders. "Trust me. You're going to find someone who sees how amazing you are, and that person is going to love you like crazy. So forget about that guy. His loss. He won't ever get to know you the way —" He blinked rapidly, gaze going off over Avery's right shoulder.

Avery stood on his tiptoes, leaning forward, desperately waiting for the end of the sentence. "The way what?"

Linc's face exploded in a ferocious sneeze that echoed down the street. He stumbled backward, shaking his head and laughing.

Avery slumped, letting the disappointment wash over him and cool his burning cheeks. "Are you going to remember this conversation in the morning?"

"Sure I am." Linc gave him a wobbly thumbs-up. "I'm drunk. I'm not wasted. I know the difference."

The cab arrived. Linc got in without *much* assistance. Avery gave the driver his address, and only realized he'd assumed Linc was coming back to his place as they pulled away from the curb. "Should we drop you off first?"

"No. I like it at your place better." Linc rested his head on the window. "You're too good for that guy."

Avery didn't reply. He was suddenly too tired and didn't want to deal with Linc's love guru routine anymore tonight.

"I'll get some blankets," Avery said as he let them into the apartment.

"Why?"

He sighed. He never minded having Linc crash at his place,

but he needed tonight to be over with. "I'll see you in the morning." He patted Linc's shoulder.

His breath caught as Linc reached up and snagged his hand, tangling their fingers together. "We can share the bed."

Still a little drunk, then.

"Fine. I'll take the couch."

"No."

Avery closed his eyes. "Please can we go to sleep? We both had a crappy day, you've had too much to drink, and I don't want to fight about this again."

"Who's fighting?" Linc grinned. "The bed is big enough for both of us. I know you only have one comforter." He tugged on his hand. "Come on."

And Avery, because he was tired, and because the sight of Oliver had reminded him how lonely he felt sometimes, and because Linc's hand around his warmed him from his palm all the way up his arm to his heart, followed him.

They both stripped down to their underwear and T-shirts. Avery did his best to look anywhere but at the hairs that curled on Linc's thighs, and how Linc filled out his shirt while Avery would only ever be bony and thin in his. They slid under the covers. The bed was more than big enough, because Avery rolled onto his side, facing away from Linc, and clung to the edge like a life raft.

"Good night," he said softly, unsurprised when the only answer was Linc's gentle snoring beside him. It vibrated over the mattress, keeping Avery awake for another hour.

———

Linc needed a moment to figure out where he was when he woke up. He was comfortable, warm without being hot, cozy under a blanket that wasn't his.

A body was wrapped around him: their legs tangled

together, arms around his stomach, and a heavy head tucked under his chin.

Morning wood pressed snuggly against his own, shifting as they breathed, rubbing softly together, making it tough to think.

He could unwind himself. Slide out, find his clothes, sneak away.

He could roll, trap Avery's soft body under him, and hump him awake so they could both enjoy themselves.

He could run his fingers through Avery's red hair and breathe him in while he was still asleep and unaware of the soft things in Linc's heart, even while his body hardened.

A shrill buzzing shattered the quiet room, and Avery rolled away from him in an instant, fumbling for the phone and shutting off the alarm. Linc turned onto his side, making sure to bunch enough blankets around his thighs to keep from embarrassing himself as the mattress lurched and Avery pulled up to his feet. He didn't say anything, and Linc kept his eyes half shut, listening to the soft sounds as Avery padded around the bedroom, appearing at the edge of Linc's hooded vision. His skin was white against the dark fabric of his T-shirt and his briefs, his ass perfect and round as he stood in front of the mirror opposite the bed. He scratched his chest and scrubbed fingers through his hair, and Linc's throat went dry with how much he wanted to touch him.

Avery left, which was a relief and a problem. Because Linc could palm himself, shuddering under the ache of his untended erection, and enjoy the sweet tension of being unable to do anything about it in someone else's bed. But then the water came on in the bathroom—the roaring whoosh of the shower—and Linc groaned at the sound of the shower curtain swishing open and shut, the mental image of Avery stripping out of the last of his clothes and stepping naked under the hot spray.

Linc wanted to be in there with him. He wanted it so much it scared him. He could picture the water sluicing over Avery's shoulders, rolling past his collarbones. The pink nipples, maybe the smattering of red hair on his chest. The soft spot under his belly button, where the hair darkened and narrowed while the water dripped farther down to—

His hips rocked into the mattress. He bit his lip and squeezed his balls, trying to stave off the desperate arousal swamping him. The flurry of thoughts and ideas, the things he could do, the sounds Avery would make if Linc was on his knees and Avery was in his mouth while the water—

"Oh, fuck." He was going to come in his shorts like he hadn't done since middle school. Then, when Avery came back from the shower, Linc would have to find a reason why he couldn't get out of bed.

Just as he was about to embarrass himself completely, the night before returned to him instead. The tall blond man with the confused frown as Linc stomped across the room like a messy giant on a mission.

"Oh, fuck," he said again, but different this time because he'd told the guy that Avery was too good for him. He'd been too drunk and too stupid to stop himself. Avery had been hurting, and Linc was too scared to be out the way Oliver and his boyfriend were. He could only protect Avery, even if it meant making an ass of himself in public with a stranger who probably thought he'd lost his mind.

He rolled, hiding his shame, but he was left facing the dresser when Avery came back. Linc should have said something. "Good morning" would do, to let Avery know he was awake. But Avery was naked except for the towel around his hips, his skin pink from the shower as he bent and opened a dresser drawer. He twisted and squirmed, pulling the clean briefs up, gifting Linc with a glimpse of his pink and freckled ass for a split second, before it was covered with dark cotton. Being this turned on was against the "just friends" bro code, but Linc was in a vulnerable spot. His dick ached between his legs again, and all he could do was silently lie there, pretending to sleep, while Avery slowly dressed himself.

Linc managed to get under control by the time a blender whined from the kitchen. Silently, he slid into his clothes from the night before. The gentle exertion brought back the smell of sweat in his shirt, the memory of the endless hours they'd spent trying to stop a fire that had already taken everything from so many people.

No wonder he'd been a mess.

Avery was pouring something green and chunky into a travel bottle when Linc entered the kitchen. Avery was in his work wardrobe: khakis, pressed shirt, his hair still damp and smooth on his head.

"I forgot, I have an early meeting with a client. Are you working today?" he asked as he gathered up papers off the dining room table and put them into his laptop bag.

"Tonight. Nine o'clock."

"You're welcome to stay here if you want. I'll probably be back at six," Avery said, still moving quickly. He nearly dropped the green shake bottle, but caught it again as he hopped on one foot to put on a shoe.

"Here." Linc took the bottle from him and pushed him toward the couch.

Avery flashed him a brief smile, before turning his attention to his laces. "I was thinking about making meatloaf tonight. Do you want to have dinner before you go to the station?"

"Sure. I might sleep for a bit this morning too." Avery's bed was a nice place to be. He gave himself a second to picture what waking up there more often would be like, with Avery pressed beside him.

"Okay." Avery did up his other shoe. "Then I'll buy extra potatoes and see you tonight." He hopped to his feet, planted a quick kiss on Linc's cheek, and went to the door.

Maybe he didn't notice what he'd done. The kiss had been so

fast, almost like a reflex. The natural extension of their cozy domestic scene.

Linc had noticed, though, and his head was full of thoughts of the way Avery smelled right before he woke up. The warm dry brush of Avery's lips on Linc's skin snapped something inside of him.

Avery was still babbling goodbyes, pulling the door open while juggling his bottle and his bag. Linc stalked toward him and slammed it shut again.

"What—" But Avery didn't get to finish before Linc turned and pressed him up against the door, fitting their mouths together instantly.

He should have been gentle. He should have asked if this was okay. Their shared orientation didn't mean Avery actually wanted this. His mouth was crooked and stiff, either confused or caught mid-sentence. Linc pulled back long enough to apologize, but Avery followed him, dropping his things to wrap himself around Linc's shoulders while his lips chased Linc's mouth before he could speak.

Good enough. Avery's kiss was the signal Linc needed to let go. He gripped Avery's hips, pushing him against the door, and Avery whimpered, hands tightening around Linc's neck to pull him closer.

The lust he'd felt in bed, temporarily banked, roared back to life. Linc slipped away, nipping at Avery's chin, sucking on the soft spot at the top of his throat. Avery's skin carried the tang of soap, and his breath caught as Linc ground against him. Tasting more of him would be so good. Get that shirt off and see if his chest was gently hairy the way Linc had been fantasizing about.

And so much more Linc wanted to do after that. He could be thirty seconds from dropping to his knees and mouthing Avery to hardness through his fly, and maybe another thirty seconds from Avery's dick in Linc's mouth while Avery pulled his hair and stared down at him in trust and adoration.

He stepped back, putting a palm over the front of his jeans, with no delusions of it making any difference to his modesty.

"What—" Avery was flushed. His hair was a mess, and his shirt was rumpled

"You should go to work." Just like that. Suddenly disheveled, so that everyone would know what Linc had done to him.

"But—"

"Go."

If Avery stayed any longer, Linc would strip him and take him down to the floor.

"You want me to leave? But this is my apartment." Avery's chest heaved under the checkered cotton of his shirt.

"Go," Linc said again.

"But you kissed me." Avery stared at him with wide eyes.

"Please," Linc rasped. "You need to go or take your clothes off. Those are your options right now."

Avery stepped back. Then his arms flailed as one of his feet skidded out from underneath him. A chunky green puddle oozed on the hardwood where his bottle had fallen. He scrambled, one hand on the doorknob. He made it through to the stairs, then back again as he snatched his laptop bag from the floor.

"I'll be—You'll—There's juice—Have a good day!"

The door slammed shut behind him. Linc stood with his eyes closed, listening to the sound of Avery's feet on the steps, then the exterior door closing. Only then did he stagger backwards, slumping down onto the couch and barely avoiding crushing the gaming headset left on one of the cushions.

Avery's saliva was drying on his chin. Linc thunked his head back against the wall.

That had been—

That had—

"Fuck."

He already knew he wouldn't be there when Avery got back.

13

*a*very—okay, it sucked to admit it—but Avery hadn't been kissed in a really long time. The incident with Oliver last year didn't count, since Avery had been the only one doing the kissing. But other than that? Years. Two of them, to be precise. He'd been on one date with one guy. At the end of the night, his date wanted to come in, and Avery was too embarrassed to admit he lived with his aunt and uncle, so they settled for making out in the guy's car.

Unfortunately, his date kissed like his tongue was a metal detector and he was checking for silver in Avery's fillings. The kiss ended abruptly when Avery jammed a finger against the gear stick. That wasn't a euphemism; he'd literally sprained a finger and had to wear a brace for a couple weeks, while lying to Aunt Brenda and Uncle Theo about what had happened. He hadn't gone out with that guy again, or anyone else.

The queer dating pool in Seacroft was tiny. He'd tried some of the apps, but so many guys online just wanted to talk about their fantasies of fucking a redhead or ignored him because he didn't have a six-pack and had stopped growing somewhere around five foot ten.

Linc would do great on the apps, with his abs and his scruffy jaw. And he definitely was a better kisser than Avery's last date. He kissed like he wanted to swallow Avery's soul, but at least he'd left the fillings alone.

The events of the day before only came back to him as he turned on his laptop. He was early, and the office was empty, but that left all the space available to fill with anxiety as the fight with Uncle Theo rattled around in his head.

The front door opened, and his uncle appeared, slowing as he saw Avery. The hesitation on his face made Avery's eyes sting.

"Good morning," Avery said.

"Morning." Uncle Theo smoothed his tie. Aunt Brenda gave it to him for Christmas a couple years ago. Avery's throat thickened at the thought of facing her the next time he went to the house. She'd ask a few specific questions, and within minutes, she'd know Avery had said he was leaving, despite the fact he'd barely decided himself. He hadn't even called Wanda back yet.

And Linc had kissed him. Avery didn't know what to do with any part of his life.

Uncle Theo smiled tightly and went into his office, shutting the door behind him. Avery exhaled slowly, planting a hand firmly on either side of his laptop. He glanced at the clock. Eight twenty-seven. Only eight hours and thirty-three minutes to go.

Meredith came in at nine. "How was your evening?" she asked with wide eyes, like she expected he'd spent the night sobbing into a bag of potato chips.

What would she say if he told her he'd woken up in the arms of a gorgeous man who'd tried to suck his face off before he left for work?

He'd also jerked off in the shower, so yeah, maybe better to keep it to himself.

"It was fine."

She nodded sympathetically. He stared at his laptop and focused on not grinning like a lunatic.

The morning was quiet. Too early in the month for many

deadlines from what few clients they had left. And the kiss with Linc left him agitated. If he went on a coffee run, the caffeine would have him vibrating through the floor by lunch hour.

And the whole time, Uncle Theo's presence loomed over his shoulder. The guilt pressed down on him like Linc had pressed him against the door, pinning him in place. Except he didn't want to be here. But at least he could do something about it, unlike, say, the heat simmering under his skin, tracing the path Linc's mouth had taken, reminding him of the pressure of Linc's hips against his.

Avery stood, rocking on his heels as his confidence fluttered. He stared at the spot on Uncle Theo's head that shone. Avery had watched it thin over the years. This man was the best thing he'd had in his life for a long time, him and Aunt Brenda. The least he could do was make a peace offering.

He knocked on the office door, heart in his throat.

"Yes?" Uncle Theo glanced up because even if he was angry, he still wouldn't shun Avery. He and Aunt Brenda had promised that from the day Avery had come to live with him. No matter what, they would be family.

"I'm still going to the job interview."

Theo nodded. "I understand."

"But I've decided I'll do the bachelor auction."

"The what?"

Avery's insides quivered. If his uncle had forgotten about the auction, then this olive branch would be as effective as one chopstick by itself. "The—the bachelor auction. The one for charity."

"Oh." Uncle Theo glanced down at his computer screen. "All right then."

"Good. I—you'll let them know?"

"I'll tell Brenda. She'll take care of it."

His apartment was empty when he got home. He was surprised how much he wasn't surprised. His disappointment was par for the course, though. One kiss and he was gone. Or had it been more than one? Where did kisses stop and start?

He called Linc's phone, but it went to voicemail, like his texts that evening and the next morning went unanswered.

———

And that was how you ended a romantic relationship before it even started and blew up a perfectly decent friendship in the process.

Linc didn't call Avery. Didn't look for him online. He worked any shift the chief would give him.

The ache in his chest consumed him, and he'd never felt so alone.

He and Brian and Vasquez were finishing breakfast in the staff lounge, which was basically a giant living room. Brian was on his laptop, clicking through screens. "Do you know how much a double stroller costs?"

Vasquez snorted. "Why would I? I'm not having kids. I like spending my money on rent and student loans instead."

Brian frowned. "You went to college?"

"A year of firefighting foundations and two years of para-medicine." She beamed. "How did you get a job here?"

"Back in my day, you answered the 'help wanted' ad."

"Shut up." She threw a paper napkin at him. "You're not ancient. You're not even a daddy yet."

"My wife calls me daddy."

"Oh my God, too much information. Scott, are you listening to this? Brian is oversharing again."

They both grinned at him, but at his scowl, their smiles faded.

"Oh," Vasquez said.

"Excuse me." Brian collected his plate and went to the dish-washer. "I need to go call Jess and see how her night was."

When Brian was gone, Vasquez shifted until they were hunched around one corner of the table. "Trouble in paradise?"

Linc sighed. "It's not like that."

"Yeah, yeah, you're not gay, he's not your boyfriend—"

"Would you keep your voice down?" He glanced at the doorway, but the station was quiet.

Vasquez rolled her eyes. "Sorry. Is it something else? You know I'm kidding about Sweet Potato, right?"

Linc chewed on his lip. The thing in his chest grated against his ribs. "I'm not out."

She nodded. "Kinda figured that."

"But I had a boyfriend once."

"It happens."

"My dad found us at a bar one night and beat the shit out of him."

She hissed. "And that's a good reason to set up shop in the closet."

He didn't need her validation. He'd held on to his fear for seven years. But now— "I kissed Avery. And then I ghosted him."

"Oh. Yeah, that's pretty bad too. Pretty stupid, actually."

He dropped his face in his hands. "I know." Avery had been hurt so much in his life, and Linc had been selfish enough to hurt him again.

"So what are you going to do about it?" Vasquez grabbed the last slice of bacon off his plate and popped it into her mouth.

He sighed. "Give him some space." Write a formal apology? He wasn't the best with words, but he'd literally kissed and ran, so, for Avery, he'd try.

"Oh, man. You have it bad." Vasquez winked.

"I do not." He did. So bad, and he wanted even more.

The alarm sounded.

"Come on, rookie."

Unfortunately, the plan to give Avery space was a spectacular failure. Seacroft was small, and suddenly Avery was everywhere.

At the supermarket. Linc was buying a week's worth of groceries for the fire station. Avery avoided eye contact and threw another bundle of celery into his cart.

At the diner. Jordan and Chelsea invited him out as some kind of peace offering. Of course Avery was also eating there, with his aunt and a balding man Linc had to assume was his uncle. Avery's aunt greeted him warmly. Avery mumbled hello and chatted with Chelsea instead.

At the dry cleaner's. The SFD was called in on an alarm that turned out to be a suspected chemical spill. The owner—who looked like he was about ninety—was out on the street corner waving his arms and telling everyone to stay back. Avery was also on the sidewalk, a dismayed expression on his face and three shirts on hangers in his hand. But by the time Linc did a preliminary walk-around and notified the neighboring store owners, Avery had disappeared.

And, finally, at the gym. They hadn't spoken in a week, though they'd somehow seen each other nearly every day. Avery walked in as Linc was finishing his second weight circuit and heading for a final cardio round on the treadmill. For the first time, Avery met his eyes. Relief bloomed in Linc's chest, then died again just as quickly when Avery slipped a pair of earphones in and walked past him.

Served him right. He focused on running, like he needed to focus on his job. And his sisters. Lacey called him twice the day before, and he hadn't had a chance to call her back. He was done moping. Time to get on with his life.

Except Avery stepped onto the treadmill right in front of his. The earbuds were still in, and he didn't glance backward as he set down his water bottle. Linc tried to look anywhere else. The TVs overhead, the guy at the front desk handing out towels. He watched the eighty-year-old man with skin like a deflated football doing chin ups like a Navy SEAL. But every time, his eyes went back to Avery.

At first, he admired the things he'd missed. The red hair. The pale skin. The determination in his spine as he set a brisk pace. Linc was on his cooldown, so he was only at five miles an hour. Avery started a bit faster and moved up quickly. He appeared intent on his run, so Linc admired the things he'd hardly let himself look at before. The shape of his calves kicking back with each stride. The bounce of his ass in his loose-fitting shorts. The flush creeping up the back of his neck as he started to sweat.

Fuck. Linc had to get out of here. His finger was on the button of his treadmill, ready to call it a day, when Avery missed his stride. One second, he was moving at seven or eight miles an hour, and then next his hands were lurching forward, grasping for the handles as the treadmill belt carried his feet out from under him. One, two stumbling steps and the orange soles of his shoes flew toward Linc.

He was off his own treadmill as Avery's chin smacked against the belt and on his knees before Avery finished hitting the carpeted floor.

———

Of course he fell. Of course. That's what he got for proving a point. He'd done his best not to think about Linc all week, which was hard because suddenly he was *everywhere.* The supermarket and the diner weren't a complete surprise—Seacroft had one place to shop and only a few decent places to eat. But what were the odds Avery's dry cleaner would initiate a natural disaster *and* the fire department would be the first people on scene for something like that?

Now he was at the gym. Avery realized avoiding Linc was impossible because they even shared a freaking gym membership. So he would prove it didn't matter. Avery could be the bigger person.

He put on his music and started the treadmill. But he couldn't shut his brain off. He was still mad. And yet behind that lurked all the things he tried not to want. Linc's mouth on his, the taste of him on Avery's tongue. The way he'd gone off on Oliver, even if he'd been wrong, when hardly anyone had ever stood up for Avery in his entire life. The firmness of his hands on Avery's shoulders as he'd told him Avery deserved someone who loved him back, and Avery had only been able to think how much he wished that person was Linc.

These thoughts tumbled through his brain as he ran. He cranked up the speed, trying to outrun them, but instead, he overstepped, kicked the plate at the front of the treadmill, and squawked as his groin pulled while his left foot slid back. His elbow banged on the rail, and his chin hit the belt. Avery smelled rubber and tasted blood as he unraveled onto the carpet, burning his knees.

"Are you okay?" Linc's hand was on Avery's back.

All Avery wanted to do was melt into the floor before his tears overflowed and he had to face Linc again. He'd been trying to be the bigger person, dammit, and instead he only proved what a disaster he was.

"Hey, Avery. Can you look at me?" Linc's voice was calm, his touch firm but gentle.

"I'm fine," Avery said.

"Did you cut yourself?" Linc's fingers were under his chin, lifting it up.

Avery blinked hard, holding back tears from the pain but mostly from the embarrassment. He tore his gaze away before it could connect with Linc's. People were watching. Some were coming toward them. They'd want to know what happened, but how was Avery supposed to explain he'd been running away from the memories of his friend-not-boyfriend who kissed him once and disappeared and who Avery was pretty sure he was half in love with anyway?

"I'm fine." He brushed away Linc's hand before it could touch his mouth, or his cheek, or stroke his shoulder while Linc told him everything would be okay.

He needed to get out.

"Avery—"

He pushed himself up to standing, ignoring the way one knee clicked and his elbow ached. He turned without so much as a thank-you.

"What happened?" a guy in a blue gym staff T-shirt asked. Avery waved him off and headed to the locker room, stopping at the fountain to rinse out his mouth and spit reddish saliva and water down the drain. His whole face was on fire, and his lip and his chin throbbed.

Linc didn't follow him, and that was a mercy. But he couldn't help but feel a little sorry about it too. If Linc had chased after him, Avery might have forgiven him, and he really wouldn't have minded.

———

The rest of the work week sucked. They lost another client, and Mr. Murphy, their biggest account, sent over an audit notice that said the IRS would be reviewing documentation for the last nine years.

"They can't do that!" Avery said. Uncle Theo only shrugged in defeat.

He finally worked up the courage to call Wanda and tell her he'd reconsidered her request.

"That's amazing!" she said. "Send me your resume and we'll talk."

"Okay." His heart fluttered in his chest at the idea of actually doing this.

"Awesome. Oh, and we're having some friends over Saturday night. It's Ronnie's birthday. You should come."

And because he was so busy being nervous about the resume thing, he agreed and totally didn't consider how "friends" also meant Vasquez's friends, especially since it was her birthday. He only realized his mistake as he walked through the front door of Wanda and Vasquez's little bungalow and his eyes connected with Linc's.

"Um," he said as Wanda approached him.

"Hey!" She threw her arms around his shoulders. "I'm so glad you came. We were just talking about you."

He hugged her back and smiled. "That's nice of you to say."

"Avery!" Vasquez joined Wanda and repeated the hugging.

"Hi. Happy birthday."

"I was so excited when Wanda said you were coming."

"Oh. Um. Thanks for inviting me." He glanced over her shoulder. Linc stood in the living room, chatting with a man who had his arm around the shoulders of a very pregnant woman.

Vasquez turned in the direction of his gaze, then rounded her attention back to Avery. She took his hand and winked. "Come meet everyone."

The small house was full of people. Avery knew a few from town, and other faces he recognized but had never spoken to. He forgot names almost as quickly as he was given them, but Vasquez introduced him to everyone as "our good friend, Avery," and everyone shook his hand and smiled like they meant it when they said they were glad to meet him.

"And this," she said, leading him up to a man with a swooshy haircut and suspenders, "is Wanda's brother Quinn."

"Hey! It's nice to meet you. I've heard a lot about you." Quinn had Wanda's fair complexion and open smile, but his eyes flashed with a look Wanda would never give Avery.

Oh boy. Quinn stepped into Avery's space, closer than even the tight quarters of the party recommended. He was tall. Taller than Linc. Avery had to tilt his head almost all the way back to see his face this close.

Quinn dropped his mouth in line with Avery's ear. "Can I get you a drink?" And yeah, Avery was a disaster who couldn't run on a treadmill, but he knew when someone was flirting with him. Mostly because—even though it happened infrequently—when it did occur, his heart hit a whole new speed. But also because Quinn's gaze was very definitely on Avery's mouth and not his eyes as he straightened up again.

"Uh, sure. A drink would be great."

"What do you want?" Quinn raised his eyebrows to accentuate he wasn't just asking about a beverage and—*wow*—he was very direct, wasn't he?

"Um, what are you having?"

Quinn winked and held out his hand. Avery hesitated. Linc was somewhere over his left shoulder. He didn't know where exactly, and he couldn't check without being totally obvious and also maybe giving Quinn a reason to lose interest.

Wait. Was he interested in Quinn's interest?

Gritting his teeth—probably a bad sign of how things were going to go for the rest of the night—he put his hand in Quinn's.

The first stop was the kitchen. Quinn showed him the alcohol and let him mix his own drink, a point for Avery's new friend in the gentleman column.

"So how do you know Wanda?" Quinn asked as they navigated to an empty sofa in the living room.

"Oh. Um, Vasquez—I mean—Veronica works with a—um—mutual friend?" The last word squeaked up into an unfortunate question.

To prove the point, Quinn laughed. "Are you asking me if that's how you all know each other?"

"No. I—Vasquez works at the fire station with a guy I know."

Yeah. A guy who he might have kissed, and who had vanished on him until Avery's limbs betrayed him in public.

"Oh, yeah? Is he here tonight?" Quinn sucked on his straw. He was handsome. Maybe a few years older than Avery. The sparkle in his gray eyes said they liked what they saw.

Avery flushed and scanned the crowd. Linc was talking to Wanda. Avery pointed nervously. "Him."

Like he'd heard, Linc's attention turned, and their eyes met. Avery held his gaze for a moment, but then glanced away, managing to take a sip of his drink without dribbling any on his shirt.

Quinn whistled. "So much tension. He's cute. Is he a friend or a *friend*?"

Avery squirmed.

"Look." Quinn's hand on his knee was gentle. His voice was kind as he spoke softly in Avery's ear. "I'm not trying to make you uncomfortable. Wanda said you might have a guy. You're adorable, so it doesn't surprise me. She also said there might be some drama."

"There's no drama," Avery said, but his eyes were on Linc again.

Quinn paused and then said, "Uh-huh. Want some help?"

"What?" Avery spun so fast their noses brushed.

Quinn grinned. "You're cute. If you were available, I'd flirt like hell with you because I can already see the tips of your ears go the perfect shade of pink when you're nervous. But if you've got something going on or, if you wish something was going on, with that handsome firefighter over there, then . . . " His fingers curled, brushing over the denim on Avery's knee. "I would be happy to stir shit up, just to remind Mr. Handsome what he's missing out on."

"He's not—" Avery bit his lip. He'd nearly said Linc wasn't out, but saying someone else wasn't out was as good as outing them. And Linc still hadn't even confirmed he was gay or bi or whatever. Avery was pretty sure he must be, with the way he'd kissed, but—

Quinn bumped against his shoulder. "We can have some fun at his expense. From those sad puppy eyes you've got going, it seems like he might have had a little fun at yours."

Avery swallowed thickly. He'd spent so much time this week cycling between hurt and anger, and here was Linc, standing there like what had happened was no big thing, like Avery was supposed to wait until Linc remembered he existed.

His eyes locked with Quinn's. "You would do that? Make him jealous?"

Quinn licked his lower lip. "Mm-hm. Totally PG-13, unless you say otherwise. We don't even have to leave the room. I'll be very attentive and get the gratification of spending my evening with someone as special as you, and you get to drive your man wild."

"He's not my man."

"If we can't get him to change his mind by the end of the night, you can have your money back."

"What m—" Avery ducked his head. "Oh. You were joking."

Quinn grinned and ran a hand down Avery's chest. "You really are adorable. If he doesn't want you, I'm happy to be next in line."

Avery buried his face between Quinn's jaw and the back of the couch. "I'm not actually very good at flirting."

Quinn's purred in his ear. "Honey, you're doing just fine."

14

*L*inc had no right to be jealous. Everything happening was his fault. And he didn't even think of himself as a jealous kind of guy. He never felt the need to stake his claim on something and accuse others of taking what was his. Maybe because his dad would fly into a rage any time he thought he'd been the least bit disrespected or challenged, and Linc had done his very best not to be like him at every possible chance.

But, holy hell, he wanted to grab the hipster who had spent all night talking to Avery by his suspenders and tell him to go sniff up someone else's hydrant.

Were hipsters even still a thing? This guy was certainly trying. Linc wore suspenders daily at work, but who wore them in real life when a belt was so much easier to deal with?

And why did he have to keep touching Avery? Every time Linc glanced toward them—more and more often as the party went on—they were pressed together. A hand on a knee, a chin on a shoulder. Hipster would say something in Avery's ear, and Avery would laugh and lean into him like they were old friends. Or more. Linc swallowed hard and kept his hand flat against his thigh as Hipster pressed a palm across Avery's chest.

"Having a good time?" Vasquez sidled up to him. Linc grunted. She grinned. "That's the spirit."

Avery and Hipster were standing in a corner. Hipster's hand slid lower, grazing Avery's hip, and he slipped a finger through one of Avery's belt loops.

Linc nearly choked on his tongue. He'd spent most of the night talking to Brian and his wife, Jess, pretending he wasn't checking on Avery's location—and the hipster's proximity—every thirty seconds. But when Jess started rubbing her low back and looking uncomfortable, Brian made their apologies and they headed out, leaving Linc nothing to do but brood.

Vasquez followed his gaze, nudging him in the ribs. "I see the Sweet Potato's having a good time."

Avery turned his face up to Hipster's and smiled. Linc's chest hurt. He had blown it, so he wasn't entitled to those smiles, but he wanted them so badly.

"Have you met Quinn?" Vasquez said.

"Who?" He scowled at her.

She bumped her chin toward the hipster. "Wanda's brother."

"Is that who he is?" Linc took a swig of his drink. He'd switched to soda about twenty minutes after Avery walked in because if he stuck with booze, he'd be embarrassing himself like he had with Oliver.

"Yup. Visiting from Raleigh. It was such a great surprise that he was coming down for this."

Sure was. Such a kind brother. Linc wanted to put him on the first bus out of the state.

"I could introduce you?" Vasquez said. "He's really friendly."

"So I see." It slipped out, the words dripping green.

"Aw." Vasquez pouted. "Are you jealous?"

"No."

"No to what?" Wanda came over.

"Scott's not jealous," Vasquez said.

"Of who?"

"Of your brother and the smoldering sweet potato."

"Oh." Wanda slid an arm around Vasquez's waist. "They're so cute, aren't they?"

"Totally. Right, Scott?"

His temper simmered beneath his skin. Quinn's hand was on Avery's hip, but instead of pushing it away, he pulled it around to the small of his back.

"I don't know what you're talking about." He should leave. He'd be a masochist to watch this.

"They look better together than I thought they would." Wanda tilted her head to one side.

"I told you."

They did look good together. Quinn was tall, but he used his height to create a barrier, like he would protect Avery from the crowd around them.

"What do you think?"

He tried to smile, tried to agree, but when he swallowed, the word got caught in his throat.

"Oh, honey." Wanda pulled Vasquez against her. "This is so painful to watch."

"Shh. It should only take another minute."

Linc frowned. "What are you talking about?"

"I think the feelings have melted his brain," Wanda stage-whispered.

"Scott. Stop being an ass. You'll feel better."

He shook his head, lips pressed together. Whatever game they were playing, he wouldn't give in.

"Quinn's kind of a manwhore, though, isn't he?" Vasquez said.

"Oh, totally. I'd love him to settle down with someone sweet like our little potato there, but he's going to play the field for a few more years."

Linc's nostrils flared, and Vasquez's smile turned evil. "Still.

If he helps Avery feel better about himself for a night, that's not a bad thing, right?"

"What did you say?" Linc wasn't able to hide his glare as his attention swung back to Vasquez and Wanda.

Wanda's mouth formed a little *O*. "Wow. I'm still only into women, but you do an excellent tall, dark, and broody."

Vasquez pinched her. "I can be tall, dark, and broody. When Quinn and Avery leave, I'll go get the stilettos."

Linc's pulse thundered in his ears at the thought of Avery and the other man going anywhere, but Wanda and Vasquez kept chattering like he wasn't even there anymore.

"Oh, V. You know how I feel about the heels. Wanna get you to kick them up in the air while I—"

"Hey," Linc growled. The two women looked up at him with twin expressions of surprised innocence.

"Yes, honey?" Wanda said.

"What do you mean he's going to help Avery feel better?"

"Well, you fucked up. And the way you've been gazing after him like a Disney prince all night, I'd say you haven't found a way to make it better," Vasquez said. "Which means poor Avery got his tender little heart squished. Wanda just asked Quinn to flirt with him a bit. Remind him that not everyone is an insensitive brute like you."

Linc's head swung back toward Avery and Quinn in horror. "So it's a pity flirt?"

"Mm. I think it's more than that now," Wanda said. "I know my brother. See his face? This stopped being a favor for his big sister at least an hour ago."

Before she even finished the sentence, Linc was pushing his way through the crowd. His emotions warred between fear for Avery—he'd be crushed when he found out Quinn's interest wasn't genuine—and rage at Vasquez. His patience was done. There would be no more pranks at work. No more good-natured teasing. He would buy no more donuts and do no more grocery runs just because he was the new guy.

Quinn glanced at him. His smirk as their eyes met set Linc's blood on fire. It roared to a blaze as Quinn dipped his head down, whispering something in Avery's ear that made him smile. He turned so they were so close they might as well be kissing. Quinn laughed, and Avery pressed his face against Quinn's shoulder. Then Avery ducked away, pushing through the crowd, perpendicular to Linc's path.

Linc changed course, trying to intercept him. He needed Avery to know what was going on. Fuck Vasquez and Wanda for meddling. Linc had screwed up everything, but Avery didn't deserve to be played like this.

He was heading up the hall. With fewer people here, Linc could move faster. "Hey!"

Avery turned. His smile would have been the best thing Linc had seen in ages, except one side of his lower lip was still swollen and scabbed from where he'd cut it at the gym. "Oh, hi."

Oh, hi? Oh. Hi? Linc's breathing was coming so fast, he was dizzy. He grabbed Avery's elbow and dragged him into what looked like a spare bedroom. Linc slammed the door shut behind them.

"What are you doing?" Avery seemed as breathless as Linc felt.

"You need to stay away from him."

"Who?" Avery asked with wide eyes.

He gritted his teeth. "The hipster. Quinn. He's not—" He exhaled, biting down on the words. Linc didn't want to break the bad news to Avery because he'd be responsible—once again—for Avery's disappointment. Again.

Avery's brows pinched together. "He's not what?"

Linc growled. "Do you even know him?"

"No." Avery bounced on his toes. "We just met. I'm getting to know him, though. He's really nice."

"He's not—he's Wanda's brother."

Avery laughed. "Yeah, I know that. She introduced us."

"But he isn't—" He pushed his fingers into his hair as he fought the urge to stalk back up the hall and tell that bastard Quinn to stay the hell away from Avery.

"Hey. Hey." Avery forced his way in front of Linc, planting his hands on his chest. "What's going on? You seem upset."

"Did he touch you? Did he hurt you or make you feel uncomfortable at all? I'll rip his arms off if he did."

"No." Avery's eyes were wide. "Why would he do that? Please don't rip his arms off. He's a blogger and a freelance writer. I don't think he has health care."

Linc paused. Something was off. Avery's palms on his chest were warm, and his eyes were bright, but not from fear. He was . . . Linc's gaze slid down to the bump on Avery's lip where he'd cut it at the gym. The cut was dark and a little raw, like he'd been tonguing at it without realizing. And the raw spot was . . . shaking? Just the barest tremor, like tension in a wire. Linc followed the movement to the corner of Avery's mouth, where the muscles quivered and spasmed and curved slightly upward.

"Are you—" Linc gasped. "Are you laughing?"

Avery stuck out his bottom lip and looked up at Linc through his lashes. The expression made Linc's anger tighten into something new. "Are you jealous?" He patted Linc's chest with one hand. "Big bad firefighter feeling left out?"

Linc gaped. "What?"

"Did it work?"

"Did what work?"

Avery lost his battle with his smile, lighting up his whole face. "Quinn. Did it work?"

The longer Linc stared, the wider Avery's smile got, until Linc worried he'd split his lip again. "You knew?"

"That he's not actually interested in me? He was very

upfront. A real gentleman." His eyebrow arched, and the unspoken *unlike some people* was deafening in the small room.

All of Linc's apologies got stuck in his throat. "Red, I—"

"Where the fuck have you been this week?"

His balls shrank about three sizes. "I'm sorry."

"It's going to take more than a sorry."

"I know."

Avery's hands moved over his chest, and Linc's T-shirt was so old and worn that he might as well have been wearing nothing. "You kissed me and you ran."

"I—" What was he supposed to say?

"Quinn's out. He's out, and he's smart and funny, and he thinks I'm smart and funny too."

"You are. Red, I—"

Avery sighed, head hanging. "But I'm interested in you, and Wanda told him so."

"You—" Linc's heart pounded with hope.

"I'm still mad. It seemed fair to make you suffer."

"Red, I'm so sorry. It's complicated. My dad . . . I . . . when I kissed you, I wasn't thinking, I—"

Avery put a finger to his lips and shushed him. "I don't want to talk right now, although we are going to get to it. But do you think we could skip to the part where we're kissing again? I'd like that a lot."

They stared at each other. Linc's mouth worked as he pieced together everything that had happened, while Avery smiled smugly and hope sparked in his eyes.

"Really?"

Avery nodded vigorously. "Now, please."

He wasn't too late.

Linc was on him in a second. One minute they were chest to chest, and the next Linc was lifting him, wrapping Avery's legs around his hips while his mouth devoured every inch of anything he could get his lips on.

"Oh, wow, I—" Avery said breathlessly. "I didn't—this worked really well."

"You're all I think about." Linc had him up against the wall, mouth on his throat. "You know that?"

"No." Avery's voice was wobbly. "No one has ever told me that before."

Linc would tell him so much more. Soft things. Dirty things. He was going to beg him for every second they could spend together tonight.

Avery's knees clenched tight to hold them together, and he moaned as Linc's lips covered his, tongue pushing into the warmth of his mouth. Linc squeezed his eyes tight, praying desperately for the strength to be the person Avery needed and deserved.

A knock sounded on the door. "Everything okay in there?"

They froze, panting.

"Don't say anything," Avery whispered. Linc squeezed Avery's ass, making him sigh.

"Scott?" Vasquez said from the hall.

"Why does she call you that?" Avery's breath on Linc's neck was hot, then cool as it blew over the spot where his tongue had been.

"Firefighter thing." And a clear reminder they were not somewhere private. Linc was seconds from tearing clothes off— his or Avery's, it didn't matter—but he would never live down getting naked in Vasquez's house. "We'll be right out!" Avery's grip around his body tightened in a gratifying way, even as Vasquez laughed in the hall.

"Okay, then."

Gently, even while everything inside him screamed not to, he set Avery down. He didn't let him go anywhere, keeping them both close together against the wall. Linc nuzzled at Avery's throat. "Can we go back to your place and figure this out?"

"No."

"Oh." Fair. He still had a lot of shit to work out on his own. Linc would need to jack off when he had a minute alone, but this second chance was more than he deserved.

Avery's fingers hooked into his belt loops and pulled them together. "But you can come back to my apartment, and we can have all the sex you want."

Linc groaned, running his hands through Avery's hair and kissing his face. "You're amazing, you know that?"

Avery laughed and pressed his cheek against Linc's collarbone. "I hope you still think so in an hour."

Linc would need so much more than an hour for what he had planned.

15

They tried to play it cool. Linc let Avery escape the bedroom first, and then he followed thirty seconds later. The hallway was empty, so maybe no one noticed. Well, no one except Vasquez. She stood with her arms crossed and one eyebrow arched as Avery and Wanda blew air kisses and said goodnight. Linc hovered far enough away to look like he was not thinking about tackling Avery onto Vasquez's living room carpet —even though he totally was. Time to go, before he abandoned all discretion entirely.

They drove in separate cars. Linc followed Avery's taillights like a beacon. His skin was a bundle of electricity, and only a miracle kept him from running a stop sign or clipping Avery's bumper in his agitation.

As they stood at Avery's front door, Linc stuffed his hands in his pockets. He'd gone home with guys, but nothing had ever felt like this. His past experiences were simple. Limited. A quick fuck and then they were strangers again. With Avery, the moment felt so full. The possibilities were overwhelming.

And the immediacy was terrifying. They wordlessly walked into the living room; Avery sucked on his injured lip, and Linc's feet suddenly felt like cement.

"Would you like something to drink?" Avery said.

"Do you have anything besides spinach water?"

Avery's nose wrinkled. "There's still a few beers left. And I have rainbow chard . . . um . . . water?"

Linc laughed. He stepped forward, letting his hands slide across Avery's hips, kissing him slowly. "Why do you drink that stuff?"

"It's good for you."

He growled as he nuzzled at Avery's ear. "Are you going to be good for me tonight?"

Avery shuddered. His body melted against Linc's. "Yes. I hope so."

He so would. He didn't have to do anything besides be who he was. Soft and eager, his mouth meeting Linc's like it was meant for kissing. It would all be so good.

"Bedroom."

"Already?" Avery squeaked.

Linc froze. "Why not?"

"I just—it's fine." He reached up to kiss Linc, but his body held something new now—a nervousness in the way Avery pressed himself closer, pushed harder. Their feet bumped together, and Linc stumbled before pulling them both upright.

"Hey. Stop."

"What?" He bit at Linc's lip, but Linc pulled his head back.

"What's wrong?" Linc said.

Avery sighed impatiently. "Nothing. You're here. I'm here. No one wants spinach water. What could be wrong?"

Linc held him close, because he didn't want Avery to think he was shutting this down, but he needed answers first. "What's wrong?" he repeated.

Avery's eyes narrowed, like he might argue, but instead, he sagged and rested his head on Linc's shoulder. His hand was underneath Linc's T-shirt, running nervous circles over his belly.

"I don't know—I've never . . . I don't know how to do this, okay?"

Linc's heart stopped. "What?"

Avery slithered out of his grasp and slumped to the couch. "I —I fooled around a bit in college. In dorm rooms. But, like. It was always—" He buried his face in his hands.

Linc was going to need more words very quickly before his head exploded with all the possibilities—good and bad. "It was what?"

"It was all so awkward. Like we thought we were in porn, except none of us had ever had sex before."

Linc wiped his mouth to hide his grin. "Okay . . . " he said slowly. "And?"

"But it was only ever blow jobs and hands."

"Are you telling me you're a virgin?" Linc might not be able to handle it, after everything else. But he would. He'd find some self-control, and he'd take it easy. It would be worth it.

"What? No. How can you say that when I just told you about the guys I've fooled around with? Just because I've never had a dick in my ass or fucked someone else, then I'm still some kind of mystical sacred sea otter?"

"Mystical—? Red, I don't even know what that means."

"It means . . . what happens if I'm not good at this?"

———

The question hung in the air, and Avery's heart did a weird thumping rhythm like a bobblehead on a dashboard.

"I'm pretty sure that's not possible," Linc said slowly.

"But it—"

Linc dragged his nose from Avery's hair to the hinge of his jaw. "Can we get some clothes off? I'll show you how great you're going to be."

"Uh. Sure." His voice was breathy, and uncertainty rattled in his chest. "But—oh!" Before he could say anything else, Linc dropped to his knees. He undid Avery's belt buckle and lifted his shirt, exposing his freckled belly button and the soft red hair below it, running into his waistband.

Linc placed a kiss along the copper trail. "I'm sorry I ran."

"It's okay." Avery dug his fingers into the upholstery, and Linc explored with his mouth.

"It's not. I'm going to make it up to you."

"You don't have to."

"I want to. I've wanted to for weeks. It's almost all I think about."

He's watching you. Can't take his eyes off you.

Quinn had told Avery that. Thinking about someone else in this moment seemed weird, but as Linc traced wet open-mouthed kisses over Avery's skin, Quinn's voice in his ear all night came back to him.

He can't stop staring. Don't look. It'll spoil the game.

Anyone in this room can see. He wants to eat you up and suck you dry. If a man looked at me like that, honey, we wouldn't make it to the door.

Linc rose, pushing Avery down to the couch and straddling him. Linc's mouth covered his, and he gasped. His fingers threaded into Linc's dark hair while their tongues chased each other.

"You have no idea how much I want you. How much I think about you."

Avery shuddered. "The morning we woke up together, I had to jerk off twice in the shower before I could come back to get dressed."

Linc rumbled. His mouth sealed over Avery's, his erection pressed against Avery's stomach. Sweat trickled down the small of his back. Avery was so warm, exhilarated and aroused, he was going to burst into flames in a minute. He pushed Linc back long enough to peel off his shirt, and Linc did the same. They needed to deal with their pants too, but the T-shirts were barely on the floor before Linc was back, pressing skin to skin. His body was so different from Avery's. Tight and muscled, his chest hair wiry and coarse where Avery's was soft and thin.

Linc seemed to like it, though. He rubbed his face on it like a cat before sucking on each of Avery's nipples.

"Oh God." Avery held him there, panting. No one had ever sucked his nipples before, and, holy shit, that needed to happen again. Often. Right now.

Linc rasped his fingernails over Avery's sides. "Wanna make you feel good." He was moving lower, mouth on Avery's sternum, his abs—or where his abs would be if he had any. His thumb stroked over Avery's erection, and Avery would have come off the couch if Linc's more sizeable body wasn't holding him down.

Linc's brown eyes were like early-morning coffee as he glanced up. He kissed Avery again, thumb still working. "Can I make you feel good?"

Avery nodded vigorously. "Yes. Yup. You can do that. I like— yes, that. Go ahead," he babbled as Linc undid the top button of his jeans, then slowly slid the zipper down. The suspense was torture. The best kind of torture.

"Lift your hips for me," Linc said gently, kissing the arc of Avery's hip.

Avery did. Linc slipped his fingers around the open jeans, and then farther in to the elastic of Avery's briefs. He asked silently with his eyebrows, and Avery nodded, arching up more, until Linc had all his clothes pulled down to his knees.

"Oh, Jesus, you're beautiful." Linc ran a finger through Avery's pubic hair, grazing the base of his erection. "I knew you'd be beautiful."

Avery's dick swelled more, imagining Linc had thought about this. About him specifically. He wasn't totally naive. Lots of people had fantasies about redheads. One of the perks of being a genetic weirdo. But the way Linc was watching him as he ran his hands over Avery's thighs and up his stomach said this wasn't just about his coloring. This was about him.

"What do you want?" Linc asked. He caressed Avery in wide circles without ever coming close enough to Avery's dick, making him squirm. "Shhh. Tell me."

"What are—" Avery swallowed. "What are my options?" Anything? Everything?

"Whatever you want." Linc kissed the sensitive spot where Avery's groin met his thigh. "I can jerk you off. Blow you. You can take my clothes off and do pretty much anything."

Oh, man. That sounded so tempting, but also like a lot of responsibility. This whole thing was right at the edge of frying Avery's brain. If he had to start making decisions, he'd melt down and wind up lying on the floor like an abandoned department store mannequin.

"Your mouth. On me." Two-word sentences were his speed right now.

Linc's tongue on the head of his penis had him closing his eyes and breathing very slowly. Some kind of feedback loop was happening between his dick and his nipples, because with every swipe of Linc's tongue, his chest tingled.

"Is that good?" Linc asked.

"Mm-hmm." He was chewing on his lip. The cut spot was sore, helping to take his arousal from thermo-nuclear back down to moderately radioactive.

His fingers dug into the couch as Linc took him into his mouth, hot and wet and slow. Oh God, so slowly. Avery's toes curled. Linc stopped before he was more than halfway down and slid back up and off, letting Avery's dick flop onto his stomach. He glanced up and chuckled. "You should see your face right now."

"What I want to see is my dick back in your mouth." And whoa, that was way bossier than he'd expected. Linc didn't seem to mind. In fact, he must have liked it, because his eyes widened. He licked a long strip up to the top of Avery's leaking cock and then swallowed him all the way down to the root in a single motion.

"Holy shit!" Avery arched, and his dick hit the back of Linc's throat, making him choke. "Sorry. Sorry."

Linc's laughter blew out through his nose, while his mouth was busy blowing Avery's mind. His fingers slipped around the inside of Avery's thigh, fondling his balls, while his tongue worked, moving up and down, dragging every molecule of Avery's consciousness into his dick.

"Oh, man. Oh." He panted, staring up at the ceiling. "That's good. Don't stop. I'm glad this is what we picked. Don't stop."

One finger slipped farther, stroking his taint. Avery's legs were still trapped in his jeans, and he strained against them, trying to give Linc more room. He squirmed. If he could slide down lower, if Linc's hand could just move a few inches farther back—

His balls tingled, and warmth spread in his lower back. Avery gasped and buried his fingers in Linc's hair, pulling hard. Linc took it as encouragement, though, and he sucked harder.

Avery panted. He needed this to—he couldn't—too soon to—

"Stop," he said, and the cool air as Linc popped off him was such a shock he nearly came anyway.

"What?"

Avery grasped his dick, squeezing hard, counting slowly. "Two times two is four. Two times four is eight. Two times eight is sixteen," he whispered like a prayer.

"What are you doing?"

"Trying not to come all over your face." He kept counting, even as Linc groaned and nuzzled at his balls. "No, stop!" Avery swatted him away, but he laughed at the same time. Linc kissed him from the arch of his left foot all the way up to his knee, past his hip—he left Avery's dick alone—to his ribs, his throat, and finally, Avery's mouth.

"You taste so good," Linc said against his lips.

"Um, thanks?" He eyed the outline of Linc's erection in his pants.

"What are you thinking?"

"I hope that fits."

Linc choked, burying his face in Avery's neck. Then he moaned when Avery slid a hand between them and gripped him, squeezing. Oh, gosh. He felt big. Avery knew he could stretch, anatomically speaking, but he wasn't sure if he actually *would*.

"We don't have to," Linc said. "I'm totally fine if it's too fast for you. Even if we just get sloppy here for a bit longer, you have no idea how much I like that idea."

But Avery wanted so much more. Virginity was a stupid concept invented by fathers trying to control their bloodline. Avery's father had abandoned his bloodline, so who the hell cared what Avery had and hadn't done with other people, or even by himself? He might not have had someone's dick in his ass, but he'd had what he needed to explore and get off on his own.

But now he wanted Linc inside him, to feel him moving. He had to know he mattered enough for Linc to want him like that.

He flipped the button open on the top of Linc's pants. "I like the idea of you inside me. I actually like it a lot."

The world tilted. Suddenly, Avery was upside down, slung over Linc's shoulder. He bounced as they made their way up the hall.

"Hey!" He squirmed. "Put me down. You don't have to carry me."

"It's my job to carry you to safety." A broad hand settled on Avery's ass. "Let me do my job, Red."

Avery sighed and relaxed. He entertained himself by

162

running his hands down Linc's back and slipping his fingers into the pockets of his jeans, squeezing. Linc walked faster.

He was deposited on his bed, flopping back. Linc stripped him quickly out of the rest of his clothes and briefs that still hung around his ankles, taking his socks with them. Then he pulled his own pants off, but left his boxer briefs on.

"No." Avery made grabby hands. "Take those off too."

Linc stretched out next to him, holding his chin in place so they could kiss long and slow. "Trust me. These are staying on for me, not for you."

"Why?"

"Just a reminder to take my time."

Avery pouted. "I'm not a kid. I know what to do."

Linc slid a hand down Avery's body until he gripped his shaft and stroked him slowly. "Oh, I know. But I'm a bit . . . primed. I don't want to hurt you."

"You won't." Avery ground against him impatiently.

"Do you have lube?"

Avery widened his eyes. "What for?"

Linc's mouth dropped open.

Avery couldn't muffle his laughter at the pained disappointment on his face. "It's in the drawer over there."

Linc grabbed Avery's ankle. They wrestled for a second, but Linc was so much bigger and stronger that his win in their tiny battle was inevitable, and when he did, he flipped Avery onto his stomach to smack his ass. Avery moaned. Spanking wasn't his kink—or he didn't think so, not really—but he'd let Linc get a little handsy if he wanted.

The bottle of lube hit the bed with a dull thud. Two condoms landed next to it.

"You just happened to have these too?" Linc said.

Avery twisted so he could scowl over his shoulder. "First, don't judge me. Maybe I like to be prepared. Condoms aren't expensive. It's easy to buy some just in case."

"And second?" Linc was kissing the soles of his feet. Avery had also never thought of himself as a foot guy either, but the scrape of stubble on the thin skin of his arches made him wonder if maybe he could be.

"And second—" He buried his face in a pillow as he finished the sentence, but the smack on his ass again had him popping back up again, yelping.

"I didn't hear that."

He growled, pulling his foot free of Linc's hand, and curled in on himself. "My aunt bought them for me as a housewarming present."

During the silence immediately following, Avery visualized Linc running for the door while Avery was left to find all his clothes again. Instead, Linc's deep laughter filled the bedroom.

"Oh my God." He stretched out over Avery, stealing another kiss or seven. "Your aunt might be my hero."

Their cocks were pressed against each other, and Avery entertained himself by flexing, rubbing them together, separated only by the thin cotton. He loved the contrasts in their bodies. Avery had always been self-conscious about his appearance. The red hair and freckles, the skinny frame that never put on bulk no matter what he did. But Linc didn't seem to mind. He explored every inch. Except the inches that mattered most.

"You're hesitating," Avery said. Linc was busy sucking marks along the inside of Avery's thigh. He already couldn't wait to look at them in the morning and remember the sight of Linc's head between his legs. But he still needed more. He jostled Linc's shoulder with his knee and received a glare in return.

"I'm taking my time."

"Come on. What are you waiting for?"

Linc bit the back of his calf. "Don't rush me."

His dick shriveled. "Do you not want to?"

Linc's head popped up at once. "Of course I do."

"Then get on with it!" He was whining now, but he didn't care.

"You're bossy."

"I'm horny, and you're still treating me like I might break. Look." He gestured at his flagging dick. "This is your fault."

His balls were in Linc's mouth in a second. One, then the other, sliding out of his lips with a pop. He sucked Avery's length down with an intensity that made his eyes roll back in his head. His stomach clenched as he cried out, "Yes. Yes. More."

A finger slipped between his legs, along his crack. Avery spread his knees while his blood boiled.

"Say yes," Linc said.

"I did."

"One more time."

Avery reached down to spread his cheeks apart. "Please fuck me with your dick."

Who knew he'd had the magic password all along? One second, Linc was all attentive and careful touches. The next, he was devouring Avery. He gasped as Linc nosed past his balls and licked a wet stripe down his taint. Linc hesitated for one last second, but Avery whined and bucked his hips and then finally —*oh, thank God, finally*—Linc pressed the flat of his tongue against Avery's hole.

"Ohhh." The word was barely a word, more like a long exhale from the depths of his chest as Linc tongued him. No one had ever done this for him before, and, yes, he was going to need it to happen a lot too, maybe even more than the nipple sucking. Each wet and warm pass sent tingling shocks all the way up his body.

"Okay?" Linc asked. He blew a stream of air across the drying spit on Avery's ass, making him tremble.

"I'll tell you when I'm not."

So Linc kept going, firming his tongue and gently pressing it inside. Avery's dick pulsed at the invasion, and he gripped himself, circling his thumb over the leaking tip.

"Yeah. Yeah. That. Keep doing that. Oh my God." Spit drooled down his ass as words fell out of his mouth. He stroked himself gently, not wanting to get too excited too quickly. Linc worked him open endlessly, tongue swirling and stretching. The lube cap shut with a faint snap. At the first cool press of Linc's finger, Avery tensed.

"Still okay?" Linc said. His finger was at Avery's entrance, but he didn't move.

"I'm fine."

Linc circled him, teasing the muscle. Instinctively, Avery lifted his hips away from the pressure.

"Do you want me to stop?"

"No."

"You've done this before. To yourself. Right?"

"Mm-hmm." Not recently. Lately he'd been more into—

Something stung inside his thigh, and he flinched. "You bit me!" But then he sighed as Linc's finger slipped inside.

"Needed you to relax."

"Biting virgins is a terrible cliché."

"I thought you weren't a virgin." Linc pushed in farther.

It was . . . Yeah, okay, the sensation was a bit weird at first. Not controlling the movement was strange, but then Linc slipped a second finger inside, and the stretch made him gulp.

"Still okay?"

"Yeah." He wanted this. He just—

Light shot out from the back of his eyes.

"Holy hell."

Linc chuckled low, sweeping over Avery's prostate. The feeling was incredible, even as he crawled back out of his brain.

"Better?" Linc said. He was back to kissing Avery's feet, brushing his lips over his ankle while he worked him open.

"Good. Yeah. So good."

Another finger, slick and wide. The stretch and pressure were still a little weird, and Avery gasped.

"You're still awfully tight. We don't have to keep going," Linc said.

Avery's eyes flew open. "I'm fine." His feet skittered out from under him when Linc hit his prostate again, and they jammed against Linc's thighs, dangerously close to his erection.

Linc laughed softly. "Careful. You need that in working order." Then he withdrew his fingers.

"What? Why did you stop." Avery lifted his head off the mattress.

"Trying something new."

Avery nearly protested as Linc stood, but then he was shucking his boxer briefs. His cock bobbed out from dark curls. Avery couldn't keep from licking his lips while Linc stroked himself.

"Oh, yeah." He chuckled softly. "You're still on board."

"So on board." Avery couldn't take his eyes off the flushed head that slid in and out of Linc's strong hand.

"Grab the lube."

Avery moved quickly to comply.

"Touch yourself. Just like I am."

Avery did. He never looked away from Linc, keeping their strokes timed together. Linc knelt on the edge of the mattress and made his way around until they were facing each other, inches apart.

"We're going to be so good together." Linc kissed him sweetly.

Avery grabbed hold of Linc's lower lip with his teeth and growled, making him laugh.

"Keep going," Linc said as he reached down and grabbed a condom. His dick was at full mast, the thick vein trailing down to the base. Avery kept jacking himself while Linc rolled the condom down and lubed himself up, then pushed himself up against the headboard, muscular legs crossed in front of him.

His grin nearly had Avery shooting all over his hand.

"Hop on," he said.

Avery had imagined it differently. In his fantasies, Linc was in charge. Pushing into him, telling him what to do.

And yet somehow, here he was in Linc's lap, head tilted down as they kissed and stroked each other. He lubed up his own fingers and slid them inside, riding them until he was comfortable.

"Yeah. Oh, fuck, you have no idea what your face looks like right now." Linc sucked on his collarbone. He was so mouthy. Avery definitely liked that.

"I'm ready."

"You so are. I can see it." He kissed Avery's chest. "Look how perfect your skin is." His words were full of something like awe. Avery always hated the way he went bright red whenever he was turned on, a beacon for everyone to see. The reaction had been especially bad as a teen trying to fly below the radar with his classmates.

Linc, though, flicking a thumb over one of Avery's nipples and dragging his fingers through the wisps of his chest hair, touched him like he was special. Like the flush on his skin was something to be admired, not hidden. "Fuck, Red, look how perfect you—" He gasped as Avery positioned himself over Linc's cock.

"I'm ready," he said, staring directly into Linc's eyes.

It took some time. He was tight, and Linc was a fistful for sure.

"That's it. That's it. You're doing so good," Linc purred in his ear, hands on his back and over his shoulders, moving all the time. "So good. You feel me? Feel me inside you?"

He did. Oh God, did he ever. The stretch was at the edge of pain. Taking Linc in, inch by inch, he felt invaded. Expanded.

He didn't know how he could take it all, but with every soft word and every slow minute, he slipped farther down and farther away from the buzz of thoughts in his head.

As Avery's ass settled in the cradle of Linc's hips, Linc groaned long and low, his cheek pressed against Avery's chest. For a second, he thought Linc might have come already, and wouldn't that suck? But then Linc sucked a nipple between his teeth and rocked his hips and oh. Oh, yeah. He was still there and ready to go.

Avery bit his lip at the drag of Linc's dick on the tight ring of his ass.

"You good?" Linc asked.

Avery could only nod as he dropped back down, focusing on remembering to breathe while Linc filled him up again. The moment was good—better even—especially the little flashes of light whenever Linc grazed his prostate. He wanted more.

Linc's hands settled on his hips. "Show me how you like it."

Avery smiled and kissed him. "You don't have to be a gentleman all the time."

The response was a powerful thrust upward. Avery cried out as Linc held him in place. "Trust me. Next time, I'm in charge."

Avery looked forward to that. But now, he set a pace. His dick bounced in front of him until Linc caught it and pumped in time with Avery's rhythm.

"Yeah. More of that." Avery ground his hips down, finding the angle he wanted.

"You do it. Make yourself come for me. I need to see it." Linc put his hands behind his head, showing off the width of his chest. Avery grazed his fingernails over Linc's nipples, toying with them the way Linc had done to him. Linc hissed, and Avery picked up the pace of his hips, pounding down as he stroked himself. His technique was messy and imperfect, but his prostate pulsed and his hand slid up and down, smoothing pre-come over his cock working in and out of his fist. The bedsprings creaked, and the headboard thumped against the wall. Linc chanted, "Yeah, yeah" over and over.

Sweat slicked down Avery's spine as the orgasm built, tightening his balls. He squeezed around Linc's cock.

"Are you close?"

"Uh-huh."

Linc's hands were back on his hips. Now he took control. "You're doing so good. So good. Can you feel how hard I am inside you?"

"Yeah," Avery whined. The pressure was building. No amount of tight squeezing or times tables was going to hold back this orgasm.

"Do you want me to come with you?"

"Yeah." He planted a hand on Linc's shoulder.

"You ready?"

"Mm." He needed everything he had to keep words coming out of his mouth. His brain was following his sweat down his spine and was about to erupt from his balls.

Linc hit a stride Avery didn't know was possible. He pulled Avery down so tight he had no range of motion, and every one of Linc's thrusts hit his prostate until his vision fuzzed and the room went white while the orgasm tore out of him. Linc buried his face in Avery's neck and held him close, pulsing in Avery's ass.

Getting disentangled took a lot of work. Linc slipped out of bed to deal with the condom, and Avery wound up doing his mannequin impression after all, limbs splayed at odd angles, basically where he'd fallen.

"I have died," he said when Linc returned. He flashed Avery a toothy grin, climbing up his body and flattening himself on top of him.

"Really?" Linc kissed him gently, with less hunger behind it.

"Mmm." He stretched, enjoying the spots they rubbed

together without expectation of anything else. He winced, though, as his ass clenched.

"You okay?" Linc said, bringing Avery with him as he shifted to his side.

"Fine. I might hurt tomorrow." That had been more intense than any finger or toy he'd ever tried in the past, stretching him beyond what he was used to.

"Sorry about that. I said I'd let you drive, and then I grabbed the stick at the last minute."

Avery laughed into the warmth of Linc's chest. "Keep your hand off my joystick."

"Please don't say that again." But he was laughing as he pulled them close, fitting Avery under his chin and throwing one heavy leg over his hip.

The room was dark and quiet. Avery's heart had slowed to a human pace, and his breathing calmed. "Linc?"

"Yeah?" Linc's voice was already heavy with sleep.

"I know about Abe."

16

Sleepy morning sex had to be Linc's second favorite thing ever. He woke up to Avery making happy little humming noises while he teased Linc's nipples with his lips and teeth, before he moved lower to take Linc's swelling cock in his mouth.

He didn't miss Avery's soft grunt, mid-blow job, as one of Linc's fingers strayed to his asshole.

Avery said he might hurt in the morning, and Linc wouldn't be surprised if he did. Working him open the night before had been an epic task, and Linc had been ready to burst by the time he was inside him. "You okay?"

Avery buzzed around his dick with a noise which might have been agreement or could just as likely have been encouragement at the way Linc's hips rocked up while Avery's tongue swirled around him.

"Red?"

Avery's head popped up and swung around to glare at him. "Am I doing something wrong?" One finger slipped between Linc's thighs to stroke his taint.

"No."

"Then don't worry about me and worry about coming

instead."

Linc bit down a laugh that became a groan when Avery slipped back over him. These little bossy moments, coupled with Avery's relative inexperience, were such a turn-on for him.

Afterward, Linc lay on his back with Avery pressed against his chest, and Linc could probably have died right here and everything would be fine.

But that wasn't how it worked.

"When did you figure it out? About Abe?"

Avery rolled his face into Linc's pecs, but his words weren't too muffled. "Only the day before yesterday."

Was that good or bad? "What gave it away?"

"You weren't talking to me. And he wasn't online either. And then—I don't know—Abraham Lincoln? And your roommate with the noisy sex life? It kind of clicked into place. I'm a little embarrassed it took as long as it did."

He was embarrassed? Linc was the one who had kissed him, promised to stick around, and then ghosted him for a week, only to have his hormones take over at the first opportunity. Nothing he had done lately was a model of good behavior.

"You have nothing to be sorry for. I should have told you from the beginning, but every time I tried, something came up, and . . . " Anything he would say next would be feeble at best.

Avery shifted, sliding over the mattress to create space between them. Linc was left feeling exposed.

"When do you think you would have told me?" Hurt flickered in his eyes for a split second before he hid it, but the flash was long enough to make Linc's insides seize.

He let out a long sigh. "The first time we played, you were just a guy with a microwave fire. And I thought . . . You were safe, online. Someone I didn't know and would probably never know and I could relax for a minute. And after that . . . I waited too long to make telling you easy." But how hard had he tried, really? Telling the truth would have been so simple. Three little words. *Avery, it's Linc.* He'd been afraid, and now he was embarrassed at being caught out, so what had he saved himself, really?

"I've been let down a lot in my life." Avery dragged his knuckles over the sheets, gaze fixed on a spot between them. "People who were supposed to be there for me weren't. People who could have been my friends laughed at me instead."

Linc lay frozen, letting Avery's words batter him. He deserved this. "I know."

"So if this is going to work—friends, more than friends, whatever—I need to know you'll at least be honest with me. Did you think I'd be angry? Over a game where we're all pretending to be someone else? I'm not actually a warrior. I wouldn't have been mad. I'm madder you didn't say anything."

The gap between them got bigger as dread tried to suck Linc down. How could he be there for Avery? How could he be what Avery needed? All he knew to do was run and dodge his sisters' phone calls. He was an expert at sharing only the details that suited him. What could he possibly give Avery?

He folded one arm behind his head and sighed heavily as he stared at the ceiling. He had one thing to give. "I'm gay." Another two little words he'd never said before. "But I'm not out."

Avery's hand froze on the sheet. "Not to anyone?"

To Mickey, once upon a time. No one since. "When I was nineteen, my boyfriend and I bought some fake IDs, took a bus to Raleigh, and went to a gay bar."

Avery tilted his chin up. "Which one? I've been to a couple of the bars in Raleigh. There's this one—"

Linc put a finger to Avery's lips, and he stilled.

"It was the best time ever. We didn't have enough money for a hotel, so we stayed out all night. We kissed and we flirted with random guys on the street, just because we could and—" He swallowed, holding back the fear. "Suddenly, my dad was there. I hadn't seen him in almost a year. He'd been in jail for a while, and when they let him out, he didn't come back home and we just thought—but he was there that night, and he saw us kissing, and he went crazy."

Avery's eyes widened. "He was your boyfriend? You told me your dad beat up some guy, but he was your boyfriend?"

Linc nodded slowly. "We were kids."

"What did you do?"

Shame gripped Linc's chest. "I tried to pull him off. I was bigger than him by then, but it was like he was possessed. My dad was screaming and Mickey was bleeding all over the place and there were cop cars coming up the street and—I was scared, so I ran." And he'd been running ever since. "Mickey got out of the hospital after a week or two. I found a few stories on the internet." The details barely qualified for regional coverage, but Linc looked everywhere and eventually found a two-paragraph summary about his father's assault charges which mentioned Mickey was recovering. "I never talked to Mickey again. And my dad . . . No one ever called me. Maybe Mickey never even said I was there. All I know is my dad went to jail, and he's been there ever since, and I—"

"It's okay." Avery kissed him, even though Linc barely wanted the comfort.

"I want to be good for you," he said, a little desperately. "I don't know how to be—"

"It's fine if you're not out. Not officially. We can still—"

"It's not fine." And he meant it. He pushed up to sit against the headboard. "You deserve more than sneaky backroom sex and a guy who won't protect you when you need it."

Avery joined him, resting his head on Linc's shoulder. "I kinda liked our sneaky almost-sex at the party last night."

Linc coughed out a thin laugh. "Red."

"It's okay. I'm tougher than I look. We don't have to be anything serious. As long as we're honest with each other." He kissed Linc's shoulder. Linc could cry at the sweetness. He didn't deserve to be let off the hook so easily.

"I'm going to try, though. It won't be like last week. No more hiding and half-truths. I'll do better." He would. He had to. Linc was done hiding. Here, anyway—in Seacroft.

"I know."

"I might be bad at it."

Avery said the same thing last night, and Linc had known he wouldn't be. But this. Letting Avery down would kill him.

"Well, you have to be bad at something. It's nice to know you're human. Look at me, I'm pretty much a walking, talking—"

Linc cut him off with another kiss, pulling him back to the mattress.

They showered together, with spent dicks and wandering hands. Avery was perfect. Freckled, pink at the edges and—after a few minutes under the spray—warm and pliant. His body in Linc's arms left him with so many ideas of things they could do in the future.

But the future was further off than he wanted to admit, because his phone was ringing from inside his jeans as they kissed and fumbled their way back to the bedroom.

"Hello?" Linc said.

"Hey, lover boy." Vasquez's voice was dry. "Have a good night?"

Linc grunted. Denying it would be pointless. She knew exactly what they had left her house to do. His chest tightened at the thought, but it flitted away as Avery, wearing only a T-shirt and briefs, slid in behind him on the bed, knees at his sides, arms around his shoulders.

"What do you want?"

"Oh, nothing." He could hear the sarcastic smile in her voice. "Brian and I were wondering if you planned on coming to work this morning. That's all."

"Shit." He lurched to his feet so fast Avery had to choose if he was going to tumble back to the mattress or cling to Linc's back like a spider monkey.

He went with the spider monkey, and Linc did not mind at all.

"I'll be right there." He smothered a laugh as Avery nibbled at his shoulder.

"Oh God, you're still there, aren't you?" Vasquez sounded pained.

"I'm on my way." He hung up before she could say anything else.

"Do you have to go?" Avery's arms tightened around him. Linc twisted, grappling until Avery faced him, legs around his hips, hands on either side of his face.

"You were amazing last night." Linc kissed him. They smelled the same now. Same soap, same morning breath. A warm, happy feeling hummed in Linc's chest. He could do this.

"I'm sorry it wasn't . . . um . . . easier."

Linc ran a hand through the bright red hair, then sat on the edge of the bed, bringing Avery onto his lap.

"I don't need it to be easy." But he very much wanted it to be Avery. He was surprised how much, given they'd only had one night together. But they fit, and not just in the way Avery felt pressed up against his chest. "As soon as my shift is over, I'll be back over here."

"Promise?" Avery straddled him and nipped at his chin.

He laughed. "Tomorrow. I'll go home and sleep for a few hours, and then I'll be right back."

"You can sleep here."

Linc groaned, shifting Avery off his lap. Avery's dick was swelling in his briefs, and Linc's erection wasn't very far behind. If he stayed here any longer, he'd never leave.

"Oh, no," Avery said, as Linc slipped into his pants.

"What?"

"I'm having dinner at my aunt and uncle's tomorrow."

"Oh." He scrambled for what to say next. Avery was slumped in defeat. If Linc touched him, they'd be back in bed.

He wasn't ready to start doing things like family dinners but— "I could—"

"It's fine." Avery waved him off. "Maybe when I'm done with work the day after?"

That was a long time from right now, but if he didn't get to work soon, they'd have all kinds of time together while Linc found a new job.

He kissed Avery one more time. "I'll see you soon."

Good thing the town was small. Linc was at the station five minutes later, rushing across the parking lot. He slowed as he spotted Brian and Vasquez leaning against the front door. They clapped slowly as he approached.

"Sorry I'm late." He rolled his eyes.

"It's fine. I told Brian you got a bit—" Vasquez bit her lip, "— carried away after he left last night."

He glanced at Brian, whose shit-eating grin was barely smaller than Vasquez's. Linc's heart kicked up. Vasquez wouldn't out him, but she was making it hard.

No, that wasn't fair. She was covering for him while his own paranoia read more into it. Let Brian think he was hungover.

They went to the equipment room. Vasquez handed them both long-handled shop brooms before she took a bottle of chrome polish and a rag from a cupboard.

"What's that for?" Linc asked.

"We're cleaning the truck bay this morning."

He glanced between them, waiting for the punchline. "All of us?"

"Well, sure. We're a team after all." She smiled sweetly at him, and he met it with a glare. Whether this was an apology for the stunt with Quinn the night before or for the shit they'd been pulling for months, one morning's worth of shared chores wasn't going to cut it.

"Scott. You're late," the chief called as they entered the bay.

"Late night, Chief," Vasquez said before he could reply.

The chief squinted at him. "Late night?"

"Vasquez's birthday." Linc stopped a half step behind her, like she might protect him. If she did, it would be worth a little more forgiveness.

"Your birthday?" the chief said.

Vasquez nodded. "Yes, sir."

"You were there too?" he said to Brian.

"Yes. It was great. They had the little meatballs on toothpicks. You know I like those, Chief."

They stood, with Brian and Vasquez still in front, while the chief eyed them all, before his gaze finally settled on Linc. "Don't be late again."

"Yes, sir."

"And how is our charitable initiative going?"

"Sir?" Linc swallowed.

"Brian told me we were going to buy a table, yes?"

Vasquez straightened. "Yes, sir."

He took a small step forward. "Well, I don't want the wife and me to be sitting on our own. So who else has bought a ticket?"

"Wanda and I will be going, sir," Vasquez said.

"And Jess and me, as long as she's up to it," Brian said. "I asked my brother and his boyfriend, but they'd already bought tickets. So we've got four more tickets sir."

The chief turned his attention to Linc again. "What about you?"

"I'll be there."

"Got someone you can bring?"

"I think so, sir?" Linc's heart thumped in his chest. A lot was happening in his brain all at once, making it hard to answer. The chief hadn't batted an eye—much—at the mention of Wanda. And Brian's brother was queer, something Linc hadn't expected. Maybe Vasquez's theory of treating everyone as bisexual until proven otherwise had some sense to it after all.

To answer the chief's question, though, the only person he wanted to come with him was Avery, and that knowledge made his knees weak with fear.

He should have called in sick this morning. Then he could have spent the day in bed with Avery and figured things out more. Except the next steps were all resting on him. He'd promised no more hiding. Avery was out. If Linc wanted to be with him, he'd need to find the courage to do the same. But making promises in the safe haven of Avery's bed was far easier than in the plain light of day.

He swallowed hard and prayed he was doing a better job of hiding his thoughts than Avery did most days. "I'll find someone, sir."

"Good." The chief nodded and spun on his heel, like that was all he'd wanted to hear. Linc had a date, and everything was right in the world.

He didn't meet Vasquez or Brian's eyes until the chief's office door was closed. Vasquez was smirking. Brian picked up his broom and went to sweep the far side of the bay.

"You okay?" Vasquez asked.

"Of course. Why wouldn't I be?"

She looked offended. "Well, how do I know? The way the two of you rushed out of the house last night, I assumed you spent the rest of the evening fucking each other's brains out."

"Shh," he hissed.

She rolled her eyes. "Brian's got a queer family. He doesn't care. Or were you thinking of bringing someone else to the auction as your date?"

Linc stopped short as she read his mind. "You still don't get to talk about my love life in public."

"Oh, so you did get laid. I was starting to think you dropped him off at the front door and then slept in to make us think something happened."

He glared at her. "Why are you on me about this?"

"Because I want you and Sweet Potato to be happy."

He was. Maybe. A tiny ember had caught the first time Avery tumbled down his front steps in a blur of red hair and fast words. "But that doesn't give you the right to—"

"He'll want to be real boyfriends." She at least dropped her voice so no one else could hear him. "Think about it. The look on his face every time he sees you. He won't be okay waiting for a booty call while you sort your shit out."

He white-knuckled his broom. "Fourteen hours ago, you were practically throwing us together. Now you want me to back off?"

"I threw him at Quinn. You're the one who decided to be brave and jump off the ledge."

He wanted to scream. But she wasn't wrong. Real boyfriends.

"Hey. Why am I the only one working?" Brian called from the other side of the bay. They both swung their heads to glare at him, and he took a step back, lifting both hands up in surrender. "Sorry. Didn't realize I was interrupting anything."

Vasquez sighed and turned her attention back to Linc. "Look, I don't mean to push."

"Yes, you do," he snapped.

"Yeah, I do. But I'm pushing as your friend, and as Avery's. I don't want to see either of you hurting."

"That's really considerate of you."

Her eyes narrowed dangerously. "Okay, fine. I'm a selfish bitch. You know he's trying to get a job with Wanda, right? If you break each other's hearts, it's going to be unbearable for the two of us."

"You and me?"

She snorted. "No. Me and Wanda."

"You *are* a selfish bitch."

She patted his shoulder. "That doesn't mean I'm wrong. Will you be able to stand up with him when it counts?"

He glared at her, but all his protests died on his tongue. He wanted to say yes. No, he *needed* to say yes. Because if he couldn't, what hope did he and Avery have?

But when Mickey needed him, he'd run. And when his sisters asked him over and over again to come home, he stayed away.

His day ruined after an amazing start, Linc grabbed his broom and swept away from Vasquez and her opinions.

———

The following evening, Avery would much rather have had Linc over, but he went to his aunt and uncle's for supper. As he entered the front hall, he would have normally shouted hello, but the silence was so thick he stopped before the word formed in his throat. He strained, listening for any indication of where they were.

As he came up the hallway, voices filtered from the back of the house. Avery crept toward them, through the kitchen, and down the hall that led to Aunt Brenda's studio.

The sound of crying stopped him just before he rounded the last corner.

"Brenda." Uncle Theo's voice was firm but patient.

"No. No." Aunt Brenda was the one crying. "You fix this. He is our son, the only one we have ever had, and if you are too stubborn to see how much you've hurt him, then you're not the man I thought you were."

"It's not that simple."

"It is. I won't let whatever spat is going on between you tear up this family."

Avery slipped back the way he'd come, trying not to make a sound. So, of course, he banged his elbow on the kitchen counter, hitting the funny bone and sending numbing pain radiating from his shoulder to his fingertips. He opened his mouth on a silent scream and kept moving away.

This wasn't right. His aunt and uncle gave him everything. They couldn't be fighting about him. They couldn't be tearing themselves apart, as she had put it, over him.

He'd call Wanda as soon as he got home and tell her something had come up, so he couldn't do the interview after all.

Wordlessly, he opened the front door and reached around until he found the doorbell. The chime sounded up the hall. "Hello? Anybody home?"

Dinner was awkward. The worst, actually. The brittle corners of Aunt Brenda's smile were painfully obvious and made his eyes sting. But nevertheless, she asked all sorts of questions about his job interview and what the company did, responding with, "Oh, that sounds exciting. Doesn't that sound exciting, Theo? I'm going to download the app and see how it works."

Uncle Theo mostly grunted and nodded and said she had all kinds of cookbooks in the kitchen, so what would they need an app for?

That dismissal made Avery clamp his jaw shut on any apologies. This wholesale refusal to understand the evolution of the world in general—and their customers specifically— was how they'd gotten to this point. So, instead, he'd pasted on a smile as bright and fake as Aunt Brenda's and told her all about the company like he was about to land his dream job.

"So what else is new?" Aunt Brenda asked when they'd exhausted the topic. Avery almost blurted out he had a boyfriend, because she'd be so happy for him. But he caught himself, because she'd want to know everything, and that meant *everything*. How did they meet? What was he like? Where had they gone on dates? When would he be coming for supper?

And that last one was the hardest to answer. What if Linc didn't want to come for supper? Or would come, but only as Avery's friend, not his boyfriend? Linc said he was going to try, but Avery couldn't push him. Unfortunately, once Aunt Brenda knew about Avery and Linc's upgraded relationship status, she'd be unavoidable.

"Nothing much." His smile was tight. He wanted to see Linc's face again and make sure this was really real before inflicting his family drama on him.

His aunt hugged him hard at the front door. "You call me as soon as your interview is over and let me know how it went."

"I will." He felt like ducking behind one of her carefully trimmed decorative shrubs and throwing up. They had never kept anything from each other, and now they were all walking on eggshells. Avery glanced over his aunt's shoulder to his uncle. His mouth was set, and he was wiping his glasses on the hem of his shirt with more focus than was strictly necessary.

"Uncle Theo," Avery said.

His uncle glanced up, squinting because his glasses were still pinched between his finger and his shirt. "Yes?"

He sighed. The single word held too much expectation, like Uncle Theo was waiting for an apology. "I'll see you tomorrow?"

"Oh. Were you planning on coming to work?"

Aunt Brenda made a strangled noise, but the color was high on her cheeks and the glare she sent her husband was murderous.

"Of course," Avery said quickly, wanting to escape any more awkwardness as fast as possible.

Back in his apartment, everything was still too quiet, but at least the added discomfort of dinnertime tension wasn't trying to suffocate him.

On a whim, he fired up the Xbox. *GatorAbe24* was in the *Winterlands* lobby.

"Hey, Red," he said, and tension eased out of Avery's shoulders.

"Hi, Abe."

"You know you could have just called me." Linc laughed.

The sound was still distorted enough that Avery could believe he hadn't recognized his voice.

"You're the one who was hanging out in an anonymous gaming lounge hoping I might show up."

"I wasn't hoping. I was—"

"Waiting for someone else?"

"No, I—" Linc sighed. "I figured if your dinner went well, you'd call and maybe I could come over."

Avery froze, staring at the hulking warrior on the screen. "And if it didn't go well?"

"Then you'd probably go home and lick your wounds in private, and I thought if I was online, we could at least catch up here."

Avery slumped back on the couch. "It was a disaster. I don't know how to fix this without hurting them or starting a fight."

"Why does it have to be you that fixes it?"

Avery blinked, staring at the ceiling. "You sound like my aunt. She and my uncle were arguing when I got there. She blames him for being a stubborn bastard."

"And is he?"

"Well, yeah. He's super old school, and the business is failing because of it."

"Then why do you have to fix it?"

He sat up again, glaring at the warrior. Avery scrunched up his face. "I thought you were supposed to be making me feel better, not asking the hard questions."

"Red, if you want me to make you feel better, you should invite me over."

Avery groaned. "I have to fix it, because they already fixed my life."

"That's a 'no' to coming over, then?"

The screens changed, so he and Linc were standing in a candlelit tunnel. He'd love to have Linc sitting next to him, but he had a lot on his mind, and Linc's mouth, his body, and his hands would be too much of a distraction. "Let's play."

"Do I get to see you tomorrow?" His voice held a note of pouting, making Avery squirm in his seat. Maybe Linc should come over after all. "You still there, Red?"

"Yeah." They moved carefully up the tunnel.

"So, tomorrow?"

"Yes." His face heated at the thought. Linc's mouth on his, on his body. His hands, his—

A troll stepped in front of them and ripped Linc's arms off.

"Oh, fuck, not again."

17

*H*aving a hot boyfriend waiting for you made the day impossibly long, especially given Linc was off work.

Lacey called after noon. "Dad's here."

Linc froze. He was washing dishes and nearly dropped his phone in the soapy water. "What do you mean?"

"He showed up this morning. Looked like he hadn't slept in days. Smelled like he hadn't showered in longer."

"Is he still there?"

She laughed bitterly. "Hell no. I told him to get lost."

He sighed. "How did he find you?"

"I didn't bother to ask."

Linc swallowed. *Say it. Say it.* He was trying to be what Avery needed. Failing to do the same for Lacey would be unfair. "Do you need me to come down?"

"No." The response was immediate, and his chest twisted in unexpected disappointment. "Just thought you'd like to know."

"Yeah. Keep me posted."

"Yeah, sure." She didn't sound like she believed him.

"Hey, Lacey?"

"Yeah?"

His heart spasmed, but he forced the words out anyway. "Do you remember Mickey?"

"The gay kid Dad beat the crap out of?" she sneered. "Why the fuck would you bring him up? This situation is shitty enough as it is without rehashing how we got into it."

Linc stared at soapy bubbles, watching them pop and disappear one by one. "Nothing. Never mind."

———

Linc went out to get groceries. When he came back, the hall outside his apartment echoed, but for once, it wasn't Jordan and Chelsea blowing off steam. Two men were having a pretty serious argument.

"So—what? You're gay now too?"

Linc froze.

"Come on, Der, don't be a jerk." Jordan's voice was hoarse.

"You are, aren't you? Shit, does Chelsea know?"

"It doesn't have anything to do with me. It's not cool for you to—"

"You better not be checking me out. We're bros, man, but that's it."

Linc rolled his eyes. Why did every straight guy think every gay guy in the world wanted them? Linc would rather fuck sandpaper than hook up with Derek.

"Don't be gross! That's not what I'm saying!" Now Jordan was starting to sound a little desperate, and Linc sighed. He and Jordan would probably never be close friends, but his roommate was doing his best to make good on his promise, and he could use some backup.

He pushed open the door, trying to keep his features neutral. Derek's scowl darkened when his gaze met Linc's, while Jordan's expression was naked relief. "Hey, guys. How's it going?"

Derek sneered. "Is it you? Did you turn my best friend gay?"

"Oh for fuck's sake, Der." Jordan rolled his eyes.

Derek strolled up to Linc, getting in his space. "Or are you still hitting it with that ginger weirdo? He probably puts out like a bitch. Moaning like a girl the whole time."

Linc's fists clenched. A sick lump hardened in his stomach. This was the moment to back down, to walk or run. Let Derek think what he wanted—Linc didn't care. But he didn't want to be that person anymore. He was tired of running, tired of hiding. He'd promised Avery he wouldn't hide.

He opened his mouth to reply.

"Get out." Jordan's voice was steady. Linc and Derek both spun toward him, the shock equal on both their faces if the way Derek's eyes bugged out of his head was anything to go on.

"Excuse me?" Derek laughed.

"Get out, Derek. If you can't not be an asshole, then you can't be here."

Linc's throat was dry, and his hands shook, but he took a step forward, shrinking the triangle he and Jordan made.

Derek's eyes swung to his, and he smirked. "Did you put him up to this?"

"I asked Jordan to be a decent human being." Linc hadn't expected him to take a stand in his own apartment, though.

"It's time for you to leave," Jordan said.

Derek glanced between them, but his bravado was fading. He could argue with Jordan as much as he wanted, but bullies like Derek knew when they were outnumbered.

He laughed once more, as he took a step back toward the door. "Whatever. Enjoy the orgy."

Linc and Jordan watched in silence as he left. His footsteps echoed down the hall

"Wow." Jordan ran a hand over his hair. "That was—"

"Yeah." Linc's heart was still shuddering in his chest.

"Sorry. I—I've been trying to drop hints. But Derek's not exactly subtle."

Linc sank to the couch. "Yeah."

Jordan stood there, rubbing his arms awkwardly. "I don't think he's going to listen to me."

"Probably not."

"But we're okay, though. Right?" His eyes were hopeful, almost like Avery's, and Linc had to smile.

"Yeah. Sure."

Jordan started pacing, walking tight laps from the couch to the kitchen and back. "That was—I mean . . . I talked down a guy who was high on I don't know what yesterday. He'd cut his head open on the curb and was talking about hopping in his car and driving to Cape Hatteras. But he was buck naked, and his pupils looked like they were the size of nickels and—"

"Sounds like a busy day."

"Yeah it was, but—" He blew out a long breath, shaking his arms from his shoulders to his fingers. "But I wasn't ever scared. He said all kind of wild things, but I knew I'd be okay. With Derek, I was scared. You didn't see him, when I first told him—I mean—I thought he was going to hit me. Like *really* hit me. And he's my friend, you know?"

Linc did. He pictured it every time he thought about telling someone about his sexuality, along with the disgust dripping from Derek's eyes.

"Thanks." He stood, shaking Jordan's hand. "For standing up to him."

"Of course!" Jordan smiled. His frame still vibrated with adrenaline. "Yeah. I mean. You're my roommate, man. I said I'd talk to him, didn't I?" He looked so proud of himself.

"Yeah."

"Yeah." Jordan nodded. "Yeah. I'm . . . I'm gonna go. See Chelsea. She's off work soon."

He'd be a raging hard-on before he even got there. But at least Linc wouldn't have to hear it.

In fairness, by the time Avery's text message came through, Linc was also practically climbing the walls.

I'm home. Still coming tonight? ;)

The winky face was an adorable temptation. Linc was showered and changed inside of ten minutes, and driving across town.

The exterior door and Avery's apartment door were both unlocked. Music played, turned up loud. As Linc pushed through the door, the sight of red hair flying and lean hips swinging as Avery danced around the living room greeted him.

He stumbled when he turned, eyes wide, chest heaving. "Hey!" He pulled his phone out and went to turn the volume down.

"No, don't." Linc laughed and started his own shake in time to the music. He still wasn't the best dancer, but in the privacy of Avery's apartment, he'd go for it. Especially if dancing meant he got to touch Avery. And then touching turned to kissing. And then they were tangled up together, limbs wound around one another, while Avery laughed against his lips.

"It's good to see you too." His mouth was hungry on Linc's.

"How'd the interview go?"

"I'll tell you later." Avery's hands slipped under his shirt, and his fingers skimmed over Linc's skin.

Linc did not mind leaving that topic for another time at all. After two days apart, and despite all the drama—from Vasquez, his sister, Derek and Jordan—the second Linc got his hands on Avery, it all dropped away.

"What do you want tonight?"

Avery hummed, nipping Linc's chin. "Why don't you take the lead, and I'll tell you when to stop."

Linc shivered. He'd been hesitant to take charge the other night, especially after Avery admitted his relative inexperience. But the memories of Avery's body around his and his soft moans as Linc filled him said he'd gotten it mostly right.

"Whatever I want?" His blood heated, running through the list in his head.

"Mm-hmm." Avery winked, like the emoji in his text, and Linc was done for.

He dropped to his knees, pressing Avery face-first against the wall. The sounds Avery made while Linc rimmed him were magic. Time to do it again.

"Oh, wow, um—" Avery said, but Linc already had a handful of the waistband of Avery's sweats and underwear and yanked them down roughly.

"Tell me to stop," he said as he kissed the dip at the base of Avery's spine.

"Don't stop, just, um—"

Linc bit at the freckled globe of Avery's ass, making him press closer against the wall, groaning. Linc spread him open, ready to get his mouth on him.

And froze.

Nestled between Avery's cheeks was some kind of sparkling blue gem.

"Oh my God," Avery said.

"What the hell is that?" Linc said, but he had a pretty good idea. He tapped it with his index finger, and Avery rose up on his toes, fingers scrabbling on the drywall. Linc did it again, to watch it dance as Avery's butt clenched.

"Um, so—"

"Something you want to tell me?" Linc ran his hands over the small of Avery's back and down his thighs, pushing the sweats below his knees.

"So, um—" Whatever Avery was up to, the plug robbed him of his power of speech. That was pretty special.

Linc caught the end of it between two fingers and tugged gently. "Do you want me to take it out?" He watched, mesmerized, as the ring of Avery's ass pulled tight over the base, while Avery squirmed and panted above him.

"Yes. No. Um . . . Can you . . . can you just . . . come back up here, for a minute?"

Linc hissed. He didn't want to go back up there. He wanted to stay here. Find out about all the magical things the sparkly toy could do and all the noises Avery would make while Linc explored. He wanted to suck him off while he played with it. Then he'd pump it in and out until Avery begged Linc to fuck him. Linc wanted to tongue Avery around it, spit dripping down his chin and Avery's balls, and finally he would pull the plug out with his teeth.

"Are you okay?" Avery glanced over his shoulder, hands still planted on the wall. Linc realized he was growling softly.

Fuck.

He rose, scooping Avery up and carrying him to the couch. If he was going to restrain himself, he needed to at least touch him. Never mind Avery's pants were still hanging around his ankles and his bare ass was tucked into Linc's lap as they sat down. Avery didn't seem to mind, though, because he kicked them off and tossed them on the floor, so Linc had to bury his face in Avery's neck to ignore Avery's half-erect cock staring at him. If he didn't, he'd start stroking him until neither of them cared what Avery had to say.

"Missed you." He planted small kisses on Avery's throat.

Avery snuggled in closer, running his fingers over Linc's jaw. "Me too."

His mouth on Linc's was still hungry, and his throat vibrated with needy little moans when Linc slid a hand between Avery's legs to run a finger over the jeweled plug. "This is pretty fancy."

"I bought it on the internet."

Linc didn't need to see Avery's face to know he'd be covered in splotches of red. He pulled him closer.

"Since the other night?" Same-day delivery was possible, but Linc hadn't realized you could get this kind of thing on Amazon. He'd been missing out.

"No. I've had it for a little while. I—"

"What?" Linc grinned and petted Avery's hair gently.

"I told you the virgin thing is stupid. I said I hadn't ever done . . . No one had ever fucked me before. But that doesn't mean I haven't . . . " He trailed off. Linc was more than fine with that, because now his head was full of images of a younger Avery, alone in his room, maybe trying to be quiet so his aunt and uncle wouldn't hear him, silently settling the plug into place. What had it felt like? Did he touch himself after? Twist it until he was hard and leaking? Jack himself off until he spurted all over the sheets while his ass pulsed around it?

"I need to fuck you," Linc said hoarsely. "So if you have something you want to talk about, now would be a good time."

Avery shuddered and nodded, pulling himself up until he was straddling him. He framed Linc's face in his hands and kissed him hard. Linc's hands went to his ass, squeezing and kneading.

"Tell me," he said as he bit Avery's bottom lip.

Avery's eyes were clenched tight. He rested his forehead against Linc's, breathing hard. "I don't like your fingers in my ass."

Linc froze, desire shriveling. "What?"

"I just . . . It's weird. It feels weird."

Linc's nose wrinkled. "It's not like I don't wash them."

"I know. It's not about that. It's hard to explain. I—"

"Did I hurt you?" They'd both been awkward, but Linc had done his best to be gentle.

"No." Avery reached for him, smothering him with kisses before he curled up on Linc's chest. "I'm making a mess of this."

"No, you aren't." Linc held him close. "Tell me what you want me to do."

"Nothing." Avery's voice was miserable.

Linc swallowed. "You don't want to have sex with me?"

"No, I do!" Avery was moving again, scrambling, practically

194

clawing at Linc's shirt. "I totally want to have sex with you. Pretty much all the time. So much you don't even know. I almost had to go jerk off in the office bathroom at lunch today, because I kept thinking about you and I couldn't—" He bit his lip.

"But you don't want my hands on your ass."

Avery took Linc's hand and slapped it down on one of his bare cheeks. "On, yes. In? Not so much."

Linc nearly laughed, but Avery looked so serious. "Okay then."

Avery's face brightened. "Okay?"

"Yeah. If you're not comfortable with it, I'm not going to force you. I'm mostly indifferent to where my fingers go anyway."

"As opposed to your dick?"

Linc couldn't stop his laugh, then. "As opposed to my dick, yes. I have very specific thoughts on where I do and do not want my dick to go."

"Me too." Avery grinned, then seemed to realize what he'd said and pulled his shirt up to bury his face in it.

Linc pulled the shirt down again to kiss Avery. "What do you want to do instead?"

"About what?"

He tapped the plug. "About this."

Avery shivered. "What do *you* want to do?"

The list of things Linc wanted to do more than watch Avery work himself open was very short.

"What about *your* fingers?" he said, voice rough.

"What about them?"

"Would you use your fingers to touch yourself? Or just the toy?"

"Oh, no, my fingers are totally cool. I don't know why it makes a difference. I mean, it's not like—oh." His eyes rounded. "Like you could watch me while I—" He sucked in a breath.

"Exactly." Linc found one of Avery's nipples and dropped his

195

head to suck on it through the thin material of Avery's T-shirt. He stiffened and arched under Linc's mouth.

"You can't see anything if your face is in my chest." Avery bit his lip and pushed back, moving on his hands until he rested against the opposite arm of the sofa. Linc sprawled along his half of the cushions, watching intently. The plug flashed and sparkled—a ridiculous bit of flair, moving in and out of view—and Avery reached behind him into a drawer of the small table by the sofa. He pulled out a bottle of lube, and Linc's throat went dry. "What's that for?"

The plug was already in, but Avery squirted lube into his palm and then turned back around, sliding down the cushions until his legs were splayed open, obscenely framing both the toy and his bobbing cock. Avery's fist closed around his erection. Linc hissed at the imagined coolness of the lube on Avery's flushed skin.

The display was delicious. So dirty. Avery wasted no time in playing with the plug. He placed a single finger on it, rocking it inside of him, and his hips rippled, sending a wave up his body.

"Oh, yeah." Linc shifted on the couch. They were barely started, and his cock was already uncomfortable in his jeans.

Avery worked himself slowly, sliding his lubed palm up and down his shaft. "What do you want to see?" His voice was almost a purr.

"Take it out. Slowly," Linc said hoarsely. Avery tilted his hips up, snagging the base between two fingers. The ring of his ass pulled tight and then released the cone-shaped end, sliding out easily. Avery sighed, still working his dick in his hand.

"You're so pretty," Linc said. "Now fuck yourself with it. Show me how you like it."

"Okay." Avery's eyes were already glassy, spots of pink spread along his cheekbones. His tongue traced the inside of his bottom lip. He hunched down farther to give himself better access and worked it back inside. He moaned as it popped past his rim again.

"Yeah." Linc dug his fingers into the upholstery, enjoying the sweet ache of his untended erection, pressing tighter against his fly. His hips rocked a little, looking for friction that wasn't there. "Yeah. That's good. You're doing good."

Avery whimpered and closed his eyes, working his cock harder. The sparkling jewel danced, even without his fingers, as his ass bunched. Linc grinned. He'd had a hunch the other night that Avery had a praise kink a mile wide. He wanted people to accept what he had to offer. Linc was only too happy to help out.

"So good," he said again. "The plug was a great idea."

Avery glanced at him. "Yeah?"

"So perfect. I could watch your greedy ass gobble it up all day."

Avery splayed his legs farther apart, putting on his show for one.

"Take it out again."

Avery did.

"Use your fingers. I want to watch you fuck yourself."

Avery found the lube bottle, slicking up two fingers. The first one slid in easily, and the second one was almost the same.

"Oh, yeah. You like that, don't you?" Linc opened the top button of his jeans before he ripped them from the inside.

"Yeah." Avery's voice was all breath.

"So do I." He undid the zipper and slipped a hand under the elastic of his shorts and stroked himself. "Oh God. You should feel this. You did this to me. Do you know that?"

Avery rocked down on his fingers. "Want you too."

"I know, Red. I've been thinking about you for two days. Your ass. Your mouth. You're so perfect for me. Look at you getting ready for me. So perfect."

"Are you going to fuck me?" Avery was all motion, hands and hips working together.

"Do you want me to?"

"Yes," he whined. Linc's dick throbbed in his hand at the sound.

"You're going to feel so good around me, Red. So warm and tight."

"Yes." Avery panted. A red flush poured from his throat and over his shoulders, painting over the freckles.

"You fit around me like you were made for me."

"Linc, I—" Avery choked on the words. Come spurted from his dick, splattering his stomach and his chest. He rocked against his fingers in erratic spasms, and Linc gripped his own dick hard, fighting back his orgasm. He hadn't meant to let Avery come so fast, but he wouldn't disappoint him by short-circuiting the fuck he'd promised.

Avery's chest heaved, and he glanced away. "Sorry."

"What for?"

He ran his fingers through the come on his torso, which was hotter than it had any right to be. "I got a bit excited."

Linc bit back a laugh. "Doesn't mean it's over."

"But I'm all sticky."

He peeled off his jeans and shorts, exposing his leaking erection. "Red. I have been waiting to do this for two days. You think a little spunk is going to turn me off now?"

Avery wrinkled his nose, but he smiled. "No."

Before he tossed his clothes to the floor, Linc fished into a pocket and pulled out a condom. He rolled it down and reached for the lube. When Avery held it out, Linc caught his wrist and tugged him over, mashing their bodies together.

"Oh my God!" Avery squawked, but he melted against Linc's mouth, biting and sucking at his lips.

"Slick me up," Linc said, and Avery hurried to comply. He squirted more than he really needed to into his palm, but the cool glide on Linc's dick was about the best thing he'd felt all day, at least until he could finally get inside Avery.

"How do you want to do this?" Linc said. When Avery shrugged, he turned him so he faced away, then tugged him backward.

"Oh." Avery trembled under his hands. He reached around, sliding his lubed fingers back into his hole. Linc breathed slowly, pressing his forehead to Avery's spine, watching the fingers slide in and out.

"Yeah. Like that. It's going to feel so good when it's me inside of you."

Avery pulled his fingers out and leaned back, reaching around to line Linc up with his ass. Linc closed his eyes and held very still, because even with all the prep, Avery was still mind-blowingly tight.

"Take your time." If Linc had his way, he'd grab Avery's hips and push him down to feel the slick rush of filling him, but instead, he let his hands wander, grazing Avery's ribs, his nipples, his cock, already half-hard again.

Avery groaned as he bottomed out.

"Okay?" Linc said, running his tongue over Avery's neck.

"Yeah."

Linc pulled Avery's thighs wide so his feet left the floor and he was mostly immobile. Avery cried out and arched against him, until his head rested on Linc's shoulder.

"Still okay?" He was trembling. They hadn't even started moving, and his orgasm was already tingling at the edges. Avery nodded vigorously and rocked against him with the little leverage he could manage. Linc held him close, planted his feet, and thrust up.

"Oh my God," Avery said.

"Yeah?" Linc thrust again, moving fast, loving the way Avery's body went limp against his, like this was the only thing he needed to sustain him. "You're so perfect," Linc said as he pumped into him. The heat between their bodies was electric.

"You're so big. Oh God, you feel so good."

"You do this to me." Linc was working hard, breathing fast. His balls were tightening, and he was going to finish too soon. "I've wanted you since the first time I saw you. Your tight body. Your mouth. Everything about you was made for me."

"Yes." Avery moaned.

Linc ran a hand over Avery's stomach, over the semi-dried come, then lower, to his erection, alive and kicking again. "You going to come again?"

"I don't know if I ca—oh God." He arched as Linc grasped him, jerking him quick and hard while his other arm held them tight together.

"You can. We can do this together. Come for me, Red. Make me—" He shouted and groaned as his own orgasm ripped out of him, spurting into the condom, buried as far into Avery's body as he could get. He nearly lost his grip on Avery's cock, but then, just as suddenly, Avery spasmed against him, mouth open on a wordless scream, and Linc's fist was covered in new lines of white come.

They gasped and panted for a long time. Avery's cock softened in Linc's hand, the spunk cooled, and all they could manage were a few lazy kisses with Avery's head twisted over his shoulder at an awkward angle.

"Holy shit," Linc said eventually.

"Uh-huh." Avery hissed, pulling himself up. As he stood, he was beautiful and obscene, like a filthy angel, back still to Linc, totally naked. He grasped one wrist over his head, tilting to the right until his spine popped. He repeated the gesture on the other left. Sweat glistened on his back, and lube shone from the inside of his thighs, making it officially the sexiest thing Linc had ever seen.

Avery turned, smile wide, spent cock drooping between his legs. His freckled stomach was smeared in come and Linc had the equal parts disgusting and desperate need to drop to his knees and lick it off. Instead, Avery trailed a hand through it like raunchy finger paint.

"Let's take a shower," he said, holding out his free hand.

Linc stretched out. "I'm pretty comfortable right here."

Avery pouted. "But I might slip and fall. You know first aid. You have to come."

"You're not going to fall." But Linc was. Falling so hard. He was probably even further gone than he knew. If Vasquez were here, she'd roll her eyes and tell him he was already fucked. Too late to be scared and back away.

"Linc?" Avery's eyes were shaded with uncertainty.

He smiled fondly. No need to worry Avery. He was everything Linc hadn't known he was looking for. Hadn't let himself look for.

"Nothing," he said with a smile. "I'll keep you safe. Don't worry."

18

———

*A*very woke up with a migraine the next morning. Not a bad one. Just a persistent throb behind his eyes that made seeing difficult, but with no nausea or ringing in his ears.

Linc, though, reacted like he was dying.

"Are you okay? You're not okay. What can I do?"

When he was worried, Linc sounded like Avery did on a good day.

"Nothing." He lay in bed with one arm flung over his eyes to block out any light.

"You have to let me do something."

He slid farther down the bed, pulling the sheets over his head. It smelled like them. Sweat and sex. Too bad he hurt too much for a repeat.

He drifted off to sleep. When he woke a few hours later, the apartment was quiet. The pain in his head was gone, and he had to squint until his eyes adjusted to the light sneaking in around the edges of his curtains, but he felt okay. He dressed quietly and checked his phone. He'd texted his uncle to say he'd be late for work, but had received no reply.

His stomach growled, which was a good sign. When his migraines were at their worst, eating was totally out of the question. Even the scent of food could send him running to the toilet. But he was hungry now. He and Linc had snacked on a few carrots and a container of leftover chicken and rice the night before, but that meager meal hadn't been much for the two of them to share. Little in Avery's house counted as edible food. His stomach growled again viciously. He'd have to grab something on the way to the office.

Except as he came down the hall, he heard the clink of bottles and the rustle of plastic. He craned his neck, and Linc—or Linc's ass, clad again in perfectly worn denim—was poking out from behind Avery's fridge door. He was tempted to smack it, but instead stepped very quietly behind him and ran his hands over the firm muscle and—

Linc yelped and flailed. His elbow swung backward. Avery tried to dodge, but the kitchen was small, and he was trapped between Linc's body and the breakfast bar.

He heard the crunch before he felt the pain. He tasted the blood before he registered the warmth dripping down his chin.

"Red!" Linc's eyes were wide.

"No. No, it's fine."

"Oh, Jesus, I think it's broken."

"It isn't. I'm fine." He tried to prove his point by inhaling, but the jolt as he went to wrinkle his nose made his migraine seem like a distant dream. "Oh my God." He wobbled, and Linc caught him.

"Shit. I'm so sorry. I didn't hear you coming." As he led Avery to the couch, Linc peeled of his shirt, thrusting it against Avery's mouth. He winced, and tears sprang to his eyes as it brushed the tip of his nose.

"I can't even smell you on this shirt," he said sadly.

Linc stared at him. "That's what you're worried about?"

Avery coughed. The pain was making him dizzy. "What were you doing in my fridge?"

"I was putting the groceries away."

"Groceries?"

"You wouldn't let me help, so I went shopping instead."

"You bought me groceries?" New tears formed in Avery's eyes, but not because of his throbbing face this time.

"And then I broke your nose!" Linc ran a hand through Avery's hair fondly, then pulled the shirt away from his face. "Let me see. Shit, it's swelling pretty badly. Do you want me to set it for you?"

"Shouldn't we go to the hospital?"

Linc sighed. "Legally, as a first responder, I should tell you yes, because we should check to make sure there's no other damage. As your boyfriend, I'm going to tell you that by the time we get there, it'll have set on its own and they'll have to break it again to put it back in place."

"Other damage? What kind of—" Avery choked and coughed. "My boyfriend?"

"Yeah." Linc cupped his cheeks in both hands. "I mean, assuming you aren't going to kick me to the curb for breaking your nose?"

"No. I really like it when you say it, though. Boyfriend." Avery's chest swelled in a rush unrelated to the swelling in his face. "It was all my fault. I shouldn't have—" He cried out as Linc's thumbs pinched the bridge of his nose and pushed toward the center sharply. "What was that?"

"It's set. Better if you don't see it coming."

He was feeling woozy again. "Is it straight?'

"Hard to say. Let me get some ice." Linc pushed off the couch. His ass was still spectacular in his jeans, but Avery hated the sight. That ass was solely responsible for the nauseating pain spreading over his eyes and up his forehead.

"Hard to say?"

"Well, it's swelling pretty fast." He grabbed one of the plastic shopping bags off the counter and pulled out ice cube trays from the freezer. "I did my best to find the center, but we won't really know until the swelling goes down. Here." He gave Avery the icy bag.

Avery laughed. "You have no shirt on."

"I broke your nose."

The ice jostled against his face, making him hiss. "The least you could do was give me the shirt off your back." He sighed. "I'm going to be all crooked now."

"Maybe." Linc wrapped one long arm around him, pulling him close but moving him gently. "If we're lucky, you'll hardly notice. First though, you'll be all swollen. Maybe a black eye or two. Shit, I'm really sorry."

"Black eye!" Avery wailed. If you asked him about broken noses on a day when his wasn't the nose in question, he'd tell you black eyes were common. But he hadn't thought about it while trying not to pass out or choke on his own blood. He pulled the ice away from his face long enough to glare at Linc while he still could. "How long am I going to be like this?"

Linc shrugged. "Dunno."

"You're the first responder. Give me your best guess."

"A few weeks?"

"A few weeks!" Oh, this was bad.

He couldn't go to work with a messed-up face. His uncle would just shake his head at this latest blunder. And what if Wanda's company wanted a second job interview? Or the—"Oh my God." Miserably, he leaned against the wall.

"Keep your head forward."

"What about the bachelor auction?"

"The what?" Linc's fingers in his hair felt nice at least.

"The bachelor auction. It's a fundraiser. Things are too bad at work to make a donation this year, so I said they could auction me off instead and now—" he raised his head long enough to wave the bag around his swollen face, "—this. No one's going to bid on a bachelor with a black eye."

The hand in his hair slipped to his back, turning in soothing circles. Avery struggled to breathe, hunched over like this, but the back rub was nice.

"I would," Linc said softly.

Avery gasped, then moaned as his blocked airways protested. The circles on his back continued. It probably looked hilarious: him slumped over, face buried in a plastic bag, clothes covered in his own blood, while his hot-as-sin shirtless boyfriend gave him a back rub. But all Avery could focus on was the shy honesty in Linc's words.

"You would?"

The circling stopped. "Sure."

"But you're not—" He swallowed and then sat up, letting the bag drop. It dripped in his lap, but he needed to see Linc for this. "You don't have to do that for me. I wouldn't force you." Avery expected them to start with small things. Drinks with Vasquez and Wanda. Maybe going to a movie. Linc bidding on him in front of the whole town was a totally different level.

Linc nodded slowly, eyes moving quickly around the apartment. "I want to. For you. For me. For whatever this is between us."

"But what about—about guys like Derek? He might be there. His dad is a bigshot with a lot of money. He'll probably bring a bunch of people."

Linc snorted, and Avery envied him. "Guys like Derek don't keep me in the closet. I do. Fear does. What my family might say does. But I think I'll be okay here. Vasquez is out, and people don't care."

"Yeah, because she'd eat them if they did."

He laughed, but then he twined his fingers between Avery's and held his gaze intently. "I'll bid on you. I'll be the one who takes you home."

Avery's heart could have burst. He tried to smile, but the pain and swelling meant it probably looked more like a deranged grimace. "As soon as my face is better, you're going to get the best blow job of your life."

Linc winced. "That would be a more attractive offer if there wasn't blood on your teeth." He squeezed Avery's hand. "Come on. Let's get you cleaned up."

———

Every time they saw each other that week, guilt gnawed at Linc's insides. The swelling was worst on the second day. He had only been able to get one eye open. On the fourth day, the bruising took over. The right side of his face turned black and purple from his nose to his eyebrow. The left side was better, with a line of sick purple-green that only spread under his eye to the ridge of his cheekbone. Once the swelling went down, they could see his nose was still reasonably straight. But even Linc found it hard to look at him for long.

So, of course, Wanda and Vasquez invited them over on day five.

When she opened the front door, Vasquez's mouth dropped open, and her eyes went wide like saucers. "Holy shit, Sweet Potato. What the hell happened to you?"

"It's nothing." Under the purples and greens, Avery's cheeks reddened.

"Like hell. Did you at least give the police a decent description of the homophobic jackass who did this to you?"

Linc was about to ask her if she'd mind letting them in when Avery said, "I did actually. Six foot one. Brown hair, brown eyes. Mid-twenties. Pecs and ass to die for. His chin is kind of scratchy when he hasn't shaved, and his elbows are super pointy when they connect with my face. But he's great in bed, so not so much with the homophobic jackass part."

If Vasquez's jaw dropped any farther, she'd dislocate it, and they'd have to call an ambulance. She stared at Avery in disbelief before her attention turned to Linc. "You?"

"It was an accident."

Her lips thinned, and she glared at him, but then Vasquez put an arm over Avery's shoulders and guided him into the house, clucking like she was his mother. "You poor little sweet potato. Let Auntie Ronnie make it better. I told him to look after you."

Linc followed slowly behind them, out of smacking range.

His phone rang in his pocket. The screen said *Lacey*. "He was here again today."

Linc glanced up the hall. Vasquez and Avery were in the kitchen. Wanda had joined them, and Avery was telling the story of his nose all over again.

"What do you mean?"

"I mean he was sitting on the porch when I got home from work."

"And?"

"He said he needed a place to stay for a few days." She sounded pissed, firing Linc's own fear and frustration.

"And you rolled out the welcome wagon?"

"Of course not. I gave him a hundred bucks and told him to go find a motel."

He closed his eyes. "You gave him money?"

"Well, what was I supposed to do? Make him dinner and unfold the couch?"

"Call the police?" The bastard needed to get lost. Old feelings, the ones telling Linc to run, threatened to strangle him.

"Hanging out on my porch isn't exactly breaking the law. And he hasn't done anything to let me get a restraining order yet."

Yet.

He looked up the hall again. Avery had his hands on

Wanda's face, thumbs over her nose. He jerked, and they all laughed, like it was the funniest thing they'd ever heard.

"Look," he said. "Don't give him any more money. He'll just spend it on cigarettes and online poker."

"What else was I supposed to do?"

He pursed his lips. He should tell her. Their father was a violent homophobe who had kept Linc looking over his shoulder for seven years. He didn't deserve any of their charity. Why would Lacey want to help him? Could Linc even trust her if she hadn't kicked their father's ass to the curb the second he'd showed up? Something wasn't adding up.

"Can I call you later?"

"Whatever." She hung up without another word.

He needed a few minutes to calm down and join the happy group inside, but Avery's laughter was turning self-conscious in the face—no pun intended—of Wanda and Vasquez's ribbing. His fingers swept over the bruises on his cheeks, and Linc strode down the hall, ready to do battle. However, Wanda and Vasquez had already noticed Avery's discomfort and stopped with the jokes. The whole experience left Linc feeling even more powerless.

Vasquez pulled out a board game. Linc wasn't much for these, but Avery's face lit up as they arranged complicated decks of cards and small cardboard circles printed to look like coins.

"I love *The Midnight Tower*. Can I be the merchant?" Avery started stacking the coins into precise piles.

"Vasquez, this is a whole geeky side of you I didn't know existed," Linc said.

She winked at him. "I am an ocean."

"Dragging men to their death?"

"Deep and mysterious."

"Keep telling yourself that."

She threw a plastic game piece at him. "You can be the peasant."

As it turned out, the peasant sucked. No money, no special skills. He was only as powerful as the fantasy community the rest of the players built around him.

Fortunately, this particular peasant was sleeping with the merchant, so he had some perks. At first, he thought the coins by his right hand were pieces he'd forgotten to count, but as Wanda and Vasquez got into a particularly vocal argument about whether a knight's spear was more powerful than an apprentice wizard's charm, cool fingers brushed against Linc's hand. As he glanced down, Avery's hand bumped against his again. Linc went to squeeze it, but instead, Avery quickly slipped something under his palm and then went back to staring straight ahead like nothing had happened. When Linc checked, he found a gold piece with a big "50" printed on it.

He leaned over to whisper in Avery's ear. "What's that for?"

Avery grinned. No amount of bruising could hide his shy pleasure as he softly replied, "Buy yourself something nice."

Linc left the piece on the table so he could brush Avery's thigh. "Is this a bribe?"

"What would it get me?" Avery shivered against his cheek.

"How's your pain?" He worked a little farther up Avery's leg. The muscles there shifted and clenched under his progress.

"On a scale of one to ten, above my neck it's about a four. Below though . . . " He took in a shaky breath.

"Yeah?" Linc leaned in closer.

"There's this . . . It's like it's throbbing and—"

"Stop getting your boy cooties all over my table!" Vasquez shouted.

Linc growled, even while his heart surged at the feeling of Avery curling into him like he could shield them from Vasquez's laughter and teasing eyes.

"I think they're really adorable," Wanda said.

"They're so cute it's disgusting," Vasquez agreed.

"They're also cheating." Wanda pointed at the fifty disc on

the table.

Avery sat up, eyes wide. "No, I—"

"Scott, the kept man is a good look for you, I'm not gonna lie."

"It's not like that," Avery said.

"Just imagine when he's the startup king of the East Coast. The man with his hands on the purse strings." Wanda bumped Vasquez and raised her eyebrows.

"I'll have you know I look really good sitting by the pool in the middle of the afternoon," Linc said.

"Oh, that reminds me," Wanda said. "Heath wants to know how you'd feel about moving to Atlanta."

The table fell silent. The multi-sided dice tumbled out of Avery's palm and clattered on the polished wood.

"Atlanta?" he said softly. Linc's stomach twisted and then soured further when Avery shot him a nervous glance. He found Avery's hand under the table and tangled their fingers together before he threw an accusatory glare at Vasquez. Her eyes widened, then rolled back in her head, before she elbowed Wanda in the ribs.

Wanda grunted. "What?" Then she gasped and her hands flew to her mouth. "Oh my God. That was really bad timing, wasn't it?"

Vasquez raised her eyebrows at Linc, as if to say *Happy now?* He squeezed Avery's hand, waiting until his eyes lifted off the table.

"Couldn't I stay in Seacroft?" he said with soft hope.

More stink eye from Vasquez, but she threw it in the direction of her partner, who only waved her off.

"I don't think so," Wanda said. "One of the reasons it's taken us so long to start hiring for this position is Heath is super old school about managing the company finances. I think he wants someone he can look in the eye when it comes to talking numbers."

Avery's hand slipped out of Linc's, making him go cold on the inside. "But I could travel? It's not that far."

Wanda bit her lip. "Maybe." If travel was actually an option, she wasn't selling it well. "But Atlanta's great. The office is small, but everyone is really friendly. There's a real cappuccino machine in the kitchen and an air hockey table in the board room because Heath hates meetings. It's a ton of fun!"

"But you work from here?" Avery said.

"Yeah, but I do the coding. Even if I worked in Atlanta, I'd be holed up in a dark room with no distractions, so it really doesn't matter where I am."

Avery still wouldn't look at Linc when he said, "Let me think about it."

The game finished with Avery holding almost every coin on the table, including all the ones he'd smuggled into Linc's pile. Apparently, that made him the winner, but no one seemed to care much at that point.

"We should go," Linc said quietly. Avery nodded beside him, but excused himself to the bathroom.

"I am so sorry," Wanda said as soon as he was out of the room. "I didn't think—"

"Yeah, babe." Vasquez crossed her arms in her chair. "You really didn't."

They both looked so torn up. Linc couldn't stay mad. He pushed back from the table, and they followed him silently to the front door.

"I'll see you at work tomorrow?" Linc said.

"Wouldn't miss it." Vasquez gave him a deflated smile.

Avery joined them, a bright smile pressing against his purplish face. "Thank you so much for having us over. We had a lot of fun."

His false cheer hurt. Linc slid an arm over his shoulder. "Come on, Red."

19

$\mathcal{T}$he drive home was mostly silent. At one point, Linc said, "I think I might have to go to Wilmington and see my sisters."

"Oh, okay." Avery struggled to find any kind of response while his mind reeled around the idea of also leaving Seacroft.

"I haven't seen them in years." Linc's gaze was fixed out the windshield, and his jaw vibrated with tension. His steely glare made the anxiety flare even brighter in Avery's brain.

"Then maybe it's time."

Linc swallowed heavily. "Yeah."

They didn't say anything after that, and Avery was ready to climb out of his skin as they pulled up in front of his apartment. He half expected Linc to kiss him goodnight and drive away, but he got out of the car and locked it.

Avery chewed on his lip. "I'm not moving to Atlanta."

Linc tapped a nail on the roof of the car. "Okay."

"I didn't think that was going to be part of the job when I interviewed."

"That's fine."

"I've never lived anywhere but North Carolina." His heart was jumping around in his chest like a hamster in a ball.

"Uh-huh." His face was shadowed. The sun had gone down hours ago, and Avery's tiny residential street wasn't well lit.

His nose itched and he wanted to scratch it, but everything still felt tight and achy. "You're not mad about it, are you?"

"About what?"

He swallowed. "About Atlanta."

"Let's go inside."

"Why?" Avery's insides were about to scramble themselves into knots.

"I'm not mad, Red. Let's go inside, because I don't want to spend the rest of the night leaning on my car."

But he kept an inch too much space between them as they crossed the street and left too many wordless seconds as Avery got the doors unlocked. Linc stayed nearby, but only when they were in the apartment did he pull Avery close.

"I'm not mad," he said again, pressing his lips to Avery's hair. The nearness, the smell of his skin—even through Avery's injured nose—helped settle him.

He sank onto the couch. "But you're something."

"It's not you. Sorry. My family—my sister, she—" Linc sighed and joined him. "Do you want the job?"

"I can't let them down."

"Wanda and Vasquez?"

"No." He glared at him. "My aunt and uncle."

"Right." Linc smoothed his hands over his thighs. Avery would prefer Linc were touching him. Honestly, he would rather do anything than have this conversation, but Linc had been extra careful with him over the last few days because of his nose. Now the question of leaving the city and the state had more or less spoiled the mood.

"My aunt didn't want me to move out. Did I ever tell you that?"

"No."

"It took her six months to listen to the idea, and then

another six months for her to stop crying any time I mentioned going to look for an apartment. I think she finally accepted it in part because this place is so close to their house."

"Well, she couldn't have expected you to live with them forever."

Avery had always known he'd move out, of course he had, but to leave entirely, out of town, out of North Carolina—they might not want him back.

The thought made him sick, irrational as it was. Very carefully, he shifted until his head was in Linc's lap, face up to avoid squashing his nose. "Do you know when I realized my parents had given up on me?"

"When?" Linc's arm came around his chest while his other hand played through Avery's hair. He did that a lot. Avery had always been self-conscious about his hair. Just one more thing to make him stand out. But he liked how much Linc was attracted to it.

"When my birthday came and they didn't do anything. I didn't think they'd actually come see me or send a gift. But I thought there would be *something*. A card. An email. My dad was never going to forgive me for being gay, but I hoped my mom might try. But she didn't."

"Shit, Red." Linc sighed. "I'm sorry."

He sniffed. "My aunt and uncle have tried so hard to make sure I never wanted for anything. They're not my parents, but they've done everything they could to get close."

"They sound like they really did."

"I never had friends in school. I wasn't from here. I talked too fast. I wasn't good at sports or anything really but math. So my aunt and uncle did everything to make me feel loved, since I didn't fit in anywhere else." And Avery did his best to be the best nephew he could for them. Always polite, always saying thank you. His lack of a social life meant he got good grades, and when

Uncle Theo had suggested Avery come work at the firm, Avery hadn't given it a second thought.

"So you want to stay here?" Linc frowned.

"How can I leave them behind? Throw everything they've done for me in their faces?"

"You're an adult. They'll understand. Your aunt and uncle care about you. They'd want you to be happy." Linc laughed bitterly. "Maybe they can give my dad some pointers."

Avery gazed up at the scratchy outline of Linc's chin in dismay. "I'm so sorry. I didn't mean—"

"It's fine." Linc pressed his index finger to Avery's mouth, then dragged it down over his lower lip. "I stopped trying to fix that situation a long time ago." Avery darted his tongue out to catch the stray finger, and Linc slipped it inside, inhaling sharply when Avery sucked it deep.

"How's your pain?" Linc said.

Avery scowled and let go of his finger. "You don't have to keep asking me that. I won't break."

Linc laughed, careful of his nose as he kissed him. "I think you already did."

He growled and was rewarded with another kiss. This was good. Nice. Having someone else in the space with him made everything easier.

If he left town, he might not have this anymore. "So what do I do about Atlanta?"

They stared at each other for a long second before Linc quietly said, "What do you want to do?"

Avery shrugged. "If the business goes down, I guess I won't have much choice."

"That's true. But if the business was doing well, and Wanda offered you the job anyway, what would you do?"

He bit his lip. The answer was so complicated. And not solely because of his family. Now he had the man with the strong fingers running steadily over his scalp to consider too.

"I'd miss you a lot," he said, hedging.

"And I'd miss you, but, Red, this thing with us is still pretty new. I wouldn't want to be the reason you decided to stay in Seacroft."

He knew he was asking for too much, but it still hurt to hear it. "Of course not." He'd be okay, though, if he had to move. Get his own apartment. Maybe get a cat for company. Make new friends in a place where his whole history wasn't an open book. That might be nice, actually.

"But," Linc said slowly, fingers still moving in his hair, keeping him still, "if you moved away, I'd come see you."

Avery tried and failed to hold down the stupid hopeful smile that broke free. "Really?"

Linc's gaze darkened. "Oh, yeah. And if that went well, then maybe we'd see what else we could do so you weren't so far away."

Now Avery did sit up. The blood rushed from his head, making his nose throb. "You would?"

Linc kissed him. "I've moved around a lot. What's one more time?"

They didn't talk much about Atlanta afterwards.

Later, when the apartment was dark and quiet and Avery's head rested on Linc's chest, listening to the steady thump of his heart, it didn't seem like that big a deal. If he left, Linc would come with him. Maybe not right away, but they were too good together to let it go. They fit together, like bits of a flat-pack sofa.

All Avery had ever wanted was someone to want him—a pathetically small goal in the grand scheme of things. Now he'd found it in Linc, and Avery wanted something else: a future with him. In Seacroft, in Atlanta. This dim basement apartment or somewhere else.

They fit. Even with Avery's babbling and migraines and his ability to create an accident out of the most mundane things, they fit.

The call came on Wednesday. Avery was staring at his computer, trying for the forty-eighth consecutive minute to figure out why the balance sheet from the equipment rental wouldn't, in fact, balance.

"You busy?" Wanda's cheeriness made him nervous.

Avery glanced at Uncle Theo's office. The black-suited people were back. "Not really."

"You got the job!"

He pushed away from his desk so fast, his wheeled chair careened and hit the wall. One of the black suits glanced over his shoulder, and Meredith snapped to her desk like she was on a bungee cord.

"You okay?"

He waved her off, hurrying for the exit. "That's—that's really great news."

"So great. Heath loved you. He thinks you'll be a great addition to the team, and I know you'll be perfect when it comes to keeping our eye on the financial ball."

The street the office faced was surprisingly busy, but everyone moved around him like he didn't exist. "That's, uh— that's really nice of you to say."

"So, we're emailing you the offer as soon as I get off the phone. I know I don't have to tell you to read it carefully and definitely let me know if you have any questions."

"Does it—" Why were words so hard? This was good news. He should be telling her how excited he was and how much he was looking forward to it. "Do I still have to move to Atlanta?"

"Not for a few months." She was talking like everything was already decided. "We know you'll need time to find a place, sublet your apartment here. But we'd like you to go down and spend the first week there. Meet the team. You know how it goes."

"I've only ever worked here." He hadn't meant to say that. The job sounded really cool. They were all about growth and being agile and quick to respond as the product evolved. Being part of something where change was a good thing would be so cool.

He'd only meant that no, he'd never actually met a team, unless you counted new clients, but they were temporary and often thrust a box of papers at him, gave him an empty desk or a spot at the table in the break room, and told him to shout if he needed anything. Would a team be the same? He envisioned a lot of hipsters in pastel button-downs and loafers. Would they see through him and know the farthest he'd ever been away from home was Bible camp in South Carolina?

"Yeah," Wanda said, because she couldn't hear the whirlpool of his mental spiral through the phone. "I'm gonna admit Heath wasn't totally sold. I think he was worried about how you'll adapt to something new. But I pointed out it said a lot about your dedication and your loyalty."

He nearly threw up on his shoes, glancing at the frosted glass window in the door of the office: *Donaldson & Associates, Chartered Accountants*. If he left, there would be no associates. Only one accountant.

So much for dedication and loyalty.

He closed his eyes, focused on breathing and not sounding like he was going to melt down in the middle of the street. "So you'll send me the email?"

"Yeah." She paused. "You're excited, right?"

His smile stretched tight to the point of pain. "Absolutely. I'll just read over it and . . . um . . . But I need to get back to work." Since he still worked there. For now.

His hands shook as he hung up. He stared at his phone, scrolling mindlessly through his social media apps right there on the sidewalk. And that was no help at all because all he got were strangers and celebrities and people he'd gone to college with but never spoken to again who told him to live his best life and also that family was everything.

How was he supposed to do both?

He was halfway to calling Linc and asking for advice when he remembered Linc was working today. He chewed on his lip. Almost lunchtime. Avery had a macaroni casserole in his freezer at home. He could drive over, grab it, and take it to the fire department. Linc would be there, and he would tell Avery what he was supposed to do.

But he'd already said he couldn't be the reason Avery stayed or went.

"Avery?"

He leapt what must have been at least a foot straight in the air. Meredith stood in the office's open doorway.

"Yeah?"

"You okay?"

"Mm-hmm." His smile still ached.

She eyed him, but when he didn't say anything else, she shrugged and held the door open. "Your uncle wants to see you."

Shit. He knew. *He knew he knew he knew*, and he was going to be so mad or disappointed or resigned, and Avery couldn't decide which was the worst possible option.

"I'll be right there."

He did one more tour on social media, but found no new inspiration. Instead, he sent a quick text to Linc.

Got the job!

Feeling like the biggest liar on the planet, he added a couple confetti emojis and a smiley face.

Uncle Theo and the two black suits were still in the office when Avery went back in. He paused at his desk and checked his computer. Wanda's email was there.

Congratulations! said the subject line.

He couldn't do this.

"Avery, come on in," Uncle Theo said as he entered the back office. "Phil. Steve. This is my nephew, Avery."

"Nice to meet you." Avery shook their hands. His palms were clammy.

"Broken nose?" one of the men said. Avery didn't actually know which one was which.

He put a hand to his black eye—now a more reptilian green. "Yeah."

"I did that once when I was about your age," Phil-Steve said. "I was in a beer league. Took a baseball to the face. Busted my nose and my cheekbone. I couldn't see properly for three weeks."

"That sounds really painful."

"You have no idea. How'd you do yours?" Phil-Steve smiled expectantly up at him.

"It's a long story." Avery glanced at Uncle Theo, whose eyes were wide with barely suppressed horror. He knew what had happened—sort of. Mostly.

Aunt Brenda had been hysterical when she'd seen Avery's face. She'd wanted to take him to the hospital to make sure no bone fragments were lodged in his brain. He'd sworn he was fine, and only a frantic phone call to Uncle Theo had saved them all a trip to the emergency room. Theo agreed with Avery's opinion that if there were bone fragments, they would have killed him days ago. But when Aunt Brenda asked what had happened, Avery said he'd slipped in the shower, because he still wasn't sure if he could announce he and Linc were a couple.

"Why don't we get to the point?" the other man—Steve-Phil? —said.

"Yes." Uncle Theo's expression was relieved. "Yes, that's a good idea. Avery, pull up a chair."

Except Uncle Theo didn't have any extra chairs. Phil-Steve and Steve-Phil had taken the two reserved for guests in Theo's office. Avery went back out to the main space, grabbed the wheeled chair, and pushed it in.

"Shut the door," Uncle Theo said as Avery reentered. He did, shooting a nervous glance at Meredith, who watched them all with intense focus, like the climax of a movie about corporate espionage.

When Avery closed the door and settled into his chair, Uncle Theo said, "I know you've seen Phil and Steve here before."

Why did it feel like he'd been called down the principal's office? Was he supposed to pick out Phil and Steve from a lineup? Finger them for spraypainting *Ms. Clayton wears combat boots* on the back of the gym wall? "Sure."

"Phil works for the bank."

"And Steve," Phil said, pointing at the man beside him, answering at least one question, "works with us on a consulting basis to help small businesses optimize their growth."

They were growing? No one bothered to inform Avery.

Uncle Theo chuckled. "What he means is they help teach stubborn old dogs new tricks."

The three of them all laughed, but Avery was still trying to follow what was going on.

"Your uncle says you have some ideas for how to build up the firm?" Steve said.

"I—" He had. He did. But if he was moving to Atlanta, it didn't matter anymore.

"Steve has convinced me that we should try them," Uncle Theo said.

"Steve has—" Avery's gaze was bouncing back and forth between them as they spoke.

"Compliance and general bookkeeping are mainstays in any firm, but if you really want to grow in the twenty-first century, you have to move beyond that."

"You do?" Avery's throat was dry. "I mean, you do. Yes. Absolutely."

"And your uncle seems to think you'd be good at leading those changes."

Avery had the weirdest feeling. Not quite déjà vu. Dread? A sense he knew where this conversation was going, but also like he'd had it a dozen times.

They had spreadsheets. Charts. Projections. Suggestions. Everything Avery had tried to pull together over the last few months but had been shut down over at every opportunity.

"And within the next five years, I think it could be very likely that you could be running a team of six or seven associates."

Smoke coming out of someone's ears was only possible in old cartoons. Otherwise, Avery would be doing it. Heat coursed under his skin, frustration pumping through his veins. Their pitch, if that's what it was, was nearly word for word the things he'd argued for. These were his ideas, shot down over and over again. But now, because a couple guys in suits and gray hair suggested it, they were doable?

"Do you understand what they're saying?" Uncle Theo asked softly.

"I think I do." Too bad for him. Avery was going to be hunting for apartments in Atlanta the minute he got home. He didn't even need to read Wanda's job offer. As long as they were paying him a livable wage, he would be booking the moving van shortly. He'd been trying too hard to be loyal and respectful, and look what he'd earned. Uncle Theo would never listen to him, but he'd listen to a couple suits, a couple *strangers*, who came in here like they could save everything. And Avery was left as some charity case the Phil-Steve machine would have to take on, just like this husk of a business.

No. Avery was done. Time for a new adventure. A big city. He could start over and be his own person.

"So, now let's talk about the transfer of ownership." Phil pulled a file folder out of his briefcase.

"The what?"

Phil spread some legal-looking documents out on the desk.

"I want to sell you the business," Uncle Theo said.

The record scratch on Avery's mounting anger was so loud, his ears nearly bled. "I'm sorry, did you just say . . . " He gaped.

"It's not much." Uncle Theo glanced down at his clasped hands. "Not as much as it could have been if we'd started this sooner, but at least this way you start with a client list and a reputation. The guys here, they've convinced me of what you've been saying all along."

"That's good, I guess." Avery dropped his gaze to his shoes; if he kept his eyes on his uncle, there would be no way to hide his thoughts.

"But the thing is, what they're talking about, what you've been talking about, it's not a fast thing. It will take energy I simply don't have anymore. In four or five years, I want to be able to take your aunt on that cruise she's been hinting at, not working on the weekends to find new clients."

"We understand," Phil said, making Avery look up again, "buying your uncle out may not be something you're in a financial situation to do at this time. Someone your age might not have the funds. That's why we've worked out a plan to help you . . . "

They talked for almost an hour. Avery rocked between stunned silence and simmering frustration. The way they described it, it all seemed so easy. The plan. The conditions on the financing. He'd be his own boss, run his own business. He'd still be in Seacroft, close to his family.

"Your aunt will be so happy," Theo said. "What do you say we sign the paperwork and then we'll close the office for the afternoon? Go celebrate, just the three of us?"

The three of them. They'd been a team for eleven years, since the day they'd come to find him. He could still have that. It would be like it was.

But was that what he wanted?

He tapped the stack of documents Phil had produced for him to sign, running a finger over the pen that lay across it. "This sounds like an amazing opportunity."

His uncle smiled. "I'm sorry it took me so long to see what you were trying to say."

Avery nodded. And leaned back in his chair. "I'm going to need some time to think about this."

———

"And so now I have to decide if I want to buy the firm or start looking for somewhere to live in Atlanta." Avery panted. His cheeks were flushed.

Linc pulled him close, letting the silence settle around them. He didn't have a good answer. On the one hand, Avery wanted to fit in somewhere so badly. This town had been his home for a long time. On the other hand, while Seacroft was imperfect, moving somewhere new would have its own problems.

"Did you talk to Wanda?" Linc asked.

Avery nodded. "Mostly. I didn't tell her everything, but she knows leaving the firm is complicated because it's family. She said she needs an answer by the end of the week."

Which was technically tomorrow, but pointing that out wouldn't wipe the miserable look off Avery's face.

They were both still half-dressed, with Linc in his jeans but no shirt, while Avery's shirt was unbuttoned and his pants undone but still on. It turned out Linc had a thing for Avery in his professional look. Making him come in his office clothes felt dirty and so tempting.

"What do you think I should do?" Avery asked.

Linc held himself still, though he wanted to squirm away. "I think you should do what feels right."

Avery's hand trailed over the front of Linc's jeans, where he was semi-hard because he couldn't *not* be aroused when they were this close.

"This feels right," Avery said.

And it did. So right. It seemed impossible that they were the same age, or very nearly anyway. Avery had such big questions and had been so few places, while Linc had made his own decisions a long time ago. Keep enough distance to feel safe, no matter what it cost. Except, in keeping that distance from his family, he'd stepped right into Avery's path. A collision like this was bound to happen; he'd known he'd finally meet someone, or even stay somewhere long enough to make friends and think about settling down.

He rolled his hips as Avery slipped his hand under Linc's waistband.

"Feels good?" He trailed a line of kisses between Linc's nipples.

"Yeah." He shimmied out of his jeans while Avery continued to stroke him.

"If I lived in Atlanta, I wouldn't be able to do this as often."

Linc bit his lip as images filled his mind. "Yeah, but imagine the reunion sex when I came to visit."

Avery swiped his thumb across Linc's slit, spreading pre-come over the sensitive head of his cock. "Are you saying it'll get boring if I stay in Seacroft?"

Boring? "Never." Not when he had miles of freckled skin to lick and kiss, when Avery's perfect long cock was there for him to suck, and his tight round ass was there for Linc to ruin.

"But it would be pretty good, right?"

"What?"

Avery smiled at him, lower lip caught between his teeth. "The reunion sex. We'd be on our own there. No one to bother us. Just you and me, living our lives. That would be pretty cool— oh!" He arched as Linc sucked him deep into his mouth.

But, as his nose brushed over the curling hairs at Avery's

groin, the image stuck. A fresh start. A bright apartment that was both of theirs. Avery's face full of expectation when Linc got off his shift, or sleepy pleasure first thing in the morning. He was so caught up—in the breathless way Avery said Linc's name as he pulled him up to kiss him, and what having that every day in a place just for them would be like—he didn't hear the drawer opening and closing. Or maybe Avery kept the lube stashed under his pillow for easy access. Instead, the only warning Linc had was the quiet click of the cap before Avery's palm closed around him.

"Oh, fuck." He bucked as the friction melted away, leaving only slick warmth.

"If we lived in separate cities, this wouldn't be my hand." Avery tugged one of Linc's nipples between his teeth. "You'd have to do it yourself. I don't know if you'd like that."

It wouldn't be as good. Not by a mile. But the separation would be short-lived. Linc couldn't be the reason Avery chose to stay or go. But if Avery went to Atlanta, Linc would be looking for a new job as soon as possible so he could follow him.

"You'd be better," he said through gritted teeth as Avery worked him up and down, twisting over the top the way he was learning Linc liked.

Avery purred against Linc's chest. He was still careful with his nose, but he let his mouth roam all over Linc's body. "I'm better?"

Linc grinned. Always fishing for the compliment, the unfettered praise. And Linc was more than happy to give it to him. "I dreamed about you last night."

"Yeah?" Avery stopped his exploration, resting his cheek on Linc's sternum so he faced down his body. Linc imagined what his dick looked like pumping in and out of Avery's fist, the head growing dark and leaking.

He had. He'd been asleep in the station dorm for more hours than normal. In his dream, he was deep inside Avery's body, and every thrust felt like the hot, tight fist wrapped around his dick right now. He'd woken up to find himself embarrassingly hard. Fortunately, no one was around, and he'd recited evacuation protocols until his erection went down.

Now, though, he could do exactly what he wanted.

"More," he growled. "I always want more from you."

Avery pushed himself down the mattress, crawling between Linc's legs. His hand slowed as he repositioned himself, and Linc squirmed at the loss of sensation.

"If I didn't live here, I wouldn't be able to do this." Avery didn't give him a chance to ask what "this" was before lapping along the seam of Linc's balls, while his hand took up its work on his shaft again.

"Fuck," Linc growled, thrusting into Avery's palm. Avery was gentle with the sensitive skin of Linc's sack: sucking each ball into his mouth, one at a time, then releasing them with a sloppy pop. A thumb pressed against his taint, before sliding along his crack and rubbing over his hole. "This okay?"

"Yeah." Linc's hips had chosen their own rhythm now. No stopping. No turning back. "Yeah, that's good, Red."

Avery traced the muscle, using the soft pad of his thumb to push in a fraction of an inch. His other hand was keeping pace with Linc, staying tight and slick as the pressure started to build at the base of his cock.

"Do you think you might let me fuck you sometime?"

The question was asked so casually, so offhand, the way Avery might have asked if the weather would be nice tomorrow, Linc almost didn't understand what he'd just said. He was so lost in the sensation, the tingling in his balls, the wet heat around his dick, and the gentle press against his ass that he nearly missed the meaning.

And then bright lights exploded behind his eyelids at the thought of Avery's long cock sliding in and out of him, holding him open. Of the burn and the stretch, Avery's hands on his lower back, holding him in place, and hot breath on Linc's neck. His orgasm was a rush, while his scream was a long, strangled thing as come spurted out of his dick, striping his stomach. His hips had curled up and Avery's tongue was on his taint and, holy shit, if Avery kept doing that, Linc might find it in himself to come again.

"Stop," he rasped, tingling with overstimulation. Avery's head popped up from between Linc's thighs, his smile as bright as Linc's orgasm. He tugged off his clothes and climbed up Linc's body, smearing come between them and not seeming to care in the least. When he was completely sprawled across Linc, he kissed him, long and hard, tongue swiping inside Linc's mouth like he was trying to claim every single inch of him.

Love. The word popped into Linc's brain, and he squashed it down immediately. Too soon, too fast. But also impossible to deny. Everything about the way he and Avery fit together felt so right.

"I've made a decision," Avery said.

"About?"

"I'm staying in Seacroft."

20

---

*L*inc left early the next morning. He had a short shift at the station, covering for a sick coworker, before he'd meet Avery at the bachelor auction. Avery's stomach was in knots about it still, but a blow job helped. A lot.

"I'll see you tonight," Linc said between kisses.

"But you'll be there, right? They know you have to leave at five?"

Linc pulled him close, pressing him against the breakfast bar so Avery had no choice but to be surrounded by him. His lover. His boyfriend. God, having this felt so good.

"I'll be there," Linc said fiercely into his ear. "Everyone will know who you're with."

Avery wriggled in happiness.

So, inevitably, he managed to drop his phone in the toilet.

The dunking wasn't his fault. Not really. Or, at least, it could have happened to anyone. One second, he was dancing around the bathroom, brushing his teeth and trying to get his hair to lie in the right direction, and the next his hip bumped against the sink. He'd propped his phone on the corner of the vanity, and the bump was enough to tip it over. In slow motion, it clacked onto the fake marble and rattled like a pinball on top of his toilet paper holder before disappearing into the bowl with a *sploosh.*

"Oh, no!" Avery said, dropping his toothbrush and drooling minty foam over his chin. He spat and rinsed, then nearly caught the side of his head on the faucet coming back up, which would have been pointless because he didn't need to hurry. His phone had already settled to the bottom of the bowl and looked pretty happy to stay there.

"No, no, no." He bobbed on his toes. His desperation was interrupted only by his disgust at the idea of thrusting his hand into the toilet bowl. When was the last time he'd cleaned it? Even if he retrieved it, would he ever be able to hold it to his face again?

The water was surprisingly cool. He didn't know why he'd expected it to be warmer. Water dripped from his hand and wrist as he pulled the phone back out and . . .

The music kept playing, like the impromptu swim break meant nothing.

"Oh, thank God." He sagged against the towel rack. There didn't appear to be any damage. His phone was a couple years old, before waterproofing came standard, but maybe he'd finally gotten lucky.

He scrubbed his hands and arms with a lot of soap, then grabbed one of the disinfecting wipes his aunt bought when he moved in to wipe down the phone. The screen flickered briefly, but when he finished, everything flashed back to life. All his apps worked, and when he texted Linc to wish him a good day, the message hovered for only a second before the checkmark popped up to indicate delivery.

Things were turning around.

He brought coffees from the diner for Meredith and himself, with a tea for Uncle Theo because he was trying to cut back on caffeine after breakfast.

"You look happy," Meredith said, taking her coffee with a smile.

"It's going to be a good day." He grinned at her. It was going to be a good *life*. He was certain of this now. Seacroft wasn't sexy, didn't have all the things a big city like Atlanta had, but it offered all the most important things Avery needed. Family. Love—he shivered at the word, but he was confident he and Linc were headed there. Someday, there would be respect too. He'd own his own business and be an established part of the community, instead of the flaky, accident-prone gay kid who had arrived in the middle of the night.

When Avery knocked on his office door, Uncle Theo was on the phone, but he motioned for him to come in. He finished his call quickly while Avery set down the tea and settled into one of the seats that Steve and Phil had taken up the previous day.

They sat silently as Uncle Theo sipped at his tea, hissing at the heat and removing the lid from the paper cup.

"So," he said.

"Yeah." Avery clasped his hands in his lap.

"I need to apologize."

He sat up straighter. "What for?"

"Your aunt gave me a good dressing down last night. I told her about our conversation, and she was not impressed."

He could picture the expression on his aunt's face. "It's a pretty fair offer, though."

Uncle Theo sipped his tea and grimaced. "She said I should have involved you in the conversations from the beginning. That apologizing after everything was settled wasn't nearly as effective in getting you to help make the decisions as soon as I knew I wanted to sell you the business."

Aunt Brenda was a very smart lady.

"But I told her you said you needed to think about it anyway. So maybe it wouldn't have made a difference when I told you. If you think you don't want to—"

"I'm in," Avery gasped. "I'm in. I'll buy the firm. I'm ready. I can do this."

The office fell into silence. Avery glanced over his shoulder. Meredith was still at her desk, but she'd turned her chair to face them. If having actual heart-eyes were possible, she would have them. She sipped her coffee with a broad smile on her face, blatantly eavesdropping through the open office door.

When Avery turned back, Uncle Theo's head was tipped to the side, and one corner of his mouth was twitching in tiny spasms. "That's good," he said softly. "That's really good, Avery."

You had to know Uncle Theo to read it right. The tiny smile. The way he opened his body up. On anyone else, it would seem restrained, bored even. For Uncle Theo, the motion was the equivalent of doing a victory dance around the office.

"So, what do we do now?" Avery asked.

"I'll call Phil. Let him know what we've agreed, and he'll bring the paperwork over."

"I have a meeting at the equipment rental this afternoon."

Uncle Theo chuckled. "Still can't get them to balance?"

"He's definitely missed something somewhere. There's no way to make the numbers add up."

The words felt good. So good. Relaxed and easy, like always, right up until the last few weeks.

"Your aunt wants me to remind you to iron your shirt before the bachelor auction tonight."

Avery rolled his eyes. "I will."

"And you'll remember to turn off the iron before you leave the apartment?"

"Yes." Although the reminder was fair. Things like that were how he'd wound up with a hot firefighter in his apartment. At the thought of Linc, he smiled a bit shyly and said, "There's something I should tell you. Well, you and Aunt Brenda."

"Oh."

"I have a boyfriend."

An excited squeal cut through the air from the outer office, and they both turned toward Meredith as she clapped gleefully, then blushed when she realized she'd been caught.

"Sorry!" she called, but then clapped some more.

Uncle Theo sighed heavily. "Is that it?"

"Is what it?"

"Your aunt will kill me if I come home with the news you've met someone and don't have any more details."

Very true. She'd want to know everything. Who he was, where he'd come from, how he and Avery met. She'd want to know his favorite meal and then she'd invite him—demand he come, really—over to the house so she could cook it for him while she grilled Linc for every detail about his history and personal life.

Avery smiled. "He's really nice. His name is Linc, and he's a firefighter. You'll meet him tonight."

Uncle Theo arched an eyebrow. "Oh, we will, will we?"

"Yup." Linc was going to bid on him, win him, and then take him home for hours of grateful boyfriend sex.

His uncle chuckled. "Well, that's enough to keep your aunt happy. But you should tell him to plan to come for dinner this weekend."

"I will."

He texted Linc when he got back to his desk.

Told my uncle. You're stuck with me now.

———

He did, in fact, nearly set his apartment on fire again, trying to do too many things at once. Iron his shirt, make a little dinner, finish an email. It wasn't the iron that got him, but the dish towel he thought he'd hung on the oven handle and had actually pinched inside the oven door. Fortunately, he caught it before the smoke got too bad. The smell wasn't as awful as the old sweet potato smell, but the towel was ruined.

Then he got spaghetti sauce on his freshly ironed shirt.

He was so late. After an extra-long visit to the equipment rental to sort out the balance sheets—turned out Mr. Graves had switched to a new invoicing program and had been billing his clients using pricing from the previous year—he'd gotten home almost two hours later than he wanted. He was supposed to be at the community center by six, and it was already five-thirty, and now he needed a fresh shirt. Also, it turned out to be laundry day, so Avery had to find the cleanest of his dirty shirts from the hamper and iron it all over again.

He made it with two minutes to spare.

Except no one was there. Well, lots of people were coming and going. A senior citizen's group doing Tai Chi. Kids dressed in Scout uniforms. No sign of bachelors, though. Or an auction.

He pulled his phone out of his pocket to double-check the details.

The screen was black. He stabbed at it with his finger, but nothing happened. Finally succumbed to its dunking, apparently.

A nice woman at the front desk let him use her computer to figure out that the auction was at the Seacroft Country Club, not the Seacroft Community Center.

So, by the time he arrived, he was super late.

Avery recognized Penny, who owned the diner downtown, as he burst through the doors. She was pacing the lobby of the country club. The second he walked in, she rushed toward him. "Avery. Where have you been? They already started the auction."

"I'm so sorry." He was sweating under his suit jacket and breathing hard.

"It's fine, come on." She tugged on his sleeve and pulled him down a hall, through a kitchen, and into a waiting area behind a curtain. Two other bachelors, guys Avery didn't recognize, were seated on hard plastic chairs. One was a little bit older than Uncle Theo and wore a suit that probably hadn't been out of his closet since some formal occasion in the eighties. The other couldn't be more than eighteen. They both gave Avery awkward smiles as he sat.

"So we're going to put you last," Penny said as she straightened his tie and smoothed his hair down like he was also below the age of majority. "Can you confirm what your prize will be?"

He blinked at her. "My prize?"

His two fellow bachelors shifted uncomfortably. His anxiety hadn't settled, and now it morphed into gurgling nervousness.

She sighed impatiently. "The auction is for a bachelor *and* an experience. Greg here is offering a session at the driving range, and Leon will take the lucky winner swing dancing."

Avery stared at Greg and Leon in horror. They glanced at their shoes like they'd failed him by not letting him know about this.

"I—" He swallowed. "I can offer a financial planning session? Household or business budgeting?"

"Oh." Her wide eyes and open mouth said the idea sounded as stupid as he thought it did, but she'd put him on the spot. She scribbled on her clipboard. "Yeah, yeah, we can do that."

Out front, a round of applause was followed by a gavel banging heavily.

"Sold!" The auctioneer sounded authentic at least.

Avery tugged on his cuffs.

"Leon, you're next." Penny helped the older gentleman up and led him toward an opening in the curtain. He shuffled along, barely lifting his feet. Hopefully, he had secret hidden talents when it came to swing dancing.

Leon sold fast. Two quick bids and the gavel fell to polite applause. Greg was already at the curtain before Penny could collect him, and then Avery was alone.

He swallowed. He wasn't nervous. Not nervous at all.

Excited. Yeah. What he was feeling wasn't anxiety. More like anticipation. He was going to walk out on that stage, and Linc would be there, sitting with the rest of the team from the fire department, and the MC would say Avery's name, and Linc would put his hand up, and everyone would know who Avery belonged to.

He tugged on his tie and straightened the rainbow clip in the middle. Uncle Theo had lent it to him.

"We're so proud of you," he'd said. Avery had tried not to cry. Everything was all coming together.

Finally.

He stretched his feet out in front of him, admiring the shiny brown shoes. They were the color of caramel and the leather was stiff, but he felt so *everything* in them. Sophisticated. Confident. Above them was a pair of striped socks. Pink and orange. Colors he'd never been allowed to wear as a kid because his father said they were for girls. Colors he'd been told he looked ugly in, just like his dad said later Avery's soul was ugly.

It wasn't. He knew that now. Had always known it, really. But now he had Linc on his arm, and the rest of the world would see it.

While trying to eat dinner and iron his shirt, he'd written an email. One he'd dreamed about for years, ever since he'd worked up the courage to ask Aunt Brenda for the address, but then had been too scared to write.

Dear Mom,

I hope you're well. Uncle Theo says he doesn't talk to you very often, but that you and Dad are in good health.

I am doing very well. I'll be taking over Uncle Theo's firm. My very own company. I'll be a business owner. Respectable. Just like you always wanted.

I have a boyfriend. His name is Lincoln. He is a firefighter. I'm telling you this not because I think you'll be happy for me, but because

I want you to know that I was right. I am gay, and nothing you could have done could have stopped or prevented that from happening.

I also want you to know I don't forgive you. I was your son, and you were supposed to love me and look after me, no matter what. I am sorry, though, for you and Dad, that you didn't know how.

I am not your son anymore. I am Theo and Brenda's, and they love me very much.

I wish you a good life.

I already have one.

Avery

On the stage, another smattering of applause sounded as a gavel banged down.

Avery hadn't sent the email. He'd thought about it, but he'd left it in his drafts, so he could read it sometimes and remind himself he was more than his parents and his history. His mother wouldn't care if he sent it, just like she hadn't cared in all the years without so much as a birthday card. He missed her, but he didn't owe her any more explanations.

He was going to build a life here. With Linc. With Theo and Brenda. And yeah, it would be quieter, smaller, maybe less exciting than it would have been in Atlanta, but it would be his, and that would be enough. He'd have other chances for adventure someday.

"Avery?"

He was on his feet before Penny could tell him it was his turn. It *was* his turn. He was going to take the stage. Maybe the fire department would whistle for him. Linc would. The heat in his eyes as he'd kissed Avery goodbye that morning said he'd do just about anything Avery wanted.

He lifted the curtain and stepped under the lights. The auctioneer said his name, and the sound of it made Avery puff out his chest. Somewhere beyond the lights, Linc was watching him and thinking what a goofball he was. Avery was Linc's goofball now.

He squinted out into the room. Aunt Brenda was there, with Uncle Theo next to her. Avery had to force his hands to his sides to keep from waving like a first grader at a school play. He strolled the edge of the stage as the auctioneer talked about the firm—soon to be *Avery's* firm—and the services it offered. He scanned the crowd, looking for the familiar sandy head. He caught sight of Wanda first, the rhinestones of her glasses twinkling in the dark. Then Vasquez, sitting to Wanda's left.

"The bidding for this fine young gentleman will begin at fifty dollars."

The seat next to Vasquez's was empty, then after that was an older man in an official looking uniform shirt. Than a woman, and another man, then—

"Do I hear fifty dollars?"

Avery's eyes slid over the faces of so many people he knew. People he'd known for years, who knew him and—

"Everyone can use a financial checkup."

Something cool poured over the back of Avery's shoulders, prickling and sharp, before it wrapped around his ribs and dug its claws in. His knees went rubbery as his toes pinched uncomfortably in his shoes.

"Do I hear—"

His desperate gaze swung back to Vasquez, then to the one empty chair.

I'll be there. Everyone will know who you're with.

Once again, Avery was alone.

21

*T*he call came at five-thirty, as Linc was driving home to change quickly before he went to the country club.

"Hello?"

"Linc?" Lilah sounded a bit breathless.

"Hey, baby sis, how's it—"

"Lacey's in the hospital."

He braked so fast the tires squealed. At least the street was empty, so he avoided being rear-ended.

"What?"

"I don't know." He could hear the sob in her voice. "I came home and there was an ambulance in the driveway and she was just lying there and—" She choked it off.

"Where are you now?"

"We're at the hospital. We just got here. Please, I need you to come. I don't know what to do."

"Okay, okay." He got the car turned around and headed toward the interstate. He gritted his teeth as his apartment building shrank in his rearview mirror. "Tell me what happened."

The details were vague and rushed. Lilah had come home,

and the paramedics were already there. Lacey was alive, but not conscious. They'd taken her to the hospital.

When he got on the highway, he turned on the Bluetooth on his phone and called Avery. The phone went straight to voicemail, so he dictated a text instead.

"Hey. I'm so sorry I'm not going to make it. My sister is in the hospital. I'll call as soon as I can."

Shit. He'd fucked up. His heart ached at the loss of all the things he would have gained tonight. The cool relief of claiming Avery as everyone watched. The knowledge this was the right thing because it was who he was. The adoration in Avery's eyes, more than enough to protect him from any judgment from the people around them.

He'd get it another way. Maybe not as big as a bachelor auction, but when he got back, he'd take Avery out somewhere. On a real date. Just the two of them. They'd sit together and Linc would put his hand on Avery's back and let his thumb turn in slow circles. Fuck anyone who saw them and thought it was wrong.

Getting to Wilmington took less time than he thought. Barely two hours later and he was pulling off the highway. All those years keeping his distance, and his sisters were closer than ever. If something was really wrong with Lacey, if he was too late to see her, speak with her, and get to know her again, he'd never forgive himself.

He rushed into the emergency ward and was given directions to Lacey's room. Lilah was waiting in the hall. She flung herself into his arms, shaking as she sobbed.

"Hey. Hey." He smoothed a hand down her hair. The strands were longer than he remembered and streaked with pink and purple.

"I didn't think you'd actually come."

His throat tightened. "Of course I'd come."

She cried a bit longer, holding on to him tight, until a voice from inside the nearest hospital room said, "Lilah! Who is that?"

He stiffened at the sound of Lacey's strong and authoritative voice. The same no-bullshit one she used on the phone. "Is she—"

Lilah nodded. "She's okay." She took his hand, and he was shocked at how tall she was. When he'd left, his baby sister had barely been in high school, and now she was all grown up. A woman whose nose bumped his chin as she hugged him one more time. "Come on."

Lacey was sitting up in bed. She wore a blue hospital gown and a scowl. Her hair was the same color he remembered, at least. The same sandy brown as his. The narrowed eyes were familiar too.

"Hey there," he said, waving his free hand, because Lilah didn't let go of his other one once, even when they were in the room.

Her scowl darkened. "What are you doing here?"

"Lilah called me. She said—"

"This?" Lacey's voice rose. "You came for this?"

He gaped. "You've been asking me to come for years."

"I would have lapsed into a diabetic coma years ago if I'd known that's what it was going to take to get my asshole brother to finally come home."

He could have argued this wasn't technically his home, that none of them lived in their hometown anymore, but there were more important issues. "A diabetic coma? You're diabetic?"

She was still glaring at him, and she crossed her arms over her chest. "How would you know?"

"She didn't know either," Lilah said, flopping into the green vinyl chair next to the bed. She stared Lacey down until her sister glanced away. "And it wasn't a coma, it was just shock."

"What do you mean, you didn't know?" Linc came around the other side of the bed.

Lacey sighed heavily. She looked older too, now that he was closer. But where Lilah had grown up, Lacey had aged. Her hair and her eyes were the same, but the lines around her mouth hadn't been there before. And she was too thin, when she'd always been a long rope of bones and muscle.

He went to brush a stray hair from her face, and she jerked her head back. "You didn't have to come."

Linc swallowed. His hand slid into his pocket, feeling for his phone. Avery still hadn't replied to his text. There would be so much make-up sex when he got back to Seacroft. But if he turned tail to check his messages again, Lacey would pounce on the advantage and probably never forgive him. "Lace. What happened?"

"It's not a big deal," she huffed.

"It is a big deal." Lilah half shouted from her chair. "You work too hard. You need to take better care of yourself."

"But I have to take care of you."

The room echoed with the silence as Linc's sisters stared each other down. He was trapped between them. Were their whole lives like this?

"What did the doctors say?" he said, trying to break the tension.

"Lincoln?"

Linc wasn't afraid of many things. He had literally been trained to run into burning buildings when all common sense would say to stay the hell away. But no amount of training could wipe away the fear that gripped his chest and squeezed so hard his heart felt like it might burst.

Slowly, he turned toward the man in the doorway.

If Lilah had grown up and Lacey had aged, then Linc's father had ...

Disintegrated? Collapsed?

He was shorter than Linc remembered. Thinner too. His hair was mostly gone and what managed to stay stuck to his scalp was a wispy yellowy gray. His skin, speckled with patchy, white stubble, hung from his face like it was too big for the bones beneath.

Linc's voice was a hoarse rasp. "Dad."

Gerry Scott held a cardboard tray with three coffee cups and a paper bag. As he shuffled into the room, Linc couldn't ignore the limp and the way his left foot turned in at an ugly angle. "I brought coffee and donuts."

Lilah growled. "For God's sake, Dad, she can't have a donut. She's diabetic."

Linc held his breath. The last time they'd been together in one place, words from any of them, in that tone, would have started a fight. The mean hiss of air through his father's teeth would tell them trouble was imminent.

Instead, though, the man before him flinched back, setting the bag down at the foot of the bed in a hurry. "No, I know that. I got a muffin too."

"That's not any better. She can't have muffins. They're full of sugar."

"Would you please stop talking about me like it's my ears and not my pancreas that stopped working? I can hear you fine," Lacey glared at her sister.

"But you can't eat that."

Their voices rose and filled the room. The whole time, Linc's dad kept his eyes and head down, as if he wanted to be anywhere else. The sight of him was almost sickening, like he was rotting from the inside out, and Linc could only stare.

Finally, a nurse came in to see what the commotion was. Her eyes widened when they landed on Linc. "Oh. You're new."

"That's my brother," Lacey said, scowling from the bed.

The nurse watched him for a second. "We don't usually like to have more than two visitors at a time." Her stare moved pointedly to each of them.

"I'll go," Lilah said finally.

"What? No." Linc glared at his dad, but he wouldn't meet Linc's eyes.

"It's fine." Lilah picked up her coat. "We left the boys with a neighbor. They're probably hungry. I'll go home and make dinner."

"Don't let Troy just eat ketchup," Lacey said.

Lilah went to the bed and kissed her older sister's forehead. "I'll call you later." She didn't acknowledge their father at all, but she squeezed Linc's hand. "Don't you dare leave until I get a chance to see you properly."

Instead of waiting for a response, Lilah walked right through the hospital room door. Linc glanced toward Lacey, picking at a blanket, and then at his dad, tearing open a packet of powdered creamer.

"Excuse me," Linc said, then rushed out the way Lilah had gone. She was only a few steps ahead of him, and he caught her shoulder before she got around the corner. "Hey. Wait."

She gave him a big smile but kept walking. "I'm so glad you're here. We really missed you." Like he'd been gone seven days, not seven years.

"What's going on?" he said.

"What do you mean?" She was carrying a small purse and rummaged inside of it.

"What do you mean, what do I mean? What the hell is going on with Dad? What the hell is he doing here?"

"Well, he found Lacey, and when he said he was her father, they let him ride in the ambulance while I got the boys settled."

Linc gripped his hair hard enough to hurt. "What do you mean he found Lacey?" What the fuck was going on? Lilah had called him, hysterical, less than three hours ago, and now they were hanging out at the hospital like it was no big thing while the ghost of their father brought them donuts and coffee? "Why are you the one leaving? Why does he get to stay?"

She sighed. "Lacey doesn't want to leave the boys alone with him."

"Fucking right. He's no babysitter."

"He's dying."

He stumbled, bumping his hip on a fire extinguisher. Pain radiated down his leg and through his gut.

"What do you mean?" A sick feeling pricked at his chest. The man in Lacey's hospital room had barely been his father. He was withered, shrunken. All this time, Linc had been running from a memory.

"Lung cancer." She shrugged and pulled out a tube of bright pink lip gloss, smearing it on with casual disinterest. "It's terminal. Lacey thinks that's why they let him out of prison."

"They kicked him loose so we can pay for his treatment?" That would be just like him. Mean and nasty in his life, a weight dragging them all down in the end.

"He's refusing treatment." She was still walking. They were through the sliding doors of the hospital, and she was talking about this like the weather.

"Wait. Stop." He grabbed her shoulder, and she shrugged him off.

"What for?"

"I don't understand."

"Yeah, well, maybe you would if you'd been here."

"Lilah, hey. Stop."

She whirled on him, pink-and-purple hair flying. "For what? So you can waltz back in like some superhero?"

"You called me."

"I didn't think you'd actually come!" Her voice cracked on a sob.

He rocked under the force of her words. Of course she hadn't. Why would she? He had done nothing but avoid them and let them down for years. Why would she expect him to change?

Except she didn't know about Avery. About his big smiles and hopeful eyes. About how Linc wanted to be the kind of person Avery thought he was. If he could be that person for Avery, then he would have to learn to be that for his sisters too.

A minivan honked. They were standing in the middle of the parking aisle. Lilah flipped the driver off, and he honked again, leaning on the horn this time. Linc put an arm around her shoulder and led her toward the cars so the van could pass.

"I'm sorry. Hey. I'm so sorry." He pulled her close.

"No, you're not. If you were sorry, you would have come back sooner. We needed you."

Fuck. Filthy sludge clogged up his guts while his baby sister sobbed in his arms in the dark parking lot.

"She was there. She was there on the stretcher and she wasn't moving, and the paramedics wouldn't let me go with her. And Dad's dying and I thought she was dead too. And if she died, then I'd have no one. I'd have the boys and no one. I'd be all by myself, Linc!" Her voice was high and her words were barely understandable, but every single one of them was like a punch. He ached. His throat, his eyes. He held her close and whispered how sorry he was over and over.

Eventually, she pushed back. Her face was puffy, and her hair was stringy. She brushed it away from her cheeks and sniffed. "Sorry."

"No." He shook his head. "This one's all on me."

Her laugh was short and hard. "Well, not all of it. Not Lacey's diabetes or Dad's cancer. But my makeup is ruined, and that's definitely your fault."

He hugged her again, and she squeezed him back. He should tell her. The apology was incomplete if she didn't understand why he'd stayed away. But she was staring up at him with cautious hope, and he couldn't be responsible for making it vanish.

"I like your hair," he said.

"Thanks."

He stayed in the parking lot until she got the car started and drove away. The old Ford had one wheel well completely rusted away, and the muffler sounded like it had about as long to live as—

"Fuck." He wrapped his arms around himself, but it didn't help.

Avery. Still no messages from Avery, and Linc needed to talk to him, now more than ever. But his call got sent to voicemail right away again.

Back in the hospital room, Lacey and his dad were dozing. His sister's eyes flickered open as Linc walked in, and she smoothed down the blankets and fought a yawn, embarrassed to be caught unguarded.

"Everything okay?" she said.

Nope. He settled into the empty chair closest to Lacey and took her hand. "Yeah. Everything's fine."

Lacey sighed. "She told you, didn't she? About him?"

"Yeah."

"It's a pretty shitty deal."

The thing Lacey hadn't said, that day on the phone when she'd called to say their dad had turned up, was suddenly made obvious in the way their dad hunched against the back of his chair. In the occasional wheezing cough pestering him, even in his sleep. In the way that he was a fraction of the man he had been, like he was being consumed.

"They making you stay here overnight?" he said, because the question was easier than talking about the giant cancer-ridden elephant in the room.

She snorted. "Yeah. For observation, they said. I'm fine."

"You're not fine. You didn't know?"

She glanced away but let him keep her hand. "How was I supposed to know? I felt like shit, but I always feel like shit. That's what happens when you have two kids and two jobs."

Another punch. "I'm sorry. For not being here."

"Yeah, yeah." She didn't smile. "I can see the mascara stains on your shirt that weren't there before. I know she's scared, but I'm not going anywhere."

His sister was a beast. A warrior. They hardly knew each other, not like adults, but that part, at least, was clear. She'd walk out of here in the morning and wrestle her diagnosis into submission as with everything else.

"I'm only a couple hours away," he said carefully. "If you need something, it's not far. I could help."

Lacey patted his hand. "You're going to have to walk the walk on that one."

She wasn't offering forgiveness, not yet, but Linc was willing to start.

He risked a glance at their sleeping father, but he hadn't woken during their entire conversation. He turned his attention back to Lacey. "I need to tell you something. About Dad. And Mickey."

Lacey grimaced. "Do we really need to rehash that?"

Linc breathed slowly, focusing on his sister, who deserved the truth, and not the old fear and shame that always blazed to life when he thought about that night. "And I need to tell you something about me. Because I was there too."

22

$\mathcal{L}$inc slept at Lacey and Lilah's on a lumpy, too-short couch. He spread out unfamiliar-smelling sheets and blankets, while Lilah got their nephews tucked into bed. Troy and Jake were five and nine. Linc remembered Jake, but he'd never seen more than pictures of Troy. Their presence —a reminder of all those years he'd missed—was worse than Lilah sobbing in his arms.

Lacey called at seven in the morning to say she was being released and needed a ride. Seven seemed early, but Linc could easily imagine her berating the nurses and doctors all night until they finally agreed to send her home. Linc drove over. He grinned as Lacey fussed and protested that she didn't need a wheelchair. The nurse said it was hospital policy and didn't back down until Lacey settled into it and allowed herself to be taken to the hospital door.

Linc's dad was there too. He didn't say anything, shuffling across the parking lot in his limping gait.

"What happened?" Linc whispered to his sister.

"Broken ankle. Never healed right. I'm not sure if they actually had doctors in prison or if they just told him to tie it off with a bedsheet."

By the time they reached the car, his dad was a long way behind them.

"Did you—" For once, Lacey looked uncertain. "Did you tell Lilah what you told me? About you and Mickey?"

Linc shook his head. "The boys were still up when I got there, and then as soon as they were asleep, she crashed too. There hasn't really been time." He'd make time, though, before he went back to Wilmington. He owed Lilah that much.

Linc made sure Lacey was comfortable and then, his feelings still tender, went around the car and held the other door open.

His dad chuckled as he reached him, patting Linc's hand over the frame. His fingers were cold and boney, like a skeleton's in a rubber glove.

At home, Lacey's boys practically tripped over each other to get down the stairs and greet her as she stepped out of the car. Troy cried a few fat tears, and Lacey passed kisses all around.

"I'm so sorry I scared you," Lacey said as she held both boys close. "I'm okay. It's okay."

"She's making them soft." His dad spoke so quietly, Linc almost didn't hear it, but when his head whipped around, his dad was already shuffling toward the house without another word.

Lilah had made pancakes, which were followed by a lot of fuss over whether or not Lacey could eat them and settled when she stuffed half a steaming pancake in her mouth and said, "Not dead yet!" around it.

The house was small, with only a breakfast bar and no table, so they sat around the living room instead. Linc sat on the sofa with the two boys. As he finished his second pancake, Troy tapped his shoulder and shyly said, "Uncle Linc?"

No one had ever called him that before. He nearly choked on his pancake.

"Yes?" he said, when he could swallow.

"Auntie Lala said you're a fireman."

"Auntie Lala?" He glanced at Lilah, squeezed into a big armchair with Lacey.

She gave a shrug. "Jake called me that when he was small, and it stuck."

He glanced back down at the little boy, watching him with big, serious eyes. "Yes. I am a fireman."

"Have you ever been in a fire?" Jake asked.

"A few."

"Are the other firefighters a bunch of hotties like on the calendars?" Lilah asked, then laughed when Lacey elbowed her. "What? He's not that far away. We could go visit."

Linc laughed along with her. It felt good. "My crew is Brian, who's kind of old and has a wife and is about to have two babies."

"Ohh." Lilah fanned herself. "A man with kids is so sexy."

Brian would be glad to hear that, at least. "And the other person on my truck is a woman. Vasquez. And she's—well, actually, she's bisexual, so she could be interested in you, but she currently has a girlfriend. I think you're out of luck on that front too."

On the other chair, by the TV, his dad scoffed. Linc had another bite of pancake.

"And what about you?" Lacey said carefully. "They've both got—um—partners. Do you have someone too?"

The living room got quiet. Linc's heart tried to thump out of his chest, and the pancake turned to glue in his throat. Lacey watched him steadily, and he knew what she was doing. He hadn't told her about Avery the night before. He'd only shared that night in Raleigh. But no doubt she still didn't trust him to tell Lilah, and he couldn't fault her for it.

But his dad was here, and awake now, and Lacey's boys too. Was this how he wanted them to think of him? Was coming out the impression he wanted to leave his nephews with on his first visit?

Avery's trusting face swam up from his memory. His wide-eyed enthusiasm, his careful hesitation when he knew he was being a geek or talking too fast but didn't know how to stop.

Linc had promised to be publicly his the night before, but they'd missed that opportunity. He hoped Avery had understood. He *would*. Avery was so dedicated to his own family. He'd get why Linc had needed to leave.

But if he couldn't be out with Avery at the auction, he could at least be out with him here.

"Actually, there is someone," he said, looking at Troy, because it felt safer than looking directly at his sisters. He swallowed, aware that he still had time to lie—or make a run for the car. "His name is Avery. He likes video games and sweet potatoes."

The seconds of silence after he said "potatoes" were the longest of his life. He focused on the sweet, nonjudgmental face of the nephew who had only met him the day before, counting slowly in his head.

One. Two. Three.

A cracking wet cough filled the room. Linc's dad was hunched over his plate, the cough shaking his whole body until Linc was sure it would split like an over-boiled egg.

His dad glanced up, wiping a string of phlegm from his lip and smiled. "Fucking queer."

"Hey!" Lacey stood so fast Lilah was flipped out of the chair with her. "We do not use that kind of language in this house."

Their father laughed again and waved her off, still wheezing. "Yeah, yeah."

"No." She strode across the room until she could poke a finger in his thin chest. "You and your shit attitude are the reason we haven't seen our brother in seven fucking years and that my sons don't know their goddamned uncle. So you can get your head out of your ass, or I will kick you to the curb so hard, you'll shit my toenails for a week."

One. Two. Three. Four.

The couch cushions were vibrating under Linc. He glanced to either side, where both boys were smothering giggles—badly—behind their hands.

"Shh," he said, but that only made them laugh harder. He pulled them against his sides, and they howled into his T-shirt.

Lacey glared at them. "This is not funny."

He shrugged while the boys squirmed against him. "What part of 'we don't use that language' were you referring to exactly?"

She scowled. "The part where there is anything wrong with being gay."

His hands tightened, and he dropped his eyes. "Oh."

"So, that's it?" Lilah said incredulously. "You're gay? That's the deep, dark secret that you've been keeping all this time?"

He opened and closed his mouth. The boys had gotten control of themselves and looked up expectantly. Linc could laugh it off. He could tell them they'd misheard and Avery was a woman. He could . . . "I guess?"

She flopped back down into her chair. "Well, that's just ridiculous."

"It is?"

"Yes." She glared at him. "I'm bi. If you'd stuck around a few more years, you'd know that."

He stared at his baby sister. "You are?"

She folded her arms over her chest. "I like who I like. What's it to you?"

"I like girls," Jake said.

"I like pizza," Troy said.

They both dissolved into laughter.

"Come here." Lacey held her arms out.

"What?" But Linc was already moving. She met him in the middle of the room, and a minute later Lilah was there too while two little bodies clung to their legs. A cough came from the corner, and they ignored it.

"Don't you stay away anymore," Lacey said.

"I won't." He'd never meant anything more in his life.

His phone rang. Thank God it rang. He needed Avery. Needed to tell him what had happened and how he was wrong to have been afraid before. He would—

Vasquez.

"Hello?" he said.

"Hello." Her voice was flat. "He says *hello*."

He laughed, a bit nervously. "Yeah. Hello. It's what people say when they answer the phone."

"Are you answering your phone from beyond the grave?"

"No. I—"

"Because dead is about the only excuse I'm going accept for what you did last night."

"What? I—"

"He is, right now, puking his guts out, and then he'll go back to curling up in a ball. And, Scott? If you're not here when he's feeling better, I will hunt you down and murder you with a ball-point pen."

If Lacey and Vasquez ever wound up in a room together, the world needed to be very afraid.

"Avery? Are you talking about Avery? Vasquez, what are you—"

"You have an hour to pull yourself out of whatever ditch you're lying in and get over here."

23

*I*n his lucid moments, Avery couldn't remember ever having a worse migraine. Although, he couldn't say how much of the nausea was the migraine and how much was the hangover. Not that it mattered when his head was over the toilet bowl and his throat was on fire.

He hadn't meant to drink so much. When he'd walked off the stage the night before, he'd *meant* to curl up under a rock and die, but then suddenly, Wanda had been there, with Vasquez beside her. One of them pressed a glass of wine in his hand. Then the drinks kept coming until he didn't care Linc had stood him up. Didn't care about the twenty-nine seconds of awkward silence before Aunt Brenda put up a paddle and shouted, "Seventy-five dollars!"

The memory of Aunt Brenda's excited wave when the gavel came down pulsed in his head and turned his brain to paste. He needed a drill, a spike, anything sharp and pointy to relieve the pressure and let it leak out of his ears or wherever else it could escape.

The second time, he didn't make it to the bathroom before he puked again.

The bitter taste of his pills lingered between his teeth, so

Vasquez must have gone to his apartment. Or maybe they were at his apartment? But no, they couldn't be. Wanda said he was too drunk to drive. She and Vasquez had brought him back to their place, and they'd played a board game involving racing plastic camels with elastics. He'd laughed his head off, knowing the laughter was only fueled by alcohol because his heart was in pieces. Everything got hazy afterwards.

A hand brushed over his forehead. Warm. Dry. He whimpered.

"Hey, Red."

Avery rolled, pulling the blanket over him and burrowing down.

Slowly, after hours—days?—the pain receded. Slowly, the pounding gavel in his head lessened. His mouth tasted like the inside of a garbage can, and the rest of him felt scooped out and shredded. When he pushed up from the mattress, his shirt smelled like booze and puke, and he stripped before it made him sick again.

He was in the little guest room. The one where Linc had hauled him up against the door and told him to stay away from Quinn. Avery had been so happy in that moment.

The hallway was quiet. He went to the bathroom, found a clean towel, and showered. Or, rather, he leaned against the cool tile and let the hot water pummel his body until he was flushed and dizzy again. The steam was so thick, he could barely see the door when he pulled the curtain back, and it took three passes with the towel before he made out his reflection in the mirror.

He shouldn't have bothered. He looked like death. A zombie. His skin was gray-green, and the stripe of bruising still hadn't faded from under one eye.

Avery sighed. He had no idea what time it was. Midday at least. He should go home. Vaguely, he remembered his aunt saying something about him coming over for dinner this weekend. Maybe tonight? He couldn't say he had other plans.

Linc hadn't been there. Avery had been trying to avoid thinking those exact words, but there it was. The one empty chair. Avery had taken one final step forward, as the last of his hope shredded itself to pieces. He'd caught Vasquez's gaze beneath the glow of the spotlight, and she'd had rage in her eyes, while Wanda shook her head sadly. She'd gone to lift her paddle, but Vasquez nudged her, and Avery was grateful for that small mercy. No need to prolong the humiliation.

He hadn't come. Might never have been planning to come in the first place, for all Avery knew.

But he was sitting on the bed when Avery walked back into his borrowed bedroom. Linc seemed impossibly big in the dark room, shoulders hunched as he twisted his fingers in his lap.

"Hey, Red."

Avery went to cross his arms over his naked chest, but the towel slipped on his hips, and he had to grab for it.

"What are you doing here?" *Where have you been?*

"Vasquez called me."

"When?" *How much do you know?*

"This morning."

He tightened the towel around his waist. Equal parts of hurt and embarrassment twisted inside him, caked in a thick muck of anger.

"Red, I'm sorry," Linc said. Every word hurt Avery's insides like glass.

"Yeah." Goose bumps rose up on his skin. Linc liked his skin. Liked to kiss it and suck on it, liked to trace his fingers over the freckles and call him beautiful. "I'd like to put some clothes on, please."

"Oh. Yeah." He reached behind him and produced a small pile. "Vasquez picked these up when she went to get your pills."

Avery stared at them. His *Winterlands* T-shirt was on the top. He didn't reach for it, because he might touch Linc's hand, and if he did, he'd very likely crumble to a pyramid of salt on the floor.

He stood still, and eventually—eighteen seconds later—Linc got the hint.

"Right." He cleared his throat. "I'll be in the kitchen."

"I'd prefer if you weren't." The solidity of his words surprised Avery. The rest of him felt milliseconds away from complete vaporization. "I'd like you to leave."

"Red, come on."

"No." Avery's eyes narrowed. "No. You don't get to call me that. You think it means anything after last night?"

"Avery."

"You humiliated me in front of literally every single person I know." His voice cracked, but he continued. "You promised me. I said you didn't have to. That I understood if you couldn't. But then *you promised me* you would be there. For me. With me. It is literally the only thing I have ever wanted in my entire life, for someone to want me, to be proud to be seen with me in public—"

"I am. Av—baby. I am. So much. Just—"

Avery took a step back. His eyes were filled with tears, but his chest was full of anger, not sadness, and it gave him a kind of power he'd never had before. "Were you even going to show up? Did you ever mean that?"

"Of course I—"

"Or was it all some joke to you? Am I some joke?"

"No—" Linc's voice was hoarse, like he might be crying too.

"I know what I am." He wrapped his arms around himself, towel be damned. If it fell, it fell. He needed the comfort, and he couldn't let Linc be the one to give it to him. He'd never trust himself again after. "I know I'm ridiculous. Poor Avery. Can't cook. Can't walk across a room without hurting himself. I don't need you to remind me in front of the whole goddamn town!"

"No. Hey. Just listen to me." Linc reached for his arm, and Avery jerked it back, banging his elbow hard against the corner of a dresser. His whole lower arm went numb, and *of course* the towel fell. He swore and grabbed for it, holding it in front of himself with his other hand, pins and needles shooting through his fingers.

"I'd like you to leave."

"But listen—"

"No!" His voice cracked again, but the word echoed off the walls. "No. I don't want to listen. You kissed me, and then you disappeared on me instead of giving us a chance to figure out how to be together. You pretended to be someone else, and I let it go because it's just a stupid video game, and I thought maybe you needed a safe space to be yourself. But now I don't know if anything you've ever told me is the truth. Was it just sex? You were looking for someone dumb enough to let you fuck them without expecting any kind of respect in return?"

"No. It was never—"

"And now this? No more forgiveness. I'm done listening to your explanations. Do you even believe yourself? No more apologies or promises. You've lost that chance."

"I'm sorry. Please." It was barely a whisper. "Please, you have to—"

"I'm moving to Atlanta."

Eight seconds.

"I thought you were staying in town?"

Avery bit the inside of his lip to keep from saying anything else. He'd made the decision in the shower. He couldn't stay. Not now. He shouldn't have said yes to his uncle in the first place. Offering to sell Avery the business was been a kind gesture. Like his aunt bidding on him last night so he didn't stand on the stage like an unwanted loser for thirty whole seconds. But he'd never learn to be his own person if he stayed in this town where he'd always feel fifteen years old.

"Please leave."

Linc shut the door softly behind him. Avery leaned against the dresser and waited for the shaking to stop.

Avery spent two days moping. His apartment had never been so tidy, which was good because he was going to have to sublet it. He checked listings for apartments in Atlanta but couldn't decide on a neighborhood. Atlanta was big. They had a transit system and everything. Before, the size seemed exciting, full of possibility. Now, it felt daunting and overwhelming.

He made some notes about questions to ask Wanda the next time they got together, but he wasn't ready to see her and Vasquez. They'd been kind to him on one of the worst nights of his adult life, but he didn't want to see their sympathetic smiles again—or go anywhere near their liquor cabinet—for a long time.

Late on Sunday afternoon, someone pounded on his door like they were being chased by a pack of wild dogs. Avery had been dozing on the purple sofa, but he rushed to the door. Only as he undid the deadbolt did it occur to him it might be Linc.

Instead, Wanda stood there.

"Are you okay?"

He stared at her, trying to make sense of her frightened eyes and her breathless words. "I was asleep."

"For how long?"

He glanced at the clock on the microwave. "Forty-five minutes?"

"I've been calling for hours. Why didn't you answer?"

"What?" He scratched at his scalp, still sleepy, then blinked. "Oh. Phone's dead. I dropped it in—um—I dropped it." Being disconnected for a few days had actually been kind of nice. Better to lick his wounds in private without the distraction of text messages and phone calls from people who probably thought they were being nice, but were only reminding him how much he needed to be taken care of like a child.

"How dead is your phone exactly?"

"Super dead. Full of water."

"Did you put it in rice?"

He'd tried that, but a quick Google search had shown if there had ever been a chance to save his phone, he'd needed to put it in rice the second he fished it out. And he didn't have rice anyway. Not like the kind you needed for wet phones. He'd bought a couple packs of instant microwave rice, but it came in a flavor packet, already pre-buttered and sort of gooey on the inside.

"You can't not have a phone. Put some clothes on."

He went to protest he was dressed, but his sweats had stains, and his T-shirt was more holes than shirt. He changed and followed her out to her car.

They drove over to the big box plaza by the highway. Avery explained what had happened to a bored customer service guy who probably heard the same story a dozen times a day. "Handsets are here. Everything with a blue sticker is covered under your current plan."

Avery picked one out and let the technician set it up.

"Turn it on," Wanda said as they went back to her car. She was watching with wide eyes, like she'd never seen this happen before, but then, once the phone was up and running and he'd scrolled through the apps a couple times, her smile faded.

"It's just a phone." He shoved it into his pocket, but pulled it back out again when it vibrated. On the screen, a single text from a number he didn't recognize popped up.

Test

"Huh." Wanda pursed her lips and showed him the same message on her phone.

"I still have to get my contacts synced up."

"Well, at least we know it works."

She drove him home. As they pulled up outside, she turned and said, "I think you should talk to Linc."

He unclipped his seat belt. "That's not a good idea." Three

days later, the humiliation of standing alone on that stage no longer made him want to vomit, but he'd be damned before he let Linc off the hook.

Wanda frowned, but she said, "Have you been looking at places in Atlanta?"

"Yeah." He couldn't put much enthusiasm behind it. His anger at Linc was warring for dominance with his ongoing guilt about the conversation he'd had to have with his aunt and uncle. His aunt had planned a celebratory dinner the day after the auction, but he'd only been able to take about two bites of her dumplings before losing his appetite. He had to confess he'd changed his mind about buying the firm. His aunt cried, and Uncle Theo had put an arm around her shoulder while telling Avery in a solemn voice that they understood and only wanted what was best for him.

They really were the best parents a person could ask for.

"You going to be okay?" Wanda asked, breaking his train of thought.

"What? Yeah." He forced a smile at her. "It'll be awesome. Fresh start." He'd probably been needing one for years. Avery tried so hard to fit in here in Seacroft, but he needed to acknowledge he'd outgrown it.

His apartment was empty and quiet. He surfed the internet, made more notes about places in Atlanta, ordered takeout, and dozed while he waited.

A steady buzzing from his kitchen counter woke him. At first, he thought someone was calling, but when he grabbed his new phone, the screen was dark. He swiped it on, and then watched as the counter on his text messages ticked upwards.

Six, seven, eight.

Must be the SIM card finally receiving missed messages from his old phone. The guy at the store hadn't been able to say for sure if he'd get them. The first few were from Wanda and his aunt.

I'm on my way! Unlock your door if you don't want me to bang it down!

Your uncle and I are just doing some shopping. Want to come for supper again? We're having ribs.

Ronnie says if you don't answer this message in the next ten minutes, we're coming over there.

Good morning, Sweet pea. Sleep okay?

Please just answer the phone so we can talk.

He frowned at the final one. His blood froze when he realized the number wasn't Wanda's or his aunt's. And the message was the last in a very long line of texts, all from one number. It went on and on. Bits and pieces caught his attention as he scrolled down.

I can't even tell you how sorry I am.

My sister's bisexual.

Cancer. He doesn't want treatment.

Please pick up the phone.

Troy has red hair. He kind of looks like you.

Are you reading these?

I'm sorry.

If you don't hear from me again, Vasquez knows where my body is buried.

Are you okay?

Shit, Red. Vasquez finally told me what happened. I'm so so sorry.

There must have been forty. Read in the correct order, the whole sequence of events all appeared so clearly. Linc's sister, the phone call. His genuine apology. The first few obviously came Friday night, proving Linc really had tried to tell him about not making it to the auction.

Linc's voicemails made Avery's eyes tear up.

"Hey. It's me. Again. Look, I know you're mad, but please. Did you read my texts? This is too important—*we're* too important—to end over a misunderstanding. I know you're angry, but please, please call me."

"Hi. Just text or something. I'm worried you've got another migraine, and no one is there to take care of you."

"Hey, I'm working today, but I'll have my phone on. Please, Avery. I'm begging here. Just send me a message so I know you're okay."

Avery stared at the phone until the screen went black again, wiping at his sniffling nose with the back of his hand. "Well, shit."

He bounced on his toes, nervous energy thrumming through his veins. *Shit, shit, shit.* He'd—well, he was still right to be hurt. Linc's explanation didn't take away the almost thirty silent seconds on that stage. But he . . . Avery might have overreacted a bit. Okay, a lot. No, not a lot, but enough. Yeah, no, he'd overreacted a lot. But how was he supposed to know about Linc's family?

"Maybe if you'd let him talk instead of kicking him out, genius." Stomping around his kitchen, he muttered and cursed, but that didn't solve anything.

He needed to fix this. He needed to talk to Linc.

24

A ferocious, early-season storm blew in that night, the kind more common in summer when the days were hotter. Winds and rains knocked down trees and power lines. A transport truck lost control on the interstate as visibility went to nothing, and eighteen other cars slammed into the pile before traffic slowed enough to avoid the accident site.

The SFD brought in every volunteer who answered the phone, whether they were on call or not, along with trucks from three other towns and counties. Linc, Vasquez, and Brian were on-site before the ambulances. The scene was a mess of twisted metal and the smell of diesel from the truck's ruptured fuel tank slowly oozing over the asphalt.

Water dripped off Linc's helmet and spattered down his jacket as he coordinated with other teams. Just when they thought the area was clear, a damn rubberneck spent too much time watching the heavy tow winch the truck back onto its axels and drove himself into the ditch.

By the time they were done, the sun was on its way up, Linc smelled like fuel and sweat, and every muscle in his body ached. He was ready to get to the station, dump his gear, and go back to his apartment to sleep for a hundred years.

But first, he unzipped his soaking, stinking jacket and fished into his uniform pants for his phone. Standard protocol said he shouldn't be looking until they were back and officially off the clock for this call, but they'd left the station hours ago, and no one was going to fault him for checking in with the real world.

Linc's phone was frustratingly blank. Not a text, not a missed call. Nothing. That his last memory of Avery would be the shattered look on his face made Linc's heart squeeze.

He caught Vasquez watching him and stuffed his phone away again while she smiled sympathetically.

"He'll call you," she said, kicking a booted foot up on the truck's frame. "I sent Wanda over yesterday to make sure he got your messages."

"Yeah." He stared out the window. The world was gray and wet. He was exhausted and sad. No matter which way he went over it, he still didn't see how he could have handled it any better. Maybe if he'd gone into the country club, found Avery, and told him what was going on, but he would have still left. And at that moment, he didn't know Lacey would be okay, so time had been crucial.

The dispatch radio crackled. Linc closed his eyes and folded his arms over his chest. The drive to the station would be too short, but at this point, he'd take any minutes of sleep he could get.

The truck veered sharply, tires squealing.

"What's going on?" Linc asked as Brian's sudden turn nearly tossed him out of his seat.

"Got a new call. Residential alarm." Brian's voice disappeared as the sirens wailed.

"What? No. Come on. Our shift ended an hour ago."

"And we're the closest truck to the call," Vasquez said.

"Can't they send someone else?" He was too tired for this.

"The other trucks have barely checked back in. They haven't inspected their gear."

"And neither have we!"

She scowled at him. He was being childish, but he'd spent hours in the rain, his boyfriend wasn't speaking to him, and he was the furthest thing from feeling helpful right now.

Vasquez sighed. "We'll go check it out. This time of day, it's probably a false alarm. If we need backup, Brian will call it in."

She was right. In firefighting, you couldn't wave a call off with "I'm not on the clock." He closed his eyes again and grumbled as Brian sped them through Seacroft's sleepy streets.

Next thing he knew, they were stopping. He opened one eye. The rain was coming down hard again. Nothing would burn for long in this weather.

Vasquez held the radio handset to her mouth. "Dispatch, this is truck seven-two. We're on-site at 171 Sand Dollar Crescent. There is nothing showing."

He sat up straight. Sand Dollar Crescent? That was—

Linc peered through the fogged-up window on his side of the truck. Through the rain was the plain white house with the converted basement that he knew only too well.

"What the fuck is this?"

Vasquez shrugged. "We got a call. You should go check it out."

Like a coward, he shook his head, and Vasquez tsked. "Standard procedure says we have to check it out, even if the initial report is nothing showing."

He stared out the window. Did he dare go in there? Vasquez was up to something. Except what if she wasn't, and Avery had a real problem?

The porch light turned on, and the front door flew open. A young man wearing only a T-shirt and sweats and with the reddest hair Linc had ever seen came flying out of the house and ran down the yard like he was being chased.

"Oh my God." Linc scrubbed his face, but he was already pushing open the door and stepping down from the truck.

"It's fine! It's fine!" Avery's voice carried over the steady drum of raindrops on the road. He was barefoot, and the water had plastered his hair to his scalp, turning it a rusty brown.

"What are you doing?" Linc said.

"It's nothing, I just—" he put his hands to his face, "—oh God, this was a bad idea. I—"

"Red." He couldn't help the nickname. Never mind Avery told him to stop using it. Just the sight of his flushed cheeks and the way his eyes widened at the word was enough for Linc to know he'd do whatever it took for Avery to forgive him.

"I—I—didn't know how—"

"Scott," Vasquez called from just inside the truck. "Are you going to check it out or not?"

Linc glanced back at Avery. "Is there a fire?"

Avery shook his head so hard, water droplets sprayed into Linc's face. "No. There was, but—I got your messages and—"

"You better go inside and make sure." Vasquez slammed the truck door shut, and the engine roared to life.

"Hey!"

She pushed the window down and poked her head into the rain. "What?"

"You're leaving?"

"False alarm. Brian and I will buy the donuts." She grinned and blew him a kiss. "Now get inside. Wanda will kill me if you both die of pneumonia."

The truck made a six-point turn in the dead-end street. Brian might have driven through the puddle right by Linc on purpose, or it might only have been that the whole street was rapidly becoming a puddle. Linc flipped him off for good measure, and Brian responded with a sharp buzz of the siren before he turned around the corner and disappeared.

Water streamed over Avery's cheeks. The last bruise under his eye was mostly gone, and his shirt was plastered to his chest.

"You look amazing," Linc said.

"I hope you think so when you find out what I've done." He blew water off the tip of his nose and shivered.

Linc put a hand on his shoulder, and the weather didn't matter at all because Avery didn't push him away. Still, he was like ice under Linc's touch. "You're freezing. Let's go inside."

Another spark of hope flared to life when Avery didn't say no.

But once they were in the apartment, the distance between them remained uncomfortable. Linc was still in his bunker pants and boots, although he'd left the coat in the truck, and Avery dripped quietly on the floor.

"I'm sorry," Avery said in a rush.

"For what?"

"I lit a match and held it under the smoke detector until the alarm went off."

Linc frowned. "You lit a match."

"Uh-huh." Avery nodded and water flew out of his hair like when a dog shook itself off at the beach. "Well. A few matches. More like twenty. It took a while."

The lecture on how dangerous that could have been would need to wait. Linc was impressed. "Most people don't have matches anymore."

"I had to go buy some. They were surprisingly hard to find."

Linc struggled to hold back a laugh while fighting to understand the logic. "But why?"

"Because I wanted to make sure you'd come."

"Red," he said softly. "I called all weekend. I sent like forty texts."

"Forty-seven. I know. But then they stopped, and I was worried—" He bit his lip. "I thought maybe—"

That Linc had given up on him? "I had to go to work."

"Oh." Then Avery glanced up, mouth curving into a smile. "Oh!"

It hurt that he would even consider Linc abandoning him so quickly. But then, hadn't he done exactly that at the auction?

"Red." He took a step forward. "I'm sorry. So sorry. I never meant to hurt you. I was trying to do the right thing for my family and I—I can't even tell you how sorry I am for what I did to you in the process."

"I know." Avery shivered again. "I did read all of your messages. A few times. I'm sorry about your dad."

That was—a very complicated topic. Linc and his dad might not ever come to an understanding, not with the time left. It didn't matter, though, not in that moment. Right now, all that mattered was Avery.

"How's your sister?" Avery asked.

"Why are you asking about my family? How are you?"

"I'm—" He gasped and nodded, like he was agreeing with a thought he hadn't put voice to. "Yeah, I'm okay."

"Still leaving for Atlanta?"

He nodded again, but his smile faded. "Yeah. It's better that way. I don't think I can actually be a grown-up in this town. I'm going to go down next weekend and look at some apartments."

"That's good. That's—" He licked his lips as he tried to find the best way to ask his question. "Could I come visit you? Once you're moved in and settled?"

Avery's smile came back, soft and perfect, as he ran a hand over the back of his head and down his neck. "Yeah. Yeah, I think I'd like that."

"Yeah?" Relief burst in Linc's chest and warmed him from the inside.

"Sure. I mean. If you still want to. I was pretty awful to you the other day."

"Oh, Jesus, Red." He couldn't help himself. Linc reached for Avery and pulled him close. They both sighed at the contact. "I deserved everything you had to say. My family is a disaster from beginning to end, but their mess doesn't excuse that way I broke my promise to you."

"But I—"

Linc kissed him. Avery would never win that argument. But he opened up for Linc, melting against his body, while Linc threaded his fingers into Avery's red hair. They were touching from chest to knee, and he could still feel too much space between them. He took one more step forward. Avery was still barefoot, while Linc was still in his boots. Avery yelped and hopped backward as Linc stepped on his toe.

"Sorry! Sorry. Are you okay?" It would be just like them to screw up this moment with a broken toe

"Fine." He shivered again. The edges of his lips were tinged with purple.

"You're really cold, aren't you?"

"Maybe a bit." His quivering chin and chattering teeth betrayed his words.

They warmed up in the shower, staying under the spray until the water turned cold. Then they stumbled toward the bed with hands and laughter, flinging back the blankets so they could curl around each other naked.

Linc could barely believe he had the stamina after the night he'd had, but relief outweighed exhaustion. They were here again, in this little basement apartment that had somehow become theirs. He came embarrassingly quickly as Avery blew him like a champ. Linc returned the favor with his tongue and the little jeweled plug until Avery was screaming his name and coming all over himself.

After, when they were warm and sleepy and spread across each other and Linc's arms and legs felt like they were turning to stone, Avery sighed quietly on his chest. "I know you said I couldn't ask you to make the decision for me. About Atlanta."

"Mm-hmm." Sleep was coming fast and made words hard.

"But." Avery traced small circles in Linc's chest hair, tangling the threads together until they pinched. "Since I've made up my mind now, do you think, maybe, instead of visiting, you might . . . I mean. Do you think—"

"Spit it out, Red."

"Just, I've been looking at apartments online. And I've seen some nice ones. But, you said once that, maybe, if it worked out, you might think about coming to Atlanta too."

Linc fought off his drowsiness. He wondered if Avery could hear the way his heart had started beating faster in his chest. "I did say that."

"Well." Avery kissed his shoulder. "Now I've decided to go. And now we've had our first big fight, and even our first make-up sex—"

"Pretty sure I'm going to need more of that in a few hours. I'm not nearly done making up with you."

"Listen." Avery bit his biceps. "I'm trying to ask you something important here."

Linc wrapped an arm around Avery and hauled him up until he was sprawled over his body. He kissed the top of Avery's head. "Yes. As soon as I can find a new job, I will move to Atlanta with you." Lacey would murder him for leaving North Carolina when they'd only just reconnected, but Atlanta to Wilmington was only a six-hour drive. He'd come up for every school play and birthday party they invited him to.

"Because it doesn't make sense for me to get an apartment for just myself if—" He froze. "Wait. What did you just say?"

Linc opened his sleepy eyes. Avery was staring at him with the most adorable mix of confusion and hope, like a golden retriever hearing a high-pitched whistle for the first time.

"Sleep now. More make-up sex after. Then we'll get online and find a place to live together in Atlanta."

"Really? But—"

"Sleep. There's time."

They had all the time in the world.

EPILOGUE

*A*very had always been good at numbers. Lately, he'd had a lot of new additions to his list of important ones.

7—the orgasms Linc gave him that rainy day in Seacroft before Avery finally said Linc was really, fully, and truly forgiven (but also because Avery was pretty sure if he got to eight, he'd die).

3—the seconds between the moment when Linc said, "And this is Avery," to his family, and a tiny red-haired body barreled into Avery's shins shouting, "Uncle Avery!"

27—the steps from the street to the front door of his new second-floor apartment in Atlanta.

1—the number of shouting matches he and Linc had wrestling the purple couch up the twenty-seven steps.

4—the orgasms Avery gave Linc as an apology for losing his cool about the couch.

43—the days it took Linc to find a job with the Atlanta Fire Rescue Department.

And finally, the newest number to add to his list:

8—the number of people he and Linc would be feeding in their apartment for Thanksgiving.

Avery pushed open the front door. "I'm back." He held the

carton of heavy cream over his head, then grimaced as he inhaled. "What's that smell?"

Linc popped up from behind the kitchen counter with a guilty expression on his face. "It's nothing."

Avery scowled. "What happened?"

Linc ran a hand through his hair. "They oozed? I don't know. I was setting the table, and there was this smell and—"

Avery pushed Linc to one side and opened the oven door. Ten sweet potatoes sat inside, and they had—well, they *had* oozed. Orange-black goo bubbled from the tiny holes Avery had meticulously punched into each potato with a fork. The goo clung to the rack and had burned to the bottom of the oven.

"Oh man," he said. "I knew we should have wrapped them in foil."

"The internet said you didn't need to."

"The internet also said we could just pop them in the microwave for five to eight minutes and they'd be cooked through, but you wouldn't let me do that, so we had to get up two hours early to do it the old-fashioned way."

"We're not microwaving anything. Not with your track record." Linc scowled at him. The expression was so frustrated, with a hint of panic at the edges, that Avery stood on his toes and kissed him.

"You're cute when you're mad."

Linc sighed. "Remind me why we're cooking Thanksgiving brunch again. No one ever cooks Thanksgiving brunch."

"Because you're working overnight, and Wanda and I have to be at the airport to catch our flight to San Francisco at eight."

"I don't see why you have to leave tonight. Or why they scheduled a meeting for tomorrow." Linc was also seriously cute when he pouted. "Who works the Friday after Thanksgiving?"

"Anyone who doesn't work in an office? You do. Everyone who works in retail."

Linc waved him off. "Yeah, yeah." He slipped an arm around

Avery's waist, pulling him close so he could kiss him. "I'm going to miss you."

Well, that was worth the oozy sweet potato. "It's only thirty-six hours. I'll be back on Saturday morning."

Linc's kisses turned hungry, and he backed Avery against the counter, grinding against him to let him know exactly much he would be missed.

"We can't." Avery laughed against his lips. "My aunt and uncle will be here any minute."

"I can be quick."

"What if your sisters get here first? Do you want to explain to the boys what you're doing to me?"

Linc dragged his jaw over the side of Avery's neck, letting stubble prickle over his skin. "I thought you might do it to me."

"Oh." Avery's eyelids fluttered, and his knees wobbled. They didn't swap very often. Avery preferred to bottom and Linc was only too happy to do the fucking, but sometimes he wanted Avery inside of him, and Avery really couldn't pass up the chance.

Linc's teeth nipped at his jaw just below his ear. "Want to feel you while you're gone."

Avery slipped his hands inside Linc's pants and under the elastic of his boxer briefs, brushing over the smooth skin of his ass. They were going to have to be fast, and the lube was down the hall, but—

He bumped against something firm and smooth where he'd been expecting the soft resistance of Linc's hole. He ran a fingertip over it, his pulse speeding up at Linc's inhale as Avery continued his slow inspection.

"What's this?" He knew. Oh, man, he totally knew, but he wanted to hear Linc say it.

"People are coming. Didn't want to waste time."

Avery nearly collapsed, tracing the edge of the silicon plug and bumping the base with a knuckle, but Linc groaned and said, "Please," like he was dying, which made everything worth it.

"I'll get the lube."

"In my pocket."

He loved this man an awful lot. Avery undid his pants and slicked himself up in seconds, while Linc dropped his jeans to below his hips and pressed back from the counter. The black plug pulled out with an obscene sound and Avery took a second to enjoy the pink flex of Linc's hole before he lined himself up and slid in.

"Oh, fuck," Linc groaned and arched back. "Oh, fuck, that's good. I needed this so bad."

Avery gripped him tight and pumped into him, wasting no time. Linc liked it hard and fast on a regular day, and the added prospect of company showing up at the apartment door spurred Avery on in a way he hadn't expected.

Linc kept up a steady stream of praise and encouragement as Avery wrapped an arm around his midsection, holding him close. "Yes. Yes, Red. Yes. That's it. I need it. Just like that. Oh, fuck, just like that."

It didn't take much like this. It never did. Not with Linc writhing and begging while his body held Avery tight and his words told Avery he was perfect in every way.

He came hard, groaning against the back of Linc's neck. The spasm of Linc's muscles around him said he was coming too.

"Oh God," Linc panted. "That was amazing. I'm so glad you had to run out to the store so I could get ready."

Avery laughed and kissed his shoulder. "You are an evil human being."

Linc stood up straight, letting Avery slip out of him with a hiss. A tea towel was clenched in Linc's fist, and he carefully pulled away from Avery's softening cock. "Guess I'll be doing laundry while you're away."

"Hello?" a voice called from the direction of the front door.

They scrambled, doing up clothes, and Avery nearly took a fist to his eye as they danced around each other. Linc dashed down the hall toward the bathroom, slamming the door shut behind him. Avery did his best to call a casual "Hi!" coming around the corner to where—*holy shit, they were all there.* Vasquez and Wanda were in the doorway, with Avery's aunt and uncle behind them, and Linc's two sisters and nephews after that.

"We were all parking at the same time," Aunt Brenda said with a smile. "Isn't that a wonderful coincidence?"

"Uh, yeah." Avery ran a hand through his hair and then over his body, making sure everything was where it should be.

Vasquez eyed him. "Where's Linc?"

Avery grinned. "Don't you mean Scott?"

She scoffed. "He's not on my truck anymore. Scott's dead to me. He's Linc now. Where is he?"

"Just in the bathroom."

"Brian sent more baby pictures." Vasquez leaned forward to kiss his cheek, dropping her voice to a hoarse whisper. "Also, your fly's down."

His face heated so much it must be bright crimson, but Vasquez smirked and led the entourage farther into the apartment, while Aunt Brenda told Avery all about how she'd decided to use mustard in her quiche recipe this time. He surreptitiously did his pants up and hoped no one noticed.

Lacey and Lilah herded the two boys toward the living room, and Troy let out a gigantic sneeze.

"Ew," Jake said. "You've got snot everywhere."

"Wash your hands," Lacey said.

"I can't." Troy glanced sadly in the direction of the kitchen sink, which was overflowing with dirty dishes from the French toast bake and the turkey bacon biscuits.

"Then use the bathroom."

"No! Linc's in there." Avery leapt forward, throwing his

278

hands wide to head Troy off. No way was he going to let the little boy walk in on Linc wiping come off the backs of his thighs and cleaning up the plug.

Aunt Brenda grabbed a small bottle off the counter. "Here's some hand sanitizer. Come here, sweetie, and let's—"

"No, that's expired. It's old. He can't—" Avery dove for it before she could hand off the bottle of lube they'd forgotten to stash.

"Hey, everyone. You're all here at once." Linc stood in the hall, looking flushed and smug. Okay, he looked well-fucked, but children were present, so Avery was keeping that bit to himself. Also, his hair was combed and his fly was done up, the bastard.

"Uncle Linc, I have to wash my hands," Troy said.

"You do? Come on down to the bathroom, little man, and let's get that taken care of."

Vasquez and Wanda were still giving Avery weird looks as he slipped the lube bottle into his pocket, but Aunt Brenda didn't seem to notice anything was off. She took control of the kitchen, enlisting Lilah's help, while Uncle Theo and Jake started a very serious conversation about whether the Falcons or the Panthers were going to win the NFC South.

"You were having sex, weren't you?"

Avery jumped. Of Linc's two sisters, Lilah was sweet, but Lacey made him nervous. She was always serious and took no bullshit.

"No." But his voice wobbled, and he could tell his face was turning bright red again.

She laughed, but kept her voice low. "I get it. It was the same for me and the boys' dad before he left. Couldn't keep my hands off him."

She walked away before he could say anything else. Linc and Troy reappeared from the bathroom, and Lacey took Troy to the balcony so they could look out over the city.

Linc wrapped his arms around Avery from behind, holding him close. There was no heat now, only happy contentment. "Everything okay?"

"Our nephew nearly washed his hands in lube."

Linc snorted and kissed the side of Avery's neck. "He takes after his uncle."

"It's been weeks since I got hurt or did something stupid in public."

And that was mostly true. The move to Atlanta had been imperfect. The big city took some adjustment, but the job kept him so busy he hadn't found time to be lonely. With Linc's arrival the previous month, everything got better. And somehow, whether because he had so much going on at work, or because he wasn't worried about an entire small town of people watching his every move, Avery's tendency to talk too much and trip while doing simple things like walking down the street had faded.

A little.

He'd dropped a potted plant off the balcony in September setting up a container garden. Fortunately, no one else had been around at the time. And he'd nearly chipped a tooth the first time he and Linc had "welcome to our new apartment" sex, but their several repeat performances had been accident free.

"Sweet pea," Aunt Brenda said. "Do you have aluminum foil? Your sweet potatoes are making a mess."

"Coming." He untangled himself from Linc's arms, even though he was sad to let go. They'd have plenty of chances to pick up where they'd left off.

"Hey." Linc pulled his hand and wound him back up for a quick kiss. "Are you happy?"

Avery smiled at him. "Of course."

"You did this, you know."

Avery flushed and rested his forehead against Linc's collarbones. "No, I didn't."

"You did. These people are all our family now, and it's because of you."

"Sweet pea!"

"Love you." Avery kissed Linc just once. He would never not love kissing him, even with their entire family watching.

"Love you too, Red."

THANK YOU

Thank you so much for reading *Hot Potato*. That's it for the Seacroft series ... for now.

Did you miss any of the earlier Seacroft Stories?

If you don't know where to start, check out *Top Shelf*, where Seb's artistic cynicism and snark are won over by Martin, the shy professor who works in the bookstore downstairs.

And then follow it up with *Cold Pressed*, where Oliver tries to ignore heartbreak and keep his life under control while starting his own business, only to have that control crumble in the hands of Nick, a smoldering bisexual dad with problems of his own.

Follow me on Amazon to be notified of new releases, or come join my Facebook readers group (facebook.com/groups/allisonsalist). Or sign up for The A-List, my monthly newsletter for new releases, giveaways, and recommendations at allisontemplebooks.com/newsletter.

The kindest thing a reader does for an author is read their book. The second kindest is to recommend it. Please take a minute to leave a review on Amazon or Goodreads, so other readers will know if this story is for them!

ABOUT THE AUTHOR

Whether I knew it then or not, I've been a writer since the second grade, when I wrote a short story about a girl and her horse. My grandmother typed it out for me and said she'd never seen so many quotation marks from a seven-year-old before. I took that as a challenge and have tried to break that record in all the stories I've taken on since then. It's good to have goals, right?

I live in Toronto with my very patient husband and the world's neediest cat. I try to split my time between writing, community theater stage management, and traveling anywhere that has good wine. Tragically, this leaves no time to clean the house.

ALSO BY ALLISON TEMPLE

Top Shelf (Seacroft Book 1)

Martin is a ghost. Well, not really, but he might as well be. Job gone, home gone, self-respect gone, and no one even seems to notice. The only person who really sees him is Seb, the artist who lives above the used bookstore.

Seb haunts the edges of Seacroft in search of beauty. He knows how to excavate the hidden value in abandoned things—whether it's in the pages of forgotten books or in Martin's stuttering attempts to rebuild his life—and transform them into works of art.

Two lost souls, Seb and Martin discover the strength they need to face eccentric townies and their dysfunctional families together. But as friendship sparks toward something more, neither man wants to risk what they've only just found. It takes two to fall in love, but it will take the whole community to bring their beauty to life.

Available on Amazon and Kindle Unlimited

(http://mybook.to/TopShelf)

Cold Pressed (Seacroft Book 2)

No strings attached is all Oliver can offer. He's hiding a broken heart that holds him back from diving into a new relationship, but he'll go on a blind date to make his family happy. Just one date, though; he doesn't have time for love to derail his plans.

Divorced and demoted to the night shift, Nick has his own problems. He's got an ex-wife who needs him and a kid with one foot in juvie. The last thing Nick needs is to butt heads—or other body parts—with a tempting hipster who wears a sad smile on their blind date.

Their chemistry can't be denied, though, in an argument or in bed. No strings sex is uncomplicated, and that's what Nick and Oliver need. But getting into bed together is one thing. Staying out of each other's hearts soon becomes so much more complicated than either one imagined.

The Pick Up

Kyle's life is going backwards. He wanted to build a bigger life for himself than Red Creek could give him, but a family crisis has forced him to return to his hometown with his six-year-old daughter. Now he's standing in the rain at his old elementary school, and his daughter's teacher, Mr. Hathaway, is lecturing him about punctuality.

Adam Hathaway is not looking for love. He's learned the hard way to keep his personal and professional life separate. But Kyle is struggling and needs a friend, and Adam wants to be that friend. He just needs to ignore his growing attraction to Kyle's goofy charm, because acting on it would mean breaking all the rules that protect his heart.

Putting down roots in this town again is not Kyle's plan. As soon as he can, he's taking his daughter and her princess costumes and moving on. The more time he spends with Adam, though, the more he thinks the quiet teacher might give him a reason to stay. Now he just has to convince Adam to take a chance on a bigger future than either of them could have planned.